Praise for
K.A. TERYNA

"A singular talent, with writing fresh and strange."
LAVIE TIDHAR
AUTHOR OF *CENTRAL STATION*

"What is most impressive here is the range of these glittering stories, from cyberpunk to folklore, generation starship to dream invasion. Again and again, I laughed in astonishment at turns of phrase and twists of the mundane into the surreal. With her brooding sense of the absurd, K.A. Teryna will teach you a new way to embrace the fantastic. I needed to read these stories—you do too!"
JAMES PATRICK KELLY
WINNER OF THE HUGO, NEBULA & LOCUS AWARDS

"K.A. Teryna's kaleidoscopic vision spans nations, worlds, and genres, delivering stories that range from sharp-eyed science fiction to dreamy myth, and all of it alive with a fiercely beating heart."
STEPHANIE FELDMAN
AUTHOR OF *SATURNALIA*

"An engaging, eclectic set of stories . . . Teryna has an interesting and vivid imagination, creating worlds and populating them with strange and captivating characters, people and otherwise. I can't tell you what these stories are like in the original Russian, but Shvartsman does a great job in capturing the beauty and the strangeness of language. If I did not know ahead of time, I would not have guessed these were not the original versions . . . These are not frivolous throw-away stories to read for a quick laugh. There is a depth to them that comes back to you later. You sink into these stories and come up for air later. When you do come up, there is a different feel to the atmosphere. It's a little richer, a little thicker and a little darker."
AMAZING STORIES

"The stories in *Black Hole Heart* refuse to be labeled. They burst from the confines of the page, swirling and switching genre gears, leaving the reader wondering what's coming next. In these pages, one finds old Russian folk tales, golems, plotting cats, children old beyond their years, generation ships, and more. Teryna balances stories about inner lives and outer space with a deftness that explains why every one of these stories has found a home in a prestigious magazine or anthology . . . Translated by Alex Shvartsman with the kind of care and dedication that allows the stories to blossom and live in our minds long after they're read, these glimpses of sometimes-dark, sometimes-hilarious worlds solidify Teryna's place on the global speculative fiction scene . . . A heady mix of genres, ideas, and worlds, *Black Hole Heart* will make you want to seek out every story Teryna has written and look out for whatever comes next."

    STRANGE HORIZONS

"Dazzling and surreal."

    THE TIMES OF LONDON
    ON "THE FARCTORY"

"K.A.Teryna perfectly matches the tone and style of those old Eastern European folktales, the ones full of blood and revenge and tragic deaths."

    ALEX BROWN
    ON "LAJOS AND HIS BEES"

BLACK
HOLE
HEART

K.A.TERYNA

BLACK HOLE HEART

AND OTHER STORIES

TRANSLATED BY
ALEX SHVARTSMAN

FAIRWOOD
PRESS
Bonney Lake, WA

BLACK HOLE HEART AND OTHER STORIES

A Fairwood Press Book
October 2025
Copyright © 2025 K.A.Teryna
Translation Copyright © 2025 Alex Shvartsman
All Rights Reserved

First Edition

Fairwood Press
21528 104th Street Court East
Bonney Lake, WA 98391
www.fairwoodpress.com

Cover art and design © K.A.Teryna
Book design by Patrick Swenson

ISBN: 978-1-958880-29-6
First Fairwood Press Edition: October 2025

Printed in the United States of America

CONTENTS

BLACK HOLE HEART

YOU WERE THIRTY-FIVE WHEN YOU PARKED YOUR PICKUP TRUCK in front of that damned diner. A single poor decision that would make you hate yourself for the rest of your life. When you think back to that moment your joints hurt, your bones ache, your teeth bite into your tongue until you taste blood. In this town, even your body behaves in an unpredictable manner.

That's why you prefer not to think of that moment at all. Anything but that.

But the treacherous memories claw their way through the tiniest chink in your mental armor, and the carefully constructed defenses tumble like a stack of alphabet blocks. You were thirty-five years old. You ordered a cup of coffee and a slice of blueberry pie.

And you stayed forever.

You were driving cross country, from the East Coast to the West. That's not such a terrible idea when all you have in the world is a rusty '39 pickup. When you left to fight in the war you had parents, a younger brother, a house near Boston, a yellow Ford, and a girlfriend named Lisa. But while you were saving the world from the Nazi menace, your parents died, and your brother gambled away your house and then left to seek better fortunes in California and took Lisa with him. Only the beat-up truck remained. How did they manage to turn a brand-new pickup into a pile of rusty metal in just three years?

The Ford was falling apart and you decided to take it on one last, three-thousand-mile road trip. Perhaps you thought that at the end of this journey you might accidentally run into Lisa while walking around on some beach in Fort Bragg, California. Stranger things have happened.

You planned to drive across America but got stuck in its heart instead, all because of the waitress. You remember her eyes—venom-green, clear-blue, fiery-orange; like a swamp, like a sea, like a sunset.

Sometimes you walk into the Double K diner and stare at the girl behind the counter. It can't possibly be the same waitress. Perhaps it's her daughter, or granddaughter. Maybe her name is also—what?—Annie?

No. That waitress's name was Ellie. *Ellie.* The black hole that has replaced your heart whispers her name.

The black hole is cold. It emits gusts of frozen wind. The black hole is treacherous. If you close your eyes even for a moment you will be trapped within it like a rabbit caught in a snare; you will fall into it, and keep falling, and when you reach the bottom you'll be thirty-five again.

"Hey, mister, where's your license plate from?"

"Those are Massachusetts plates, doll. Who taught you to make such excellent coffee?"

You were never a good liar, but the girl's blushing cheeks are all the reward you wanted for your awkward compliment.

"I'm sorry, mister, but blueberry pie won't be ready for another thirty minutes. The long haul truckers bought out the morning batch—they're a hungry lot! Would you like to try Ma Gray's signature pudding instead?"

"I'll wait for the pie, doll. I'm in no hurry."

Thirty minutes is long enough to pin your life to this town like a rare butterfly to a wooden pinning block.

You could say: "Screw the pie, dear. To be honest, I never liked pie. The coffee is great, but it's time for me to move along."

You could leave a five-dollar bill on the counter. Such a generous tip is well beyond your means, but that girl's eyes are awfully pretty.

"Have a good day, babe," you could've said as you walk out into the scorching Kansas afternoon and toward your yellow pickup.

Instead you tell her, "I'm in no hurry."

And now you never have to rush anywhere again.

Someone gently taps you on your shoulder. You open your eyes.

"What do you say, mayor? I think this is an excellent idea!"

It's the sheriff. He stares at you without blinking. You have no idea what he's talking about, but he's waiting for you to respond.

"Sure," you say. "Sure."

There are bits and pieces of memories jumbled in your head. You seem to recall that you knew him when he was a boy. He was a decent quarterback. You were barely a mediocre coach.

The Bay of Pigs. The Moon landing. Sunflowers. An awkward attempt to kiss the unattractive librarian. Lonely nights at the movie theater. Bingo in the evenings. So many lies gathered in the trash bin of your memory.

None of that was real. None of that *will* be real.

There are two dots connected by the straight line: point A and point B. Then and now. Point A, when you were thirty-five years old with your entire life ahead of you. Point B, when you're a hundred and your life somehow never began.

Between those points is a black hole sixty-five years wide.

Sometimes you walk into the Double K diner and stare at the girl behind the counter. You want to ask her just one question, but you order the awful swill they call coffee instead.

Why ask the question when you already know the answer?

You close your eyes as an old man and when you open them a moment later you're thirty-five again.

"Listen, babe," you say. "What if I don't wait for the damn pie? What if I drive away, get on the road right now, in my fine yellow truck?"

"The pie is delicious, mister. If you don't try it, you'll regret it for the rest of your life."

"What if I *like* life-long regrets? Maybe collecting them is my hobby. Maybe I'm a regret connoisseur."

"Then you should go, mister. It will be an outstanding regret. Pride of your collection."

You get up. You should leave a tip, but you have no change and a fiver is way too much. When you grasp the handle of the front door, she calls after you.

"I'll tell you what's gonna happen, mister. You'll get into your broken-down Ford and you'll keep pressing the gas pedal until your foot falls asleep. You'll drive fifteen hundred miles in something like thirty hours. Fresh air and an open road: it will be the happiest thirty hours of your life. You'll drive your truck to its death, like messengers did to their horses on the Pony Express in 1861. It will be a worthy end for this clunker. You'll arrive in Fort Bragg, California and head straight for the beach. There you'll find large pebbles smoothed by the waves over thousands of years, the whisper of the ocean, the cries of seagulls, and the most stunning sunset you've ever seen.

"You'll decide, right there and then, that the time has come to begin anew. After all, you're good with your hands and with your brain both, more than can be said of most people your age. You'll think that maybe you should move to New York and try to make it big in advertising.

"That's when they'll show up.

"It will be an incredible, impossible coincidence. If you happen to be a card player, mister, you'll know what I mean. It'll be like being dealt a straight flush in the game with the highest possible stakes. Three to seven of clubs. Imagine yourself, holding those cards, trying not to show excitement, to keep your poker face. Fanning the cards slowly, carefully, arranging them out of order: six, three, four, seven, five. All clubs. You won't believe your eyes. Your hands will shake. The greatest windfall of luck in your life, and the bitterest disappointment, because all of your opponents will fold their cards, one by one, before the betting even opens.

"Yeah, mister, this will be the most useless straight flush in your life. First you will hear the familiar laugh. Then you will see the pebbles that your brother Charlie is tossing into the ocean. Then you will see him. Charlie will not have changed at all. He will have laughed like a man who never faced death. And Lisa—Lisa will look even better than you remember. You loved her long hair, but the new, shorter cut will make her even prettier, will make it impossible for you to look away. They will kiss, and that kiss—believe me—will tear a hole through your heart. That kiss will strike true where the German sniper missed.

"This beach, this ocean, this sunset—it will be all for them, with you merely a bystander, a card drawn by mistake. Perhaps, you'll think, you should have never returned from the war.

"You will reach into your pocket and draw a Colt—the same one you used to shoot two krauts point blank during a battle in '44—a fine weapon. You will draw this Colt faster than one can say *matryoshka*, a stupid word you learned from an old Russian doctor. You won't aim. It would be ludicrous to aim at your own brother and at the woman you love. You'll simply fire, again and again, at the sunset, at the ocean, at the pebbles, and at the seagulls.

"Charlie will die instantly, before he realizes what's happening, a smile still on his face. He will be buried with that smile, and will rot like that, smiling as California worms feast on his flesh.

"Lisa will die slowly, painfully. She will die staring right at you. Tenderness, multiplied by the three hundred and seventeen minutes of happiness from the first night you shared together, divided by ninety-nine thousand seven hundred and twenty-three minutes of loneliness—that's what her gaze will look like."

The waitress—Ellie, was it?—goes back to wiping down the counter as though you aren't there, as though you've never been there at all.

You slowly let go of the door handle and ask, trying to feign indifference: "What did you say, doll?"

"I said pie's ready, mister. Maybe you should stay a while? Unless, of course, you're in a rush."

"Bring on the pie, doll. I'm in no hurry."

SONGS OF THE SNOW WHALE

UMILYK: FABLE OF THE MOTHER OF WHITE WHALES

"THEY SAY THE BLIZZARD ON R'EVAVA IS THE WRATH OF THE SNOW whale. It beats its tail against the infinite surface of the Milky Way and shakes loose small snowflakes that cover the island," said Umilyk.

"In all of the Soviet Union snow is an atmospheric phenomenon, and only in Chukotka is it a cosmic one," added Borisov.

"Not even in the whole of Chukotka, but on R'evava. For what is Chukotka but a word? An administrative unit, a geometric shape marked on a map with a ruler. To listen to those cartographers, they think even Magadan will pass for Chukotka."

"Those are some rabid cartographers. Don't listen to them. Listen to me. Better yet, tell us what makes your R'evava so special? Why is snow an aggregate state of water everywhere else, but it turns into shards of eternity on this island?" asked Borisov.

Before answering, Umilyk looked over the room with a certain degree of tenderness. Everything here was right and calibrated, so it was no shame to entertain guests.

Even a group of guests as peculiar as this.

A young woman with light, almost white hair and dead eyes, eyes which looked the way they do when the last of the tears have run out. Even through several layers of clothing, Umilyk could clearly see that the woman was with child. The habits of pregnant women change: they must now protect more than just themselves. And even if their taste for life dissipates along with those last tears, the maternal instinct remains.

A tall bald man in glasses with thick lenses looked like a professor, and enunciated his Russian words with an exaggerated care. Umilyk already knew that this man was from Poland and that he was no professor, but some sort of a musician.

The second man, with a rough pockmarked face, a constant smirk, and unruly hair, was a reporter from Moscow who was in such a hurry to return to the mainland that he'd traveled from Kytoorken to R'evava, only to find a blizzard instead of the scheduled helicopter.

But the presence that seemed strangest to Umilyk was that of the old woman. She crouched near the entrance in such a manner that it seemed she was ready to get up and leave as soon as the storm would pass. Her name was Navetyn and she'd lived for a hundred, if not two hundred, winters, or so those who were born and grew up on R'evava had told Umilyk. Umilyk himself was a "lifer"—a slang word from the lexicon of Soviet officials who occasionally wandered as far as R'evava. He'd spent nearly thirty years here. When Umilyk had first arrived, Navetyn was already old, like the island itself.

Her yaranga stood apart from everyone else's dwellings. On occasion, Umilyk thought that when Navetyn died it would be a while before anyone found out. But she was in no hurry to die; on the contrary, she impressed with her sharp mind and a clear sense of time. She always knew in advance about a successful hunt, and when the whaleboats returned filled with fat prey, Navetyn waited for them at the shore with her pekul knife. She was as dexterous as the best workers in the cutting brigade and her presence was always welcome.

Which made it even more surprising that Navetyn had turned up at the village at such an inopportune time, an hour before the first November blizzard.

A village was an overstatement. There were no administrative buildings or even a culture club on all of R'evava. The weather station was the center of life, and that's where the group had gathered, waiting for flying weather.

Umilyk sighed. Providing visitors with local flavor was not a task mentioned in the job description, but it was no less important than keeping an accurate meteorological log.

"Once upon a time, there lived other tribes in the north alongside the Luoravetlan Peoples: walrus people, bearded seal people, and even whale people. Men of these tribes married human women and so propagated their intelligent kind. One time, a great whale, the mother of white whales, arrived in these lands, and she took a Luoravetlan hunter as her husband. All the great whale wanted was to teach her first husband a lesson, for he was the headstrong snow whale that swims the Milky Way and whose song people hear on the border between reality and dreams.

"But the children the great whale had with her Luoravetlan hunter were as precious to her as the white whale's. When the children grew up they prayed: Mother, we can't swim with you into the ocean but there's no room for us here. All the best land is occupied by other people, what should we do? The great whale listened to those pleas, sighed, and turned herself into an island so that her children would have a land of their own. This island was named R'evava. She left only one command to her children, and those words are passed from generation to generation: white whales are brothers, and one doesn't kill their brother. They say that the great whale herself sometimes appears to the island residents in human form, to see how her children are faring.

"This is why the great snow whale always singles out R'evava, and why he brings the blizzard. He comes in search of his wife, who left him for a human man and his children."

BORISOV: THE TALE OF A WHALER

The blizzard howled outside and beat against walls and tiny windows, tapping on the roof like a northern giant probing for a weak spot in a dilapidated dwelling.

Borisov could see right through the caretaker. He noticed the moment when the duty of entertaining uninvited guests became something more intimate and important to him. For a moment it seemed to Borisov that he'd glimpsed the huge eye of the snow whale through the tiny window of the weather station and the eye stared, unblinking, directly at him.

He recalled how much he was looking forward to this trip: a special feeling somewhere below the solar plexus. It was similar to an attraction to a woman but icier, a chill spreading through the blood and tingling fingertips with tiny needles. In this manner, thought Borisov, are born the letters that he would later build into words. He definitely needed a typewriter. An Olympia, the object of special pride and secret devotion, awaited Borisov in Moscow. He hated writing longhand as his handwriting was terrible, the beauty of ideas and clarity of thought becoming lost in his chicken scratch. But it would've been ridiculous to drag the Olympia north. Borisov imagined himself with the Olympia on a whaler motorboat and grinned, then grew gloomy. He was used to tracing his line of thought like a fisherman, who carefully pulls his line so as not to frighten his prey. Before the fish surfaces, the fisherman already knows by its weight and manner whether he's about to see a catfish, a pike, or even a sturgeon.

Borisov knew which story had made him gloomy.

There was no excitement left, no special feeling anticipating his homecoming. His desire to come home was businesslike, casual, like the wish to sleep in one's own bed after a long flight. This feeling was also reminiscent of a relationship with a woman: the romance was at an end, the attraction was over, everything there was to know about her had already been discovered and understood, and exactly as much of himself shared as he was willing to, and no more. Borisov knew he would never return to Chukotka and that made him a little sad. But it was the memory of Ettyn that hung over him like a dark cloud.

"This is all very beautiful," said Borisov, "until it results in someone's death."

Out of the corner of his eye he noticed the girl wrapped in the dawn shawl shudder. She couldn't seem to get warm, despite the hot rooms of the weather station and strong hot tea proffered by the caretaker. The Polish man didn't look at him; he kept fiddling with his miniature vargan mouth harp. The old woman in the corner stared simultaneously at Borisov and deep into her internal abyss. Umilyk raised his eyebrows politely.

"There used to be a hunter in Kytoorken. He was very young, still a boy, but tall, very tall for Chukotka, if the honored Umilyk will forgive me."

Umilyk shrugged as if to say, what's there to forgive? It is true that I'm short of stature.

"The boy was named Ettyn and he was a whaler."

Borisov recalled how difficult it had been to convince the foreman to take him along on a whale hunt. Ettyn had helped him, and he'd done so selflessly, merely for the delight of communicating with the person who'd come all the way from Moscow. Ettyn had learned the word "jovial" from Borisov and had liked it so much that he'd stuck it into every other phrase. A cargo cult, Borisov had thought contemptuously then. Now he was ashamed of his contempt.

"When the harpoon hits the whale, the tip opens. The whale dives to the bottom but the deed is done, a float called a pikh-pikh follows the harpoon into the water. And the more harpoons strike the whale, the more floats there are, which makes it more difficult for the whale to dive. That whale fought like mad, he ripped the first two harpoons out and the sea became stained with whale blood, but the hunters were inexorable. Each of them, with perhaps the exception of Ettyn, had dealt with dozens or even hundreds of whales in their lifetimes. They couldn't be surprised by the survival instinct of a single underwater beast."

Borisov's cadence was measured, unhurried. When he seemed to be losing his train of thought, his imagination pictured the Olympia on a huge, totally empty desk. Under the glass-covered tabletop there were scraps and clippings of Borisov's life: ticket stubs, newspaper clippings, napkins, and even one Aldan computer punch card. For as long as he could remember, whenever he'd position his fingers at the keys, the words would reemerge. As if they'd been stored in the fingertips and the typewriter keyboard was the means of extracting them and giving them form.

At the moment, that form was the whale.

"It was impossible to see the whale itself in all that blood and roiling. It was clear only that this was a lygirgev,"—here Borisov gave in to the temptation to use a fancy word. He tasted it as he looked at the faces of his listeners and imagined a different set of faces: sophisticated and well-fed Muscovites.

"A bowhead whale," Umilyk explained to the woman and the Polish man.

"The Ettyn boy's harpoon was the last to strike the whale. Next came the carbines."

Borisov had read about how the Soviet whalers went mad. The letters of the man who wrote about this weren't living and convincing, and his statistics didn't give form to feeling: Borisov had read but hadn't understood. He understood on the day when he watched an enormous and clearly intelligent creature fight for its life. It was like deicide: a seditious thought Borisov hid away, for it was only appropriate to express in secret drafts.

One could only imagine the picture of industrial slaughter, and it was an intellectual effort akin to recreating a seascape painting from a child's pencil sketch. Borisov winced and mentally crossed out this comparison. It was tinged with the sort of condescension for the indigenous people that Borisov was hoping to avoid. But it seemed that sickness didn't ask for permission before entering his mind.

Borisov's own eyewitness account of the slaughter as a means of folk harvest was sloppily recorded in his notebook so he could bring it to life with the help of his Olympia later.

"When the boats towed the carcass to the island and the tractor dragged it ashore, it became apparent that the whale was enormous, and that it was white. You know, when people mention the white whale, one imagines a snow-white color like in our comrade's tale. Of course the whale was not literally white, but it was apparent to everyone from the first glance that this whale was special. This was also apparent to Ettyn. Do you understand what happened? It's a very simple story. A boy goes on his first whale hunt and the hunt is successful, the boy throws a harpoon and the harpoon finds its target. The whale is caught. And then it becomes clear that, according to grandma's tales, this is a special whale. A forbidden whale. That its death brings misfortune to the entire clan. And instead of the joy of a successful initiation, the boy experiences some completely different feelings."

"What happened to him?" the young woman asked, alarmed.

Borisov shrugged.

"Several days later, alone and unarmed, he undertook the task of driving off a bear and her cubs that had come close to a store. It was a foolish and terrible death. They shot the bear, of course. Even the hunting inspector recognized the shooting as justified— which is quite a rarity, by the way. It's usually punishable by a fine to the tune of several thousand rubles. You might blame youthful maximalism, but I knew him. Ettyn was entirely different. He was a good hunter and a thoughtful young man, except in cases that dealt with such legends. And if something caused him to act rashly, it was the weight of guilt imposed by primitive tales."

Borisov had come to Kytoorken to write about the beauty of indigenous fishing and its meaningfulness as compared to the soulless commercial slaughter by the whaler crews.

But the story hadn't come together. The Ettyn boy hadn't fitted into the pre-conceived structure; his dead body had ruined the composition. The words had collapsed under this weight. It seemed: remove the boy, and everything would work, but Borisov knew that the essay must be honest. He couldn't excise the boy and hope the essay would survive such a surgery. Ettyn himself had told him about the whale people, and in those stories a human was something like a whale's soul, its intelligent part, which could take physical form and leave the whale body at will—but not for long.

Without its "inner human" the whale lost its cognizance and became a mindless mass of muscle.

He couldn't remove the boy from the story about the Chukotka whale fishing: the essay would become lifeless and wild.

"Perhaps the boy was born on R'evava?" the Polish man suddenly asked, clearly enunciating each word. These seemed to be the first words he'd uttered since they all introduced themselves. "Is that why you came to this island?"

Borisov said nothing. Then Krzysztof added, "I also have a story about a whale."

KRZYSZTOF: MEMORIES OF THE ETHNOGRAPHER

Krzysztof didn't really understand why he'd interjected into this conversation. Words had been Jacek's domain. Krzysztof didn't like words, which is why he put in so much effort into overcoming them. But, even having added two more languages to his native Polish, he was no match for Jacek.

"You seem to think that faith in such things is the lot of naïve people unspoiled by civilization. My brother had two PhDs; he traveled across half the world and wrote several books. Jacek Tominski. Perhaps you've read his *Whale Songs*. He believed that at least one white whale—such as is described by the residents of R'evava—exists."

The caretaker nodded. "He was a great man. No one listened to stories better than him."

Krzysztof looked at Umilyk in surprise. He understood better and better why his brother had come to love these people. It was like leaving a smog-filled, dusty city, a dodgy society obsessed with mutual profit, compromises, and things left unspoken, and heading out to the simple and clear edge of the world.

Umilyk had noted the most important detail: no one listened

to stories better than Jacek. It had always been so. There was a storytelling talent, and there was a talent as a listener. The way Jacek listened, he could turn anyone into a talented storyteller. Jacek could suss out a true melody in the white noise of anyone's most awkward narrative. He could see it, touch it, clear it up, and admire it.

When he'd lacked words as a child, Krzysztof had played the piano. His fingers caressed the keys. Jacek had listened, and then told the story, and Krzysztof was amazed at how his brother had fished the words out from the current of the melody, like fish from the river.

"Jacek and I hadn't seen each other in many years. He wrote me letters regularly. I replied inconsistently and grudgingly, but even in my abbreviated style my brother managed to glean everything important. He wasn't counting on my own insight, so he described everything willingly and in great detail. That, and not my sensitivity or attention to my brother's hobbies, is the reason I know quite a bit about Řevava and the white whales. You see, people here believe that anyone who was born on the island and lived a worthy life won't die, won't become a pile of ash in a Soviet crematorium or a stack of rotting bones in Soviet ground; won't remain a portrait of an exemplary production worker on a factory wall or a few lines in the local or even a Moscow newspaper. No, they believe that white whales will come for the good people. It seems it always remained a mystery to me whether my brother was a good person. He never finished writing his last letter. This is all that I have left of him."

Krzysztof took the small vargan from his pocket, which Jacek had sent him a few years ago. Seemingly Jacek had nothing like that in mind, but Krzysztof considered it a matter of honor to learn this language, also. Too bad his brother would never hear him play.

"You came to pick up your brother's body?" the young woman asked quietly. Only now did Krzysztof realize she'd been carefully following their conversation, and even participating in it with her silence.

"The Chukchi people have this capacious word: enan-ot-kynatyk. It means, 'to carry the decedent on a sleigh while sitting astride them.' I don't think these wonderful people imply something greater here—some sort of metaphysical depths. But I see those. I think it's about the importance of letting our dead go, instead of dragging them along as a weight. I came here to let my brother go. There's no body left, and maybe that's for the best. First, I won't have to ride astride him on a sleigh. Second, I absolutely do not want to see him dead. People change too much in death. It's not surprising that death gives birth to most of the myths."

"Do you have two university degrees, too? You speak very well."

"Not at all; I'm just a musician. A humble pianist. And a bit of a parrot. My brother used to speak and write me letters smoothly; I'm merely repeating after him. It seems to be my destiny to repeat others' melodies and words. But I promised you a whale story. Here I will also act as a parrot: the story isn't mine.

"You've read *Moby Dick*, of course? A great book. My brother loved it very much. And, of course, he had a theory. Jacek had a theory about everything. When they say a person is looking for patterns everywhere, they're talking about my brother.

"The Chukchi have the concept of teryky, a shapeshifter. This is usually used to describe a person taken by the tundra. Such a person becomes wild and loses themselves.

"Imagine a whale person who's lost their human component. Won't they become a teryky? And if so, will people call them Moby Dick?"

"Would that make your brother Ahab?"

Krzysztof thought it over, his chin down to his chest.

"Perhaps not. I'd say, Ahab's opposite. Do you know why the boy who killed the white whale lost his mind from grief? It's not because he killed a brother. That is a knowable human motive which people practice on a daily basis. But, as our loved ones lose their substance and form as they leave us and it becomes replaced with idealized features, so do our legends with time become gods. You see, people desperately need gods. This is, as your expression goes, fundamental to their moral compass. A god is not necessarily an incorporeal bearded old man in the sky. It's not necessarily a young man on a cross. Sometimes a god is a flesh-and-blood person whom you've designated as your judge. And sometimes, it's an enormous white whale. That's what happened to that boy. He killed his god."

Krzysztof fiddled with his vargan for a time. His fingers felt the instrument coming to life, inspired either by the conversation or by the storm outside the window.

"My brother wasn't concerned with gods. Jacek believed in white whales, but he wanted to meet them as an equal. Person to person."

"To meet them how?"

"It seems there's no method other than to wait. At least, that's what my brother thought. Unfortunately, he ran out of time."

Krzysztof quit resisting and let the vargan take over. When he clenched it with his teeth the sound seemed to be born on its own, even before his fingers touched the reed. Focused on the emerging melody he didn't immediately notice that the old woman had joined the conversation.

The old woman spoke quietly and Krzysztof couldn't make out the words. After a moment he realized that even if he could hear her, he wouldn't have understood: the old woman was speaking the Chukchi language.

Umilyk began to translate quickly and smoothly, as though he'd been waiting for her to speak.

"Navetyn says that she has a story about a whale," he said.

The old woman's voice sounded like she'd picked up the vargan melody, chewed it with her toothless mouth, and then weaved it into a narrative thread. Krzysztof closed his eyes and suddenly felt what he thought his brother had felt. The voice lulled, even more noticeably due to Krzysztof not understanding the words. And yet he did seem to understand them, their meaning and spirit, their melody; seemed to dive into that river and then the current took him away before the caretaker spoke, translating the old woman's words into Russian.

NAVETYN: THE LEGEND OF THE WOMAN LOVED BY A WHALE

There lived a woman in the village of Nunak who had no husband. On rare occasions such women become huntresses, and they say there are no better huntresses than these. The bearded seal does not like the smell of a man, but he lets women approach closer. This is because a long time ago the seal tribe was equal to the humans, and the seal people took human wives. They still remember this.

The woman from Nunak was no huntress. Her pekul was rusty and the kerker and kamleika clothing she sewed were only fit for a shapeshifting bear.

But the woman knew many strange songs, and she taught these songs to others. There was a special song to make it snow, and another to make it stop. A song for a calm night, and a song to summon a pusa seal.

When hunters would return with a bearded seal, harbor seal, or a whale, the woman would take her rusty pekul and come for her share; no one dared to say anything to her.

The woman lived alone; she walked along the shore in solitude, and she sang.

The songs the woman sang were passed on to her by her grandmother, but the purpose for some was not known. At times the purpose was clear from the components of the melody: the woman recognized in her song the elements of snow and night and silence, and knew that this song was for a restful winter slumber, such that it would allow one to wake up full of energy and joy.

One song she could not understand. It weaved together the blizzard and whale calls, but the woman could not make sense of this combination.

One evening, at the edge of dusk, during the days of November blizzard, the woman stood on a rock and sang. She saw all the signs of the oncoming storm, but she didn't rush home. She decided to see whether the song would work if sung during the blizzard.

And then it was too late: the blizzard crashed upon the earth and the world disappeared. The song dissipated in the howl of the wind, and the woman realized she could not find her way home.

Then the stranger came. He said: I will guide you. He took her by the hand and led her through the storm, and when the gusts of wind were especially strong he stopped and hugged the woman tightly, shielding her with his body. And the wind had no power over him.

He led her home, and he stayed the night, then left in the morning.

Ever since then the man had come almost every night, until the woman was with child.

One time the woman had followed him all the way to the sea, and had seen the body of an enormous white whale towering over the shore. When the man approached him, the whale had opened his mouth and the man had walked inside.

That's how the woman had found out that she'd become the wife of a whale person.

This didn't change anything in their lives: the woman sang her songs, and the man came when she called. Sometimes he stayed the night, sometimes two. But never more than three. He said that he could not leave his whale body for too long. Without a soul the whale would grow bored, become unpredictable and violent, lose his mind.

But it so happened that the woman fell ill. Neither the shaman potions nor the seal fat would help. Nothing could warm her. The woman lay in the middle of the well-heated living area of the yaranga, wrapped in bear furs, and it seemed she would be covered in a layer of ice at any moment. The people of Nunak did not know the reasons for her illness and therefore could not help. But the reason was that the child in her belly was a snow whale and he needed special songs to grow peacefully and not to accidentally kill his mother.

The whale-father stayed with his human wife and sang to her these songs. While he was near, the whale cub in her belly calmed down and the woman became warm and comfortable. A day went by, then another, then a third, and a tenth. Finally the danger had passed and the woman regained consciousness. She stepped out of the yaranga to get meat for dinner from the icebox, and she saw the people of Nunak celebrating and sharpening their knives. The news came that the hunters had harpooned an enormous white whale, which brought joy to the entire village. The woman rushed back to the yaranga, but it was too late. Her husband was no longer there; a small pile of snow was all that remained of him.

The old woman stopped talking, and so did Umilyk.

Umilyk knew that his retelling was akin to carrying snow in a sieve through a hot yaranga. Awkward and impractical, but when there's no choice it's better to bring however much would make it through.

A transparent and thoughtful silence hung in the room. Only then did Umilyk realize that the blizzard outside had stopped.

"What happened to her?"

It was the woman with dead eyes who spoke. Umilyk had seen her follow Navetyn's tale with great interest, but didn't think she'd dare to ask a question. And when the old woman replied, he was surprised even more. Although the old woman's tone was grouchy, Umilyk thought that if her words were given form, they would emanate warmth.

Umilyk translated: "This is a simple story, as comrade Borisov says. The woman who carries a snow whale within her, becomes a part of the whale tribe herself. Of course, the mother of white whales came for her."

"And the people of Nanuk simply let her go?" Borisov asked skeptically. "This woman knew many important songs. Surely they understood the benefits of her presence."

The old woman spoke a short phrase and Umilyk hesitated for a moment, seeking the right words. For some reason he thought it important that the translation should sound equally poetic.

"Everything in this world has its own song: the people of

Nunak forgot about the woman as soon as the snow powdered the traces of her footsteps."

Borisov laughed and turned to Olga. "Well then, it's your turn. Do you have a story about a whale?"

OLGA: A STORY ABOUT A WHALE

"Do you have a story about a whale?" the Muscovite had asked, and his smarmy tone had made her shrink. It was like a scalpel cutting skin, to see what was inside.

The boy in her belly shifted. She somehow knew with certainty that it was a boy. Maybe because Aiwe had said so, and he always spoke the truth.

This child knew everything about her, and, it seemed, he really wanted to live. She felt him kick any time her thoughts strayed in the wrong direction. In those moments it seemed the darkness she'd fallen into after Aiwe's death didn't quite recede, but rather gained dimensions and depth.

No one is to blame, the doctor had said. Aiwe's heart stopped first, and a few seconds later the beam fell from his weakened hand and crushed the big, strong, handsome Aiwe.

The doctor was short and skinny and very young, and Olga could see herself from three years ago in his gray eyes. She was like that during her early days in this monochrome world that seemed so flat, demonstrative, unreal—like a hastily erected prop for a movie about life in the far north.

But when it came to his area of expertise, the doctor transformed; his voice gained confidence, and his mannerisms became harsh. Olga noted in passing how she would enjoy watching a professional metamorphosis like that under different circumstances. But now, it was as though the automated registrar of what was happening wouldn't turn off, and she watched from the sidelines, wrapped in darkness and grief.

Grief can have different tastes. Olga's grief had an aftertaste of whale fat: the day Aiwe had died, a whaler brigade from Kytoorken had returned from a bountiful hunt. It was a major event and a holiday for the entire village.

Of course she'd heard about the boy from the Muscovite's story. So very young, he'd tried to scare off a bear and her cubs alone. A tragic death. Except Olga hadn't known he was a whaler and that the Kytoorken whale prize was, in part, his accomplishment.

After Aiwe had died, reality became something like an avant-garde black-and-white film, some weird French production with experiments by the director and cameraman. Olga kept losing the narrative thread and finding herself in the center of various events. Here was Aiwe's death certificate, and arguments with officials who didn't know where to record the man who was not written into any of their thick books; here she was in the school director's tiny office—indifferent but inexorable, she had no strength to remain in Kytoorken; here she was at the post office, making a long distance call to Tashlinsk, her mother's accusatory tone when she found out about the pregnancy; here was Umilyk serving her tea, and Borisov with his story, and Krzysztof, and the old Chukchi woman.

Somewhere in-between all that were the nausea, melancholy, nightmares, and the endless kicks in the stomach. She had no time for the young hunter, whose death, it turned out, was tacked on with a red thread to her own life. Olga imagined how in some other small Chukotka village someone was drinking tea and mentioning her Aiwe's death in passing, as an afterthought. This always happened with the dead: they left behind only brief threads of conversation, someone's unreliable memories and, with any luck, photographs. What sort of cadaver could be put together from such materials? The boy from the Muscovite's story appeared wholly alive. Olga could easily imagine him, and could seemingly even hear his voice in the song of the blizzard. Could she so deftly create a verbal portrait of Aiwe for their son?

"Do you have a story about a whale?"

Aiwe had brought her to the shore and they'd watched the whale. Olga hadn't known how to see it at all, but Aiwe had showed her where to look and how to see. He'd told her to listen to the whale song. Olga had listened in earnest, and he'd hugged her and told her that she must listen not with her ears, but with her heart.

Now Olga thought she had no heart left. Above the spot where her boy's tiny heart beat there was a cold emptiness.

Aiwe had appeared out of nowhere; one day he'd walked into her night school and said, "I heard your voice and came to see." Since then he'd come every evening, hadn't asked for anything, hadn't courted her, and hadn't flirted. Olga didn't even understand how it came to be that he'd become the most important person in her life.

How did it come to be that, by leaving, Aiwe had taken her life with him? Olga felt herself a shadow that had no place in any of the usual worlds.

She realized that she couldn't remain in Kytoorken, but her native Tashlinsk seemed alien and flat. Olga felt stuck between two worlds, the higher and the lower, and rejected by both. Sometimes she overcame the feeling of utter foolishness and asked the boy in her belly: where to?

"Do you have a story about a whale?"

Sometimes she listened the way Aiwe had taught her. Not with her ears, but with her heart, even if only its tatters remained. And when she listened like that, she thought she could hear her boy. He sang the way the whales sing.

The old Chukchi woman, Navetyn, was now singing, too. Her whispers intertwined with the moans of the vargan, mixed together, tamed it. Everything disappeared: the people, the weather station, the waiting, the questions. Only the blizzard and the voice of the great mother of white whales remained, and it called to her: come with me.

R'EVAVA, THE WHALE-ISLAND

Umilyk stepped out onto the porch to catch a glimpse of the snow whale's tail as it swam away into the darkness.

The silence after a blizzard is a special time, and a state of mind. As if the entire world stops and freezes. And it listens: what now? Did it survive? Is it whole? Are the north and south poles still in their place?

The silence after a blizzard is so piercing that it seems possible to hear the thoughts and aspirations of all nearby creatures. This silence binds them all together into a single net. Umilyk listened to the stars; they rejoiced at the return of the snow whale. He listened to the sea calming under fast ice; he could seemingly even hear the helicopter preparing for flight in the distant town of Pevek.

Umilyk heard Borisov's thoughts. Borisov, who stepped onto the porch after him, was sad in the way a hunter is sad after an unsuccessful hunt.

Krzysztof stepped outside and from his gait and the movement of the air, Umilyk realized that the musician was fascinated by the beauty around him. Krzysztof had already put away the vargan, but the melody still sounded in his thoughts.

Umilyk wondered whether he should tell the Polish man that he'd seen his brother talk to the sea on the final day of his life. Had seen him board a whaleboat on his way to meet a whale. Had seen the storm being born on the horizon. If he should say that he still wasn't certain whether he should have stopped him.

Instead, he said: "You know, this was the first time in thirty years that I witnessed such a long telling by the old Navetyn. What a story, huh?"

"Navetyn?" Borisov asked absentmindedly. It was clear that his thoughts were already in Pevek, in Magadan, in Moscow.

Umilyk glanced at Krzysztof who only raised his eyebrows in solidarity with Borisov's question.

"The helicopter is almost here," said Umilyk, to change the subject. The image of Navetyn in his mind grew dim and out of focus, as it happens when you don't see someone you know for a long time.

"Listen," the Muscovite voiced a concern. "I was told another passenger would be joining us, a teacher from Kytoorken. We

aren't going to wait for her, since she couldn't be bothered to arrive on time, are we?"

Umilyk shook his head. For another moment he listened to
the sound of receding footsteps—the almost inaudible steps of an
old woman and a young one. And then he stared at the gloomy
sky, catching a few stray snowflakes with his face—the final greet-
ing from the snow whale.

THE ERRATA

SATURN

DANNY HAD MADE THE PLAN SOUND SIMPLE.

We'd steal the shuttle, he said. It had been arranged.

The trajectory had been calculated. He'd had an expert for that.

The rest would be simple, he said. You get it, he said.

Danny loved to hint at some special contacts of his. He tended to say things like, "For those who get it," or "You and me, we don't need things explained to us." When he talked like that, it alleviated all desire to double-check and clarify, because that would make whoever asked the question immediately fall out of the circle of people in-the-know created by Danny, to lose the special club membership granted to them on credit.

It seemed Danny had everything pre-planned and thought through. There was no reason not to believe him. Quite the opposite; Alik really *wanted* to believe him. The Saturn idea was just the breath of fresh air Alik needed in the timeless vacuum of the *Errata*.

One of Mom's favorite authors had written that a person's soul lagged behind by several days when one traveled between the continents. What about space travel, then? Alik kept wondering if his soul had shaken loose a few years back, during liftoff. Now was its chance to catch up.

Obviously, Alik never shared his thoughts about time and especially souls with Danny or any of the others. Only Mom might have understood such things.

It was best if she didn't know about Saturn.

BOOKS

Mom was diminutive and thin, and reminded Alik of a hungry lizard. Sometimes it seemed as though she satiated her hunger by devouring words. She sat still on a stool, hunched in an impossible position under the light of a tiny lamp, and read voraciously. Or maybe it was the other way around, and the words used Mom to satiate their own hunger, by pulling her so deep into the realm of books that Alik thought one day he wouldn't be able to call her back.

The books were everywhere. The books were predators.

There's this theory: people didn't domesticate wheat; wheat used people to spread itself across the globe.

Now the Earth was dying, and who knew what role the insidious plant had played in that? Certainly not Alik. He existed on the periphery of the information cycle, where any available information had already been torn to shreds and chewed up many times over. Where you could only see a chaotic pile of speculation and rumor, with no way to figure out the truth.

Alik couldn't be certain whether wheat was treacherous, but he had long understood books to be just that.

Without taking protective measures, you became their slave. They stole your time and your space. They drove you crazy. They drove Mom crazy, and she had used up almost the entire baggage allowance for both herself and Alik by packing books. Suppose,

Alik thought, they even offered something in return. But it was something incomprehensive and intangible, something that had no price tag and no use.

Uma the cat was categorically opposed to his viewpoint. She valued the books highly and slept exclusively while perched atop a pile of them.

THE SHIP

Mom was sure that the ship had gotten its name by mistake—ironic as that may be.

The previous ships had all been named after goddesses. Alik recalled *Aurora, Freya*, and *Lada*, but there were others, too. Always female names. As though, having exhausted their resources on war and play, male gods had irritably scattered the remnants of humanity, while goddesses gathered it in their palms and carried it gently across the boundless darkness of the universe.

According to Mom, *Errata* was neither a woman nor a goddess, nor a proper noun, or even truly a singular noun. It was a list of errors that had been glued onto the end of a book in the old days. But here and now, the *Errata* gained both a feminine gender and the status as a savior deity. Perhaps someone had confused her with Hecate, and they have our thanks, Mom would say.

The *Errata* was enormous. It was not merely an ark, but a flying city. Alik and his mom were assigned a tiny cabin on the Zeta deck. Zeta meant the backend, which was clear to anyone. Except to Mom, with her irritating habit of seeing the silver lining in everything. "So we're all the way in the back," she would say. "That means things can't get any worse."

Back on Earth, Mom's library had occupied the living room and timidly extended its tentacles into the rest of the apartment. Here the library's small embassy—only a few hundred volumes—took up almost all available space. At first the books were stacked in sloppy piles, then the good man Gorchin had built shelves for them out of "decommissioned" polymer panels. Mom had sewn a jacket for his young daughter as a thank you. It turned out that in the future they chose by leaving Earth, social mechanics from the distant past—such as barter—worked best.

ZETA

Mom's vocation became yet another form of dead weight aboard the *Errata*—no one needed historians in space.

The new ecosystem could use accountants. Once commerce and trade become the main form of human activity, there's always a need for people who know how to balance the books.

Within two years, the Zeta deck had turned into an enormous marketplace. It was a process rather than an event, but Alik fully understood it only after the *Errata* had swung around Venus and headed back. Alik was eleven at the time; he remembered Earth clearly and hadn't yet grown tired of this new, hermetically sealed world.

Mom refused to learn accounting. She could do many things with her hands: sew, knit, repair things, cook. She lacked the most important skill necessary for surviving in the Zeta marketplace: the ability to sell her skills. Having worked as a cashier, courier, mover, and cleaner, Mom had been relieved to undergo the training that was being advertised via leaflets and become a technician.

Zetans considered this to be a dirty and unworthy vocation. They couldn't understand why anyone would prefer to break a sweat servicing the less-than-ideal and ironically error-beset systems of the *Errata* when they could do what humans were created to do: trade. Gorchin declared that trade would exist forever, even if only two people and a stack of polypropylene panels remained aboard the ship. Mom retorted that a third person was necessary: someone to patch up the ship and ensure it could continue to fly.

HUNGER

"What would you have brought?" Mom had asked him.

Over the course of five years aboard the *Errata*, Alik changed his answer several times. The first idea to prove untenable was to fill the luggage with extra power sources for the VR station. Danny had done just that, and Alik was extremely jealous at first. Danny managed to stretch out his supply of batteries for almost five years, by turning on his VR terminal less and less frequently, which made every minute more valuable. But now, as they approached Saturn, he had a worse time of it than those on the public energy rations who were weaned from Earth addictions cold turkey, five years ago.

Energy on the *Errata* was parceled out more stingily as the ship traveled farther from the Sun. Dim lights in the hallways, no public electrical outlets, and strict personal limits. Everyone was free to decide how to spend their allocation. For example, one could exchange a day in VR for a month of living in a dark cabin.

There was also another kind of hunger. It was especially difficult early on, when Mom couldn't assimilate in this new world, with its evenly parceled spaces and clear boundaries. On the Zeta deck the difference between wellbeing and lack thereof was much more noticeable than on the vast Earth. The wise cat Uma, who didn't love people at the best of times, was now avoiding them altogether, making an exception only for Mom and Alik. In those days Alik wished that instead of books they would've packed the same weight in canned food. Mom guiltily said that canned food would run out, but the books were forever. Alik was not especially comforted by that, but ultimately Mom had turned out to be right. Over the course of five years, even the most frugal had run out of their personal supplies of Earth food.

Surprisingly, it was during those hunger-filled days that Alik came to appreciate what were seemingly the most useless of Mom's books—the cookbooks. Why drag into the unknown the recipes no one could ever cook, for lack of the right ingredients? And yet those recipes and the photographs depicting the prepared dishes surprisingly managed to comfort Alik in those hungry days.

TIME

The *Errata's* weird trajectory, where it raced toward the Sun and around Venus in order to achieve sufficient acceleration and escape faster, mystified Alik and instilled him with a sort of terror. Returning to Earth after this gravitational maneuver seemed to him like a form of time travel, and he kept waiting for the sighting of another *Errata* to be announced. The one at the beginning of its journey and headed toward Venus with another Alik onboard, two years younger and not yet fully aware that life had irrevocably changed.

And then they saw the Earth. Residents of the Zeta deck didn't usually see such things. Their days and nights were spent in the deep labyrinth of corridors. But this was a special occasion, and Mom brought Alik into the recreational zone of the upper decks, where images of receding Earth were transmitted onto huge screens.

Surprisingly, the *Errata* had its share of jumpers.

Alik heard of them back on Earth. Any ship that found itself in the vicinity of Earth after its gravitational maneuver around Venus had some people aboard who wanted to go back. Two years spent as sardines in a tin can were sufficient to realize their withering thirst for freedom and solid ground under their feet.

Few jumpers managed not to miss Earth entirely. Fewer still landed successfully. After the first several incidents, the arks tightened the control over their fleet of descent vehicles, but the jumpers managed to build their own shuttles in secret, out of whatever supplies they could find.

It was here and not in the moment of liftoff that a clear line delineating the past and the future existed for Alik. The past was left behind on Earth, with the jumpers carrying its last remaining crumbs in their fragile dinghies. The future was distant, somewhere on New Earth, which was a long journey away. Perhaps thousands of years long.

There was no here and now. Only timelessness.

THE SARCOPHAGI

Rows of suspended animation sarcophagi occupied the vast dark halls on the Alpha deck. Heroes slept within. Heroes akin to King Arthur in Avalon, or Commander Suvorov in the secret cave, or King Gesar in his hidden realm. Those heroes of old Earth slept the troubled sleep awaiting some future calamity where their strength would once again be needed. The new heroes slept deeply and had no intention of saving anyone. On the contrary, they entrusted the saving of their own lives to other people.

Movement between decks was limited by regulations, and the Alpha deck was strictly off limits. Alik, like all Zetans, had mastered the secrets of the service corridors in the early years of the journey. Alik was certain that those prohibitions were meant for adults. A child is permitted to make mistakes because they aren't expected to suffer any real punishment. It's after we grow up that we realize we only ever truly lived when we were children.

Alik would look upon the faces of these sleeping people and try to understand what made them more worthy of New Earth than him, his mother, or Uma. It was said the sarcophagi were occupied by major scientists and talented artists, but Gorchin grumbled that all the truly gifted people left Earth on ships named after goddesses. That, in lieu of the intellectual elite, this list of errors contained only rich cowards.

Trapped in their sarcophagi, those people could neither confirm nor deny the accusation. By the time they woke up, Gorchin, Mom, Alik, and Uma would be long gone. For now, their faces remained calm and serene.

If they were lucky, their sleep wasn't troubled by dreams.

JUPITER JACKETS

Few Zeta kids attended school. In a world where success is defined solely by one's ability to eat one's fill, every child was an extra pair of working hands.

Somehow, the enclosed space of the *Errata* also erected barriers for the imagination, locked up thoughts and cut off dreams. This, too, was an effect of timelessness. If the future won't come soon, and when it does, it will only come for those people on the Alpha deck and not for everyone else, then what's the point of dreaming? Any dream would be entrapped in a tiny matchbox racing through space toward the unknown.

The *Errata* would always need new engineers, biologists, and astrophysicists, Mom said. Alik focused on the word "need." How did that differ from the consumer culture of the Zeta deck?

There was the Jupiter jacket incident, where the cultures of the Zeta deck and the ship overall had gloriously clashed. The jackets appeared all over the marketplace when the *Errata* was passing by Jupiter. They were bought and sold, and fortunes were made. Everybody wanted to have one. Rumors circulated that the Jupiter cloth had a truly cosmic origin. That people on the decks above had deployed a special device to capture nearby meteorites, pulverize the ensnared matter into dust, and use this dust to print super strong meteorite cloth. That's what made those jackets glow gently in the dark.

There was a raid, and all the Jupiter jackets were confiscated: from the warehouses, from the sellers, and from those people who carelessly walked around wearing their purchases. Turns out it wasn't any sort of meteorite cloth, but some cunning thief finding their way into the sealed storage decks, where clothing for the colonists was stored.

There was nothing surprising about this; much of what was sold on the Zeta deck had similar origins. Even—Alik suspected— the supposedly decommissioned panels Gorchin had used to build Mom's bookshelves.

Aboard the *Errata* one could only live by serving somebody else's future, or by stealing from it. Alik was sickened by this realization.

Funny thing about the Jupiter jackets: upper deck people put their heads together and decided to distribute the jackets to the technicians—free of charge.

DREAMS

Alik slept uneasily.

He formulated the following explanation for his nightmares: the absorbers had malfunctioned due to the excess or lack of carbon dioxide. He began to suffocate, his heart raced, and his brain instantly came up with the plot that would explain those symptoms.

The alternative was to admit that Alik still pined for the Earth he could never return to.

Most of the time he dreamed about the days when they had been packing for the journey. It was a torturous dream, where Alik badly needed to bring along one of his naïve childish treasures: a plastic dinosaur, a slingshot, a matchbox filled with ball bearings—but he could never find them in the chaos of the preparations. In some of his dreams Mom would fly away and forget to bring Alik with her. He woke up feeling light, like all was right with the world. This feeling instantly disappeared, replaced by the shame and heaviness of the entire *Errata*, as though it wasn't the ship that carried Alik across the void, but rather it was Alik who was expected to carry the ship.

He'd experienced something similar back on Earth, when Dad had died. In his dreams, Dad performed everyday tasks: he washed dishes, returned home from picking mushrooms in the forest, played with Uma when she had still been a kitten. He'd see Alik and inquire gently: why did you bury me alive? It's fine, he added. Everything is going to be fine now. Alik would wake up endlessly happy, and then feel the realization of his father's death as deeply as he had the first time.

DEMON

Alik never talked to strangers about Mom's books. He could've turned her decision to bring them into a joke, but he was certain it would still result in pitying glances, and Alik hated to be pitied.

Later, it turned out he would garner no sympathy, but it was best not to speak about the books after all.

This happened the day he met Demon—one of those special contacts Danny would always mention. Demon was seventeen, a grown man, which made Danny proud of their friendship.

Danny assured them that he'd personally come up with the Saturn flyby idea. But, listening to Demon, Alik couldn't help but recall Mephistopheles. Demon had nudged gently, gradually, toward the correct understanding and the grandness of this adventure. He made it seem like the flyby was a historical necessity and a once-in-a-lifetime chance that only an idiot would pass up. Demon couldn't come along—he had work and important social obligations—they'd understand about those when they grew up. But he was ready to help in any way he could.

One small detail: despite his deepest sympathy for their cause, Demon's services weren't free. After all, he said, I'm risking as much as the rest of you. Perhaps more. As the great Keynes would say, how are you going to pay for this?

Danny's answer was to bring Demon to his father's office.

The office wasn't much at first glance: a tiny closet with a table, a chair, and a desk lamp. And a shelf of books. A tiny shelf with a half-dozen tomes.

The way Demon stared greedily at the shelf taught Alik two things. First, Danny had made a serious mistake by bringing Demon here. Second, the books were worth something in this new world after all. They were worth a lot.

Demon almost immediately pulled himself together and said that yes, as a favor, he'd be willing to accept the payment in books. But these weren't enough. One more book would do it.

Someone said, "We'll find one more." Alik realized that he was the one speaking those words.

THE PLAN

Steal the shuttle. Do a flyby according to the trajectory calculated in advance. Celebrate the New Year out there, while enjoying the view of the icy rings of Saturn. Use the planet's gravity to accelerate toward the *Errata* and catch up to it. Return as heroes and remember this adventure for the rest of their lives. Danny had been attending the navigation club for a year and a half now, and how difficult was any of this for someone with a brain and a pair of capable hands, anyway?

Alik listened to all of this with some doubt and even a bit of irony. For example, wasn't it foolish to celebrate the Earth New Year so far away from Earth orbit? Shouldn't they switch over to the Saturn calendar? New Year would come along rarely, but the good news was that, by the local timekeeping, they'd never grow old.

And then Mom said something that stuck with him.

Back on Earth, the horoscope had been an innocent pastime for her, a cause to share some laughs. A collection of the best predictions fit into a thick notebook. It was filled with pasted newspaper clippings from when she was young, when there was still a place for newspapers and clippings in anyone's reality.

Aboard the *Errata*, this notebook became the basis for her own system. By some convoluted method apparent only to herself, Mom counted pages and lines, divided them by dates of birth and multiplied by the day of the week, subtracted anxiety and added dreams. The result was presented to the questioner in all seriousness. There were plenty of people who would come to Mom in order to learn their fate. In changing times people are always more likely to believe in magic, miracles, and horoscopes, Mom would say. Why not console them in their search? But Alik could see that Mom herself was starting to believe that here, aboard the

Errata, the horoscopes had gained some additional significance. All of these ascending Saturns and Jupiters in retrograde were now within an arm's reach. And that meant something.

Alik usually had no trouble disregarding this nonsense. But one thing—not so much a prediction than a pronouncement, dug its claws into his consciousness, reminding of itself every now and again.

Mom had said, "You shouldn't celebrate the New Year at home."

At some point the puzzle pieces clicked into place: his search for meaning, Danny painting rosy pictures of their plans, Demon's promises, Mom's horoscope. As though Fate, easily avoided on the spacious Earth, waited for him around every corner in the narrow corridors of the *Errata*. It held up a sign pointing at Saturn: *Go that way.*

LOT 17

Alik didn't plan on saying goodbye to Mom; she would detect the tiniest falsehood in his voice. In the morning, as she got ready for work, he lay in bed with his nose toward the wall and listened to his racing heart.

When Mom left, Alik suddenly and sharply regretted that he didn't at least turn around and glance at her for what might have been the last time.

As certain as Danny was of their success, space was space. After all, Alik had joined this adventure so he could feel alive. And a person never feels as alive as when they're at the edge of death.

The dispatch told Alik that Mom was working on Lot 17 that day. A tattered paper map hung on the wall nearby, and Alik discovered by studying this map that Lot 17 had been exposed to vacuum as recently as a week ago, but now it was possible to reach it without a spacesuit.

For some reason, and despite Mom's encouragement, Alik had never visited the border lots before. Chasing its launch window, the *Errata* had left Earth half-baked. Alik was used to seeing this through the eyes of Gorchin and other residents of Zeta who took the fact that the ship was incomplete as a sure sign of the universe's personal antipathy toward each and every one of them.

Alik followed strange paths getting to Lot 17. He screwed something up and found himself near the ceiling of a cavernous space. He cautiously looked down as he made his way to the edge of a jutting metal beam. He felt like a character from the "Lunch atop a Skyscraper" photograph, a copy of which hung in their cabin.

He heard discontented rumbling behind him. He turned to find Uma the cat perched atop the neighboring beam, her front paws dangling over the abyss. This was a great spot to watch people while hiding from them.

There was no New York City below, but the view was no less majestic. Huge forklifts and walking cranes moved smoothly. On the walls and floor, hanging on cables under the ceiling, on beams and dividers, people were working. They fired up their welding tools, laughed, quarreled. In front of Alik's eyes they clawed back space from the infinite universe. They didn't do it for some future generations or the strangers sleeping in sarcophagi, but for themselves. For their children. For Alik.

Alik had never been to a place like this and now he was astounded. How was it possible to live among all this and never notice?

This was the *Errata* as his Mom saw it. And, apparently, so did Uma. Perhaps everyone else did, too? Except Alik, who had wandered within a stone's throw of this miracle and had never realized it.

Alik couldn't see Mom from up there, but he suddenly realized he didn't need to.

THE DOCKS

The narrow, poorly lit corridors appeared to Alik in a different light. They regained the sense of wonder that had been lost somewhere en route between Earth and Venus. In the early days he would stop in some random corridor and think, *I'm in space!*

He could've simply never showed up at the docks, but Alik had given his word and, like a magnet, this promise pulled him toward the shuttles. Besides, this was a rare chance to visit an area where people like Alik weren't normally allowed.

Still, he felt a timid hope that the code Demon had provided wouldn't work, and the door wouldn't open.

The code worked. The second one, too.

The corridors by the docks were empty. They had probably been much better-guarded when the ship had passed by Earth. Or perhaps it had to do with the upcoming holiday. Holidays tend to make people relax. As though nothing bad could ever happen during a holiday.

He felt troubled for some reason. Perhaps this is how a plastic hockey player might feel having left his usual track on the toy hockey field. The childish feeling of being able to do what he pleased with no consequences evaporated, as though his decision had changed his status. He was no longer a kid.

Demon seemed nervous as he waited by the eleventh gate.

Alik proffered a book to Demon. This was the price of his freedom. He'd changed his mind about coming along, but the book was promised as part of the payment for everyone. He decided not to say goodbye to the other boys—it would be a long and inappropriate conversation.

You chickened out, Demon declared. Alik merely waved him off. He wasn't about to try and explain the miracle he'd recently witnessed, or talk about time and souls. Especially since he didn't understand those things very well himself, he only felt them.

Alik headed back, feeling deep regret over the loss of the book. Not because he now knew its price in the world of the *Errata*, but because this particular book was precious to him. He'd picked it because he considered this book to be his. An ancient edition with pages falling out which had been reassembled and painstakingly stitched. A little girl and a smiling cat were depicted on the cover. Mom used to read it when Alik was little, so he'd fall asleep. And his name was similar to the name of the girl from the book. He was a bit annoyed at the similarity at first, but the girl had proved herself to be quite clever, so it was okay.

HERE AND NOW

Alik never heard the footsteps behind him. He suddenly found himself on the floor, and only then felt the pain of being hit and then hit again in the kidney. Along with the pain came desperate clarity. Some people never experience this in their entire lives: to clearly, and in great detail, see the mechanisms of the surrounding world, or at least a minor part of it. That's when Alik realized he was about to die, because this sort of insight was only revealed in the moments preceding death.

He turned around and saw Demon, scared and angry, and saw the intertwined reasons and motives. Demon was the man of timelessness, the same sort of man Alik had almost become, too. A tiny grain of dust within the matchbox floating in endless darkness. A plastic hockey player who only knew how to move within the track cut out for him in the toy hockey field. We're the same as our world. And our world is the same as us.

Now it was perfectly clear that Demon was only interested in precious books. He'd never even considered that Danny and the boys might succeed, that their shuttle might do a flyby of Saturn and successfully return to the *Errata*. By now Alik realized this was a mad plan. He wondered if Demon might've been connected to the jumpers who fled to Earth three years ago.

Alik had a bit of experience fighting in the corridors of the Zeta deck. His sweep was clumsy, but Demon stumbled and Alik managed to get up and take a few steps. A thought stopped him: he could get away, but then the boys would perish.

He could scream—Danny would hear him. But would he decide that their plot was uncovered and ship security was after them? Would the warning only accelerate their liftoff?

Not knowing what he was doing, Alik began to sing, badly and loudly, making up the melody as he went:

> "Beware the Jabberwock, my son!
>   The jaws that bite, the claws that catch!
> Beware the Jubjub bird, and shun
>   The frumious Bandersnatch!"

A blow to the solar plexus shut him up as it knocked the wind out of him. Another blow to the teeth and a hail of random other blows followed. He fell again and rolled, trying to cover his head.

Out of the corner of his eye, Alik noticed a bright spot: Uma the cat had snuck after him to the docks and now awaited the outcome of the battle with lazy indifference. Goodbye, Uma.

Perhaps he'd underestimated her antipathy toward people. When Devil swung again, Uma lunged at his face with impeccable aim and dug her claws in. Demon howled.

Then Alik heard voices. He thought it was Danny and the others, but maybe it was someone else. Perhaps the entire ship were gathering here to watch time return to Alik. And it *was* returning.

Alik felt the texture of the here and now. Something he thought had been irrevocably lost, dissolved in memories of the past and worries about the future. Life was here and now, trickling through his fingers in little streams of blood, warm and salty to the touch. This is what's called synesthesia, Alik recalled. Maybe that's what one's soul felt like, after a long period of absence. He tried to smile, but a mere attempt sent waves of terrible pain through his entire body.

THE CLOCK

When he opened his eyes, Alik thought for a brief moment that he was inside a sarcophagus on the Alpha deck. He saw the world through a volume of water that filled the glass sarcophagus Alik was floating in, upright. His first thought was: not now. Not after time had returned, filled his blood and given him meaning. Alik tried to hit the glass; maybe it wasn't too late? He didn't have the strength. Also, he could make out the room—greenish through the prism of the regenerative liquid—and realized his mistake. He was in the medical bay on one of the upper decks. Of course, no one planned to send him into a thousand-year-long sleep. They were only trying to heal him.

Mom slept in the chair in the corner, wrapped in a Jupiter jacket. A digital clock displayed numbers above her head. 23:59 turned to 00:00 and the sounds of cheering emanated tentatively and then louder and louder from somewhere beyond the wall.

Uma the cat sat on the floor directly opposite Alik and looked at him with undisguised curiosity. She probably mistook him for a large, ridiculous fish.

Alik waved at her.

UNTILTED

FIRSTLY, MY NAME IS MARCUS.

Grandma sumtimes calls me Marcy. Marcy is a girls name.

I should make her stop caling me by a girls name. But I cant. She washed my soiled diapers when I was litle. She didnt sleep nites. She personaly received me from the stork. She pulled me from the cabbage patch. She did loads of other stuff for me too.

So I cant make her. I can only ask. Ask her not to call me Marcy in front of polite society. (That's how Grandma says it: "In front of polite society.") Also, not to call me Bunny.

But sumtimes she forgets. Sumtimes she calls me Marcy. Or Bunny. I roll my eyes and make "that face," and she apologizes and buys icecream.

She calls me "Marco Polo" only when she wants to needle me. Like when I did sumthing wrong. One time, after she did that, I called her an old crone. She was very upset.

Secondly, write your name at the bottom.

Thirdly: I AM SERIOUS.

P.S. Ostriches.

Ostriches? What do ostriches have to do with anything, Marcus thought.

The note turned out even dumber than usual. But sometimes you have to do dumb things in order to achieve clever results.

Marcus rips the sheet from his notepad. On the back, it says "October 17" and "Homework" in neat letters, very different from the chicken scratch of the note. That's because he wrote the note just now, while riding on the metro station escalator, but the date he wrote back home, on Grandma's desk, under her stern gaze. Not the real her, but her portrait where she's still young, sporting a killer hairdo and a smartly starched shirt.

The rest of the back of the sheet is blank. He never finished the composition about autumn.

The escalator has almost reached the bottom, and time is running out.

Marcus reviews the note. Everything seems in place, exactly as it should be. Even the "October 17" and "Homework" written on the back. Even the mention of "soiled diapers," which Grandma would have raised her eyebrow at. Sorry, Grandma. It's necessary.

Everything is in place. All that's missing is the title. Every important document has an official title, like "Report" or "Declaration" or "Certificate." In this case he could go with an "Agreement" or even a "Contract." But too much honesty can be a bad thing in what he's attempting. Sometimes it's better to do without a title. He writes at the top of the page in large, messy letters: "UNTILTED."

Perfect. The letters form a pattern, whisper urgently to each other, grasp at each other as if getting ready for a circle dance.

Marcus jumps off the escalator and shoves the notepad into his backpack as he runs. His steps echo across the empty station, but are quickly drowned out by the sound of an approaching train. His heart skips. Is he too late?

No. The train arrives on the right side of the platform. He needs the left.

He sees the girl—woman?—standing at the very edge of the platform, staring into the darkness of the tunnel.

She's probably too old to be in high school. Marcus isn't good at estimating people's ages. Some dress like teenagers well into their fifties while others look like young retirees while they're still attending school. Some, like Grandma, glow as though they're filled to the brim with fireflies, while others are filled only with darkness and bitter smoke from an extinguished candle.

The woman across the platform is among the latter. She looks like a sad outer shell of a nesting doll after someone removed everything inside.

He follows her because he needs a guide.

The underpass at Serpukhovsky Square is too long to cross on one's own. Almost endless. It's poorly lit, and although it seems harmless, no one in their right mind should brave it alone.

Marcus knows: underpasses lie in wait, stalking lonely pedestrians whose disappearance would not be noticed by the passers-by. And once an underpass captures its victim, it never lets go. At first one wouldn't even notice that anything is wrong. They'd walk on and on, barely registering that the underpass seems longer than usual. Then they'd realize that there is no exit ahead. They'd turn around and see only darkness.

Marcus feels relatively safe in short underpasses, even when he's alone. He can walk and talk on a cell phone. Even if his interlocutor doesn't see him, their voice is a decent anchor. But the Serpukhovsky Square underpass is too long. Also, the battery in Marcus's phone is dead.

That's why he needs a guide.

She walks past him, shoulders slumped, face hidden under a hood.

Marcus follows, then overtakes her and walks a few steps in front of her, making sure she can see him. He turns around often. After all, that's an honest bargain: she guides him, and he guides her.

When they cross the underpass, she lingers a few moments and turns toward the metro station. She is almost out of sight when Marcus realizes he had to catch up to her right away.

*

A gust of wind from the tunnel caresses her blond hair. Marcus can't see her face, but he's sure she isn't smiling. He's certain she hasn't smiled for a long time.

Marcus feels her pain. Not as though he's experiencing it himself; it's more like watching a YouTube video of a dying dog. (What kind of a person films and posts a thing like that?)

From within the tunnel he can already hear the oncoming train. He can see the glimmers from its headlights reflecting against the rails. Marcus takes a deep breath and approaches the woman. He touches her arm gently to gain her attention, and offers her the note.

These days it's naïve to assume that a person would accept something from a stranger. This might never work on the street in daylight. But there's something about the empty subway platform at night that makes Marcus believe she'll take the note. Then it will be up to the words. They have to work. They must.

The nesting doll turns and looks at him with a mix of surprise and confusion. She accepts the note.

The train rumbles as it enters the station and comes to a stop.

The train leaves the station and she's still reading the note trying to make sense of it. Did a child hand it to her?

She was certain she'd go through with it until the last moment. It would be easy to take just one step. She could have jumped out a window—that's even easier, especially after a few glasses of Chardonnay. She couldn't cut her veins, but stepping through a window? Sure. It's only a single step, same as here.

But there's something showy about jumping from a window. Something hysterical. "People will talk," her mother would have said.

It may seem there's nothing more showy and hysterical than stepping in front of an oncoming train, but Dahlia knows this not to be the case. Metro is such a lonely place, even in the middle of the day, in the middle of a crowd. Especially so at night.

She left her wallet at home. No one will recognize her. No one will search for her. Just another faceless statistic lost among the ones and zeroes of some database. Used to be a one, now a zero.

But she couldn't do it in front of the child. Where did he come from, so late at night?

An old man pushes his cart out of the train car. He looks at Dahlia suspiciously, mutters something under his breath. The wheels of his cart squeak unpleasantly.

Dahlia realizes she's shaking. Her head is swimming. Her feet feel weak. She needs to sit down. She was certain she'd go through with it, until the last moment.

She programmed herself to do it step by step, like the Curiosity Rover. Fly to Mars. Collect data. Send data home. Period. What does the rover do if it flies to Mars, but Mars isn't there?

The rover reads Marcus's note.

Please stand clear of the closing doors. Next stop, Tulskaya Station.

Marcus holds his breath like he always does when someone is reading one of his notes. It's a little like a papier-mâché volcano school project: you set off the chemical reaction and don't really expect it to work, but it always does.

The words are like that. They seem stupid, naïve. Childish. All the typos, the asides—they seem like nonsense, as though Marcus wrote them while suffering from a Tourette's episode. They shouldn't work but, like the volcano, they do.

This is why Marcus hates writing essays. It requires too much effort to string words together that make sense. In the end, they are just words. In the end, the volcano doesn't erupt.

Marcus can tell exactly when she reaches the line about the ostriches. He offers her a ballpoint pen with a chewed plastic cap. Grandma's vintage pen, made back in the Soviet times.

I hope she's like the girls from school, thinks Marcus, because schoolgirls like to write their names on sheets of paper.

They also like to draw hearts and kittens, but mostly they like to write their names.

The boy patiently waits for her to finish reading. He is small and wiry, and wears an old-fashioned checkered coat. The sort of coat parents like, but show it to a school bully and it will set them off like waving a red rag in front of a bull. He wears a huge blue backpack, square and silly-looking. A striped hat with a pompon.

Without really knowing why, Dahlia signs the note. The pen puts a small hole through the paper on the last letter.

Should the rover return to Earth if it fails to locate Mars? Can it?

Dahlia looks at the boy. He stares back silently.

She has to break the silence, so she says, "Now what?" Her voice is drowned out by the oncoming train on the opposite platform.

The boy looks at his watch and says, "Cat."

"What?"

Please stand clear of the closing doors. Next stop, Polyanka Station.

"Cat!" he shouts over the announcement.

So, she heard right. "What do you mean, 'cat'?" She asks the question realizing there can be no logical answer here. One of them must be nuts.

He waits for the noise of the departing train to abate, then explains with a note of long-suffering indulgence in his voice: "It's exactly midnight now, so the new day has begun." He looks at her, realizes she needs more details. The notes of indulgence in his voice crescendo into a symphony. "You know, like when you move into a new apartment, you have to let the cat in first. For luck. *Capisce?*"

New day? New apartment? Cat for luck? This smacks of sur- realism. Maybe she's gorged on too much Chardonnay and fell asleep? Or perhaps she took that step after all and is lying on the tracks right now like a broken doll, her dying brain hallucinating this conversation?

"Are you insane?"

"Grandma says I'm not."

He gently takes the note from her and folds it over several times.

"What do you need my name for?"

Another train is approaching. It beckons.

Not in front of the child!

"Maybe I need it to steal your soul with voodoo. I'm kidding! Strictly speaking, I don't need your name at all. In fact, you shouldn't give out your name to strangers like this, next time. How do you know I'm not dangerous?" Then he adds, "I'm going to call you Nesting Doll. Do you like it?"

"Then I'll call you Marcy."

"Ha! Fine, then." After a brief silence: "Just so you know, you signed the contract."

He says "contract" in a way that makes Dahlia certain he'd write it with a capital C. Or in all caps.

Thirdly: I AM SERIOUS.

It's like with a stray puppy: it finds you in the street and looks at you in that begging manner that only dogs can master. If you give it a piece of bread or even just glance at it, it'll be ready to follow you to the ends of the earth. One glance and the puppy will make the decision for the both of you.

You're forced to take the bus just so it can't follow you, even though you're only one stop away from home. You rationalize this to yourself: the puppy belongs to someone and you don't want it to get lost following you around. This sort of inner monolog is tiresome and painful and it ruins your day: far better never to look at the stray puppy—and certainly not to give it bread—in the first place.

It's really difficult not to ask, "What contract?" But she manages it. She marches toward the escalator.

The Nesting Doll—no, Dahlia, what an unusual name—forges ahead, her gaze filled with a hellish mix of anguish, exhaustion, and curiosity. She seems unhappy to be curious (as though she could presently be happy about anything at all), but there isn't anything she can do about that. It's the words in the note. They bewitch her.

They ride the escalator up. Dahlia begins walking up the stairs—some people are always in a rush, the speed of the escalator isn't enough for them—but Marcus slides past her, stops a couple of steps ahead of her and turns to face her. The height of the steps places them eye to eye.

"You're a quick one," she says.

"Sure am."

"Okay, fine. What's the point of this contract? Not to call you Marcy?"

"That too."

"Why would anyone call a boy that?"

"It's because I'm adorable, like a girl. Everyone wants to pinch my cheeks."

"I don't."

"You just don't know me yet."

She looks like an actor who studied her lines and dressed the part of Guildenstern only to enter the stage and find herself in the middle of a science fiction play about scientists studying cell division. The actors and the audience all stare at her waiting for some clever twist, but all she's got is the "Happy, in that we are not over-happy" line.

"How old are you?" she asks.

"What, are you gonna ask me who I want to be when I grow up next?"

"I couldn't care less."

Yeah, right. Every single adult he talks to for more than a few moments invariably asks that question.

She looks at the note in his hand. Marcus also looks at it. Seemingly realizes what she's thinking.

"If you're wondering about the misspellings, they're intentional. Part of the plan. Wanna know why?" She is quiet, but not in the leave-me-alone way, so Marcus continues. "First, to divert the focus of your attention. Cognitive dissonance. Our brains are designed to zero in on errors and paradoxes, and weird stuff. It's like shock therapy for your mind. Drunk sailors riding zebras, that sort of thing."

He could have diverted her attention in some other way too. Like maybe pull down his pants and pee onto the rails. But then Dahlia probably wouldn't be talking to him now. At the moment, she's looking at him as though he did pee on the rails. A typical adult reaction to his theories.

"That worked," she says. "I missed my train. So, congratulations on all your success."

"You should congratulate me on the fact that I changed your mind about jumping in front of that train."

"I didn't . . ." She trails off. Frowns. But she doesn't turn away.

"I know you didn't *really* change your mind. But, let's say, you've rescheduled the performance."

"So . . . now what?"

Marcus shrugs. The next and most important step is more difficult to explain. Important steps are like that, not easily expressed in words.

He says, "I'm going to rid you of your pain."

I'm going to rid you of your pain. That's what he said.

Little liar.

Dahlia knows this to be impossible.

They say time heals all wounds. But she knows time is more like a doctor: it diagnoses you, writes you prescriptions, and schedules follow-up visits. But it doesn't *heal.*

Time prescribes you pain killers and vitamins, and you gullibly buy them and swallow them by the handful. By the time all your money is gone, you realize that the pain killers are no longer having their effect, and the vitamins make your stomach turn. You realize that the pain only got worse. That you can't avoid thinking about it.

You can't stop remembering, again and again—until you find

yourself at the metro platform, waiting for the train to arrive so you can take one final step.

The nurse said something about "FD." The doctor replied, "I see it." Dahlia was on the exam table for the ultrasound, the doctor moving the probe across her belly covered in cold, sticky goo. Then the doctor told her to get dressed and handed her a napkin.

Dahlia had hated ultrasounds since she was a kid. The procedure always invoked something scary and dangerous. When the doctor explained that "FD" meant "fetal demise," her childhood fears became realized.

She didn't respond, and the doctor told her, "You're holding up great. Don't despair—you can still have kids."

She stepped outside and saw women with protruding bellies—third trimester—hiding behind the gazebo while they smoked and gossiped. That's when she began to cry.

She wasn't holding up well at all.

Andrej said, "Everything will be all right, dear. We'll try again. Time heals all wounds."

He couldn't have known that it would never be all right again.

She locked herself in the bedroom and stared at the wallpaper patterns.

From behind the door, he said, "I have to go to work." He asked, "Can I come in and give you a kiss?"

"Go away," she told him.

And then some unhinged manager shot up their office. Of course, Andrej tried to stop him. Three gunshot wounds to the chest. There wasn't even time to call an ambulance.

All because the last thing she said to him was "Go away."

If only she had let him in.

If only he had come in and kissed her, she would have told him, "Stay. Let's look for patterns in the wallpaper together."

If only.

*

"I can help you, but first you have to help me," he says.

"It was stolen from me," he says.

"You signed the contract," he says.

Then he tells her, "At least walk me through the underpass," and she thinks of stray puppies and she can't refuse him. It's one in the morning, it's dark and cold, and who knows if there isn't some maniac hiding in the shadows. When they exit the subway onto the street he tells her, "The hotel isn't far away." She thinks that's reasonable: walk him to the hotel so he realizes his plan is no good and agrees to go home, or at least tells her his parents' phone number.

They amble down some unfamiliar alley, snow in their faces. Dahlia doesn't even know where they are anymore: still near Serpukhovskaya Metro station or all the way in Saint Petersburg.

"You're definitely crazy," she says.

"Grandma says I'm not."

"Is your grandma a psychiatrist?"

"My grandma's dead."

Uncomfortable silence.

"I'm sorry."

"We're almost there," Marcus says.

Dahlia realizes the subway is closed for the night, so she can't complete the program of her Mars rover even if she wanted to. She could call a taxi and go home, drink her Chardonnay (there's probably still a bottle left in the fridge) and then step out of the window. But her apartment is only on the third floor. She won't feel better if she breaks her back.

Or she could spend the night staring at the patterns of her wallpaper again. They won't be comforting; she'll catch glimpses of the eyes and teeth of the monsters hidden within.

It's as though Marcus hears her thoughts. "You signed the contract," he says.

He looks at her sternly and she capitulates. "Fine. What are you trying to find?"

*

Grandma told him, "Don't cry, kiddo. Everything will be fine."

He really was a kid back then. About four years old. *Old*. By that logic, he'll one day be seventy years *young*.

It was all the swing set's fault. One of those squeaking monsters that can be found on every playground, irritating anyone within earshot. Except for kids, because kids aren't bothered by the annoying noises. Kids are themselves the source of all things loud and unbearable.

The very existence of this swing set irritated Marcus. It was a trial. A test. The older kids, including the first-grader, told him that no one on the playground was considered a person until they swung all the way around. Marcus didn't know how to do this. He was afraid. But he tried anyway.

He doesn't remember what happened exactly, other than flying into the prickly embrace of a bush and then suffering a hellish pain in his knee. And the knowledge that nothing will ever be okay again.

Then he cried hysterically.

Grandma treated the bruises with rubbing alcohol, but he didn't feel better. Maybe it wasn't the skinned knee, maybe it was his wounded pride. Because when he flew into the bush, the older kids laughed like they expected him to fail. Someone said, "Wheee!" and added, "Cosmonaut!"

Grandma pulled a box from the shelf and told him, "Look. There will be magic." But the right thing to say would have been, "Listen."

She turned the key several times and opened the lid.

Marcus heard music. For a moment, he felt as though instead of sitting on a stool in the kitchen with puffy eyes and a skinned knee he was lying on his back on the surface of a huge ocean, with miles of warm saltwater underneath. A gentle sun warmed his face and slow waves rocked him and carried him somewhere far away.

Grandma closed the box.

Incredible! The knee didn't hurt anymore. At all. Even the

rubbing alcohol didn't sting. Better yet, the memory of the embarrassing fall dissipated and faded away. It was like a scene featuring a bunch of strangers he saw in an old photograph. It no longer ate at him.

He didn't understand what was happening at first.

He visited Grandma in her room. She was in bed, drowning in pillows and blankets—pre-war artifacts she might have received as wedding gifts. She often asked him to read to her, and Marcus always did. He read from *Gone with the Wind*, a terribly boring book.

Grandma grew tired quickly.

There was something wrong with Marcus too, but he didn't understand what it was. It felt as though a monster nested in his chest, putting pressure on his heart. The monster made it difficult to breathe. He constantly wanted to cry. But why? He wasn't the one who was ill.

Mom asked why he wasn't visiting Grandma. He said, "I am."

He would peek into her room, see her lying there without moving, breathing heavily. He would run away, hide in the closet among coats and jackets, and cry.

One time, an ambulance came. Paramedics said Grandma should go to the hospital.

Grandma said no. She said, "I want to die at home."

But no one listened to her. Mom hugged her from one side. The paramedic supported her from the other. They led her to the front door.

Marcus hid in the closet and watched through the crack in the door. He couldn't bear to see Grandma like this. But he also couldn't bear to look away.

It was intolerably painful.

Grandma stopped. She turned and looked, seemingly, right at him. As though she knew he was there. She said, "I'm not going to fight you all, damn it." Surprisingly, she smiled. It was a pained, pale smile, but it was a smile.

And then she said, "Let's sit for a moment." And, "Bring me the music box."

Marcus wondered if she was talking to him, but Mom went and got it.

Marcus thought, why didn't I think of that? And neither did Grandma? Why suffer when you can hide the pain away in the music box?

Grandma leaned over the music box, whispered something, and turned the key. She opened the box.

Marcus thought, now everything is going to be fine. He felt light and unburdened, as though someone had scooped out all his pain and fear.

And then he woke up, and Mom told him that Grandma had passed away in the hospital.

Something was wrong, but at first, he didn't realize it.

There was a funeral followed by a wake. Strange people milled around the apartment. They patted him on the head, pitied him. They said, "Poor boy, you loved your grandmother so very much."

But he didn't feel a thing. It was as though she'd gone to the store, or left on vacation. Nothing to mourn.

He felt the others mourn. Grandma's friend was in hysterics but he somehow knew that while she was sad, she wasn't quite as upset as she made it seem. On the other hand, an old neighbor who would occasionally go with grandma for long walks in the park was far more distraught than he let show.

Far more distraught than Mom was.

But how could Marcus blame Mom if he felt nothing himself? Grandma was dead and he wanted to cry, really wanted to, but he couldn't.

He also caught himself beginning to forget some of the details about her, as though she had been some insignificant stranger. An unfamiliar old woman in someone's photo journal.

And then he realized: the music box.

She hadn't hidden away her pain. She'd hidden *his* pain.

He also realized he wanted his pain back.

He found the music box and turned the key. It played "Polonaise Farewell" by Oginski and nothing else happened. His pain didn't come back. He punched the music box, shook it, wound it up all the way. Nothing. The stupid box didn't work.

Later he picked up a kitten in the yard. It was dirty, wet, and scared. He gave it a saucer of milk and wrapped it in Mom's Angora wool blanket. But the kitten wouldn't stop trembling. Whenever Marcus let it go, it hid in the farthest corner under the bed.

Marcus thought that perhaps the music would calm it down. He found the music box in the desk drawer, turned the key and opened it. The box played only a few notes of the polonaise before it stopped, but that was enough. After hearing the music, the kitten climbed out from under the bed and lapped the milk. Marcus's knee hurt for several days afterward.

That's how he learned that you can't simply put the pain away in the music box, or retrieve it. You can only trade one pain for another.

And then the music box disappeared.

Marcus finishes the note and shows it to Dahlia. It says:

I am cold and my cellfone batery died and I have to wait for Mom. Please may I wait inside?

Also please can I have sum TEA?

Dahlia looks at Marcus skeptically, then at the night desk clerk, whom she can clearly see through the window. This plan might have worked if the clerk were female. Better yet, an older woman. But behind the counter she sees a young man, the unyielding sort who follows rules to the letter in hopes of accelerating his climb up the corporate ladder, or at least earning a bonus. It's unlikely that the company handbook covers letting strange children warm up in the lobby, let alone making them tea.

"You're underestimating the power of words," says Marcus. "Here I go."

Dahlia wants to stop him, to say that she doesn't believe this plan will work, that this is all madness and that she's done, but Marcus marches inside and looks pleadingly at the clerk as he hands him the note. And then the clerk is pointing Marcus toward the couch in the lobby and heads somewhere deeper into the bowels of the hotel. She can hardly believe it.

While Dahlia ponders if perhaps she should make her escape now that the night clerk seems to have taken responsibility for the child and she no longer has the excuse of "I can't leave him alone on the street at night," Marcus retrieves the key he needs from its slot behind the counter, runs out the front door and drags Dahlia inside.

He hands her a flashlight and tells her to point it down, and then she is inside and the door closes behind her, and she wonders, how the hell does he do that?

The hotel room is cool and smells pleasantly of men's cologne.

Dahlia leans with her back against the door, behind which she can hear the boy's receding footsteps.

She clicks the flashlight on. Its dim beam barely penetrates the darkness. A useless toy. She feels along the wall for a switch and flips it on. Let there be light.

There's an open suitcase on the floor, shirts and socks hanging over all four of its edges as though they were crawling to freedom, but Dahlia's presence forced them to temporarily play dead. Andrej would never be this messy, she thought. Her own suitcase might look like this, but Andrej always packed with neat, practical efficiency.

Dahlia hates going through other people's things. Even when she was a kid she never looked in her mom's handbag without asking. More than anything, she wants to grab the little troublemaker by his shirttails, and make him rummage through these clothes himself. She chases away the cowardly idea of leaving and telling Marcus that she searched the room and found no music box.

After all, she's bound by contract. No one forced her to write her name on that silly piece of paper. No one but her is to blame for ending up in this stupid situation. But then, her bloody corpse lying on the rails would have been even more stupid. And even more scary.

She recalls the game she used to play as a child, whenever she was alone and bored, waiting for something. She could pretend she was a little princess, transplanted to a strange world by the power of unknowable magic. Or, perhaps, she's an alien invader who sneaks into the neighborhood library to get her hands on the valuable tome about the adventures of Tarzan.

Neither scenario quite fits her current predicament. Perhaps she's James Bond, set out to save the world from her latest nemesis. If so, then her clothes are chockfull of cool spy gadgets and she isn't afraid of this room's tenant. Also, if she were James Bond, she'd be buzzed on martinis and ready to overcome any obstacle.

She looks inside the wardrobe, the nightstand, the fridge. She checks under the pillow, the mattress, the bed. She even tries the windowsill behind the curtain and moves the painting on the wall, looking for a hidden safe. She pushes the clothes in the suitcase around with the tail end of her flashlight.

Nothing. There's no music box. Even James Bond is powerless in this predicament.

Dahlia turns off the light and gets ready to make her escape when she remembers the restroom. Maybe the box is hidden inside the toilet tank? As she's checking the tank, she hears the front door creak. She hears cautious footsteps. Someone enters the hotel room, stops in front of the restroom door. She hears breathing. Dahlia waits, motionless. From the corner of her eye, she catches a glimpse of herself in the mirror: a ridiculous, disheveled woman in an unkempt down jacket, holding the flashlight above her head like a club.

She can't stop herself from snorting.

Marcus whispers from behind the door, "Are you in the bathroom?" Without waiting for a response, he opens the door. "Quit wasting time." He sounds cheerful. He seems like he's barely holding himself back from giving her a hug. He must've been afraid she would split.

The elevator dings in the corridor.

Marcus's face turns somber. "It's him."

She doesn't have to ask who he means. The tenant of this room has become synonymous with something scary and relentless.

There's a sound of approaching footsteps, softened by the hallway's carpet but distinct in the quiet of the night. Dahlia thinks, maybe this is somebody else, headed to another room. Marcus isn't so optimistic. He turns off the light, grabs her by the hand and pulls her toward the closet. She stumbles over the suitcase in the dark. They get inside the closet. Marcus pulls its door closed just as the front door is opening.

Marcus thinks maybe he should not have turned off the light. Or at least shouldn't have shut the closet door tight. Inside the dark closet, he feels the same way he does in a dark underpass.

Perhaps closets are branches of the underpass. Small field offices. Especially the closet that belongs to That Man.

As well as That Man, himself.

He showed up out of nowhere, looking like he was put together from the faults and flaws of ten different people. People who got chewed up and swallowed by the underpass.

What if the underpass is hunting him?

What if this is a trap?

What if That Man appeared just so he could lure Marcus here?

What if That Man isn't a man at all, but a golem, a Frankenstein's monster built out of flaws? Built out of all the things Marcus hates?

Marcus thinks it may not help that there are two of them, so long as each of them feels alone. Perhaps the underpass is capable of swallowing both of them at once. Perhaps they'll never get out of here alive.

Marcus squeezes Dahlia's hand.

*

Dahlia thinks she was probably wrong: lying dead on the tracks would be preferable to this.

And then the lights come on and an unfamiliar voice says, "Come out, Marcus. I know you're there."

Marcus squeezes her hand tighter as though to say: Don't answer. He can't possibly know I'm here.

"You come out too, young lady," the voice adds.

"This is ridiculous," says Dahlia.

"Not at all," says Marcus.

"It is. Haven't you heard of Occam's razor?"

"I'm too young to shave. Just kidding. Yeah, I heard of it. Outdated thinking. The world is much more complex than it appears."

"Okay, suppose you're right. Suppose dinosaurs never existed and all those bones and skulls and stuff are fake. Who do you think is behind that? Who benefits?"

They're sitting in the hotel lobby. This deep scientific discussion is a passable distraction for Dahlia, so she doesn't have to think about what happened upstairs. About how she helped a child break into a stranger's room. Perhaps she wouldn't feel so bad if the stranger had shouted at her. She could've shouted back, could've gotten into an argument. The great thing about arguments is that even if you begin with the full knowledge that you're wrong, when you keep it up long enough you begin to buy into your own statements until you're certain there is no version of truth other than your own.

But the man calmly introduced himself as Igor. He said that Marcus's mother would be there in twenty minutes. And that they could wait at reception. That the night clerk had tea and cookies. And that he, Igor, would gladly invite them to wait in the room, except he is certain Marcus wouldn't assent.

Marcus exited the closet with all the dignity of a crown prince who was caught in the act of playing the ukulele, and left the room without saying a word to Igor.

So, they're sitting in the lobby and Marcus is eating a cookie, folding a magazine page into a paper dinosaur, and saying utter nonsense.

"There are lots of options. At a minimum, it benefits the paleontologists. What a wonderful idea, to make up their own profession! I bet they have a secret society, with initiation rites and decoder rings. They get grants, business trips, plenty of fresh air working outdoors. I mean, I'm not judging. It's not like they were the first to do something like this."

"Oh? And who was the first?"

"That's obvious: mathematicians! Physics, chemistry, the exact sciences—I get that. They study the real world. But math is pure abstraction. Hi, Mom!"

Marcus switches the subject so smoothly, for a second Dahlia thinks this may be another one of his games. She turns around.

"Mom, this is Dahlia. Dahlia, Mom."

Dahlia thinks back to when her own mother brought her to school for the first time. How she stared at all the other moms, evaluating them.

Everyone else's mom was dressed and made up according to the latest fashion, wearing fancy haircuts and designer purses. Her own mom seemed out of place, like an old Ford sedan that mistakenly drove onto the floor of the auto show displaying the latest sports cars.

Marcus's mom would have been a Lexus or even a Lamborghini of that group. She was tall, pretty, very well put together. Even after spending half a night searching for her son, her makeup was perfect.

Marcus's mom doesn't look at Dahlia. She looks at Marcus. Silently.

Dahlia knows this silent treatment. Her own mother used it when fifteen-year-old Dahlia didn't come home one evening. Mom stayed up all night waiting for her, then worked her shift at the warehouse. And when she came home and saw her sleepy, hung-over daughter, she didn't say one word. Despite her fiery temperament, there was no "You're punished." No "You're ground-ed." Only a tired silence.

The silence grows awkward.

Finally, Marcus's mom says, "Dahlia, thank you for watching after Mark."

That's how she says it: Mark. This version wasn't on Marcus's list. It takes Dahlia a moment to realize she's talking about him.

She should say something, but she's afraid. She fears that the evening will end, they will leave and she will be alone with her thoughts.

Marcus's mom says, "I bought a really nice Darjeeling today. How do you feel about it?"

Dahlia has no idea what Darjeeling is, but she feels fine about it. Just fine.

The wind blows snowflakes through the open window.

Marcus finishes his bowl of soup in silence, with a dignified submissiveness of a political prisoner, and is sent to bed.

In the kitchen, his mom, Vika, nervously smokes a long thin cigarette as she talks.

Dahlia drinks tea and listens.

Dahlia can't help but think the kitchen suits its owner: ev-erything here is new, clean, shiny. Impersonal. But then she sees a string of dried mushrooms hanging on a nail. It draws her eye and makes her comfortable, a humanizing touch among the un-bearable sterility of perfection.

Vika says, "He's just like my mother. She used to bring home all manner of critters. Healed them and fed them and warmed them up. People, too. Like she knew when they needed it, if you know what I mean?"

Then Vika says, "I don't blame you for getting involved. It's impossible to say no to Mark. Mother was the only one who could rein him in."

Dahlia doesn't respond and it doesn't seem like her response is needed. She's trying to figure out whether this woman realizes that her son is hiding behind the door, listening. He must be, if she learned anything about him at all this evening.

"Mother's death is really hard on him."

(*No, but I'd like it to be*, Marcus thinks. He's sitting on the floor in the corridor, his cheek plastered against the kitchen door. He's wearing pajamas with kittens and bunnies on them.)

Vika says, "It was to be expected. Mark doesn't accept Igor. Doesn't want to let him in."

Dahlia thinks *doesn't accept* is putting it mildly.

"Too many shocks in too short a period of time," says Vika. "Igor and I were going to get married. Did Mark tell you? We had to postpone it. Not that it's going to bring her back."

Dahlia thinks: I can't judge her. I understand exactly what she means. She remembers what it was like to love someone. When the rest of the world and its details, large and small, seemed insignificant and unimportant.

"Do you know what he was looking for? At Igor's?" Vika asks.

"Why don't you ask him?"

"Have you tried asking him anything?"

Dahlia thinks there's no harm in telling her. The look on this woman's face is proof enough she's ready to hear any answer. If she says Marcus planned kidnapping and murder, Vika might not be surprised.

"He wanted to find some sort of a music box. He thought it was hidden at the hotel."

"Oh my God."

Dahlia is waiting for Vika to add something, but she doesn't. Instead, she puts out the cigarette and banishes the ashtray to the balcony. Then she calls out, "Mark, bring me my bag."

Clearly, she knows her son pretty well, after all.

There's a patter of bare feet in the corridor.

Vika says, "One thing I don't get. How did he know? He never asks anything, but always seems to know everything."

Marcus enters carrying a large checkered leather bag—fancy and feminine, the sort Dahlia would never buy—he carries it carefully in extended arms, as though it's a ticking bomb.

Vika rummages through the bag, pulling out a wallet, keys, glasses, some book, a screwdriver, lipstick, a few ballpoint pens, a notepad. And, finally, a music box.

"Igor did have it," she explains. "He took it to a shop to get the winding mechanism repaired."

"Did he wind it?" asks Marcus.

"I don't think so."

"It's a simple question. Did he wind it, or didn't he?"

"I specifically asked him not to."

Her answer seems to satisfy Marcus. He hugs the box to his chest like a pet and takes a step toward the door.

"Don't you want to say anything?"

"What should I say?"

"Igor spent a week looking for a repairman who would agree to fix the clockwork in his presence, so Igor could be certain no one would listen to your precious polonaise."

"Did he find one?"

"As you can see."

"What can I say? He's a responsible person." Marcus leaves.

Dahlia watches him go. So, this is how the evening ends. The story resolves itself. "Thank you for the tea," she says. "It was delicious. I think it's time for me to go."

"I'll call you a taxi," Vika offers.

"No need. I'll walk a bit, and the Metro is going to open soon."

Dahlia is in the hall outside Marcus's apartment. She presses her forehead against the window and watches the snowflakes fall. The door behind her opens. Marcus comes out, clad in kittens and bunnies. Dressed like this, he looks like a regular little boy, which is really what he is. Dahlia understands, seeing him like this, how one might call him Marcy.

He's holding the music box.

Marcus says, "You didn't think our adventure was over?"

Dahlia doesn't respond. It's almost dawn. A new day is starting, and it holds nothing good in store for her. In the morning, the events of this night will seem like a silly dream. Marcus will stay here, with his naïve belief in miracles. She'll leave.

But her pain will remain, growing ever darker.

Marcus turns the key. Something inside the music box comes alive, creaks and clicks. He says, "Before I do this, I have to warn you: there are side effects. For example, you will experience the desire to help old ladies cross at intersections, and to feed stray kittens."

"That doesn't sound so bad. What else?"

"With time, you'll want your pain back. I know what I'm talking about. Without pain, there's no memory. And to get it back, you'll have to really love someone. That's how the magic works."

On a flight of stairs in a strange building, in an unfamiliar neighborhood, this is what a little boy wearing kittens-and-bunnies pajamas is saying to her. Unbelievable.

Thirdly: I AM SERIOUS.

She badly wants to interrupt him, to make him stop. To shout at him. To make him forget about his stupid magic. To tell him that the world isn't black and white: it's gray and there's no escaping that. That he knows nothing about pain, and to stop torturing her.

But if his mom is able to tolerate his idiosyncrasies and not say things like that to him, then Dahlia can, too. So, she says nothing. She waits for him to finish his monolog so she can leave.

Marcus leans over the music box and whispers something. Dahlia can't quite make out the words. But that doesn't matter. Because he opens the lid, and the box begins to play "Polonaise Farewell."

She feels light and unburdened. As though someone had scooped out all her darkness and pain. As though gentle waves are carrying her away.

They sit together on the staircase, atop Dahlia's jacket. Marcus wraps himself in a large sweater which his mom brought out and silently handed to him before returning to the apartment. What an incredible woman!

Dahlia hugs Marcus and pats him on his head. He's almost not crying anymore. Dahlia understands that he needed those tears. And that he needed her, so he could cry them. Still, she refuses to believe that she would ever want her pain back, now that it's trapped inside the music box.

Meanwhile, Marcus thinks that Dahlia doesn't really understand much about "city love and sausage slices" as Grandma used to put it.

And that, one day, she will.

MORPHEUS

"THE KEY IS NOT TO TRAUMATIZE THE FISH."

Grandpa always treated the fish with a certain level of empathy. Even now he gently pushes a minnow onto the hook. He passes the line under its gill with precise, carefully measured motion, tucks the hook into the eyelet that's sticking out through the minnow's mouth, pulls it back, and admires his handiwork. A double hook protrudes from the minnow's mouth like a dazzling metal mustache.

I watch Grandpa's hands, but his movements are too familiar; my focus slides off them as they fade into the background. I see only the minnow or, to be precise, its eyes. They aren't empty as fish eyes ought to be. They're filled with longing and doom.

I recall the boiled hake they served us in kindergarten, a long time ago. I never ate it; didn't even want to look at it. The black film that covered the inner walls of the fish belly seemed to me the gates of the abyss. The same abyss that surrounds me now. The sounds of the nighttime river fade and are replaced with the sounds of the cafeteria—the clinking of spoons against plates, the unsteady rumble of children's voices, the admonishing calls of the teachers: *Nekrasov, hold your fork right; Fedina, settle down and eat quietly!*

"Pass me the next one," says Grandpa.

I'm at the river again.

The bucket of live bait stands nearby. It emits a suspicious rustle, as though the minnows, having despaired of trying to escape the trap at the lid, are now attempting to gnaw through the bottom. But I can't get distracted before I solve the Rubik's cube. I keep turning it, keep repeating the algorithms which my consciousness has long forgotten, but which my fingers remember. I can't seem to solve it; each algorithm I try returns a fish pattern at the top layer.

I can't open the bucket before I solve the cube. In it, under the scratched-up plastic cover and among the minnows hides the knowledge that Grandpa can't be here, because he died a long time ago. I know this, the minnows know this, even the pikes that swim somewhere underneath the boat know this. Only Grandpa doesn't know.

I feel the same longing I saw in the eyes of the fish. Doom blends with air and I breathe the mixture in. It collects somewhere in my lungs like a lump of bitterness one might wake up with after uneasy sleep.

Wake up.

I look at my watch. Research papers on the subject recommend checking the watch, looking away, then checking it again. If the hands display completely different times then the solution is clear: you're asleep. In my case there are no hands on the watch at all. The time is never o'clock.

I see other signs, too. The sky is too low; it's almost possible to reach up and tear off a piece of a cloud, perhaps made of cotton or foam. Instead of the familiar dachas, untidy three-story buildings appear on the shore across the river. They look like an abandoned summer camp or resort. Beyond them rise the horned silhouettes of slagheaps.

This is a dream.

The realization doesn't strike; it builds gradually over several steps: yes, I'm asleep and the cube hasn't been solved; I'm asleep, which is why the cube refuses to be solved, and Grandpa keeps waiting for me to pass him live bait; I'm asleep; there is no cube, no fish, and no Grandpa.

But Grandpa is there, and he's still waiting. The boat sways gently on the waves of the river. Somewhere, the seagulls caw churlishly.

I must wake up. Not because of the river, the seagulls, or fishing—which I can't stand—but because of sleep itself and of my realization. I can't recall why being asleep is a bad thing, but the foreboding of something unkind lingers at the edge of my mind.

I must wake up, before it's too late.

I could take flight, puncture the low sky, and escape this evening shrouded in the shadow of something terrifying; but I take pity on my grandfather, even if he's long dead. I don't want the wounded sky to fall into the river, to crush the cardboard boat, and the cardboard Grandpa in the boat, and the cardboard minnows in the bucket.

I rise from my seat, lean my hands against the side of the boat, close my eyes, and slide into the water. Let Grandpa stay alive a bit longer, at least here. While submerged, I hear grumbling from above, the sort Grandpa used to break the monotony of fishing. His voice becomes diluted in the murky depths until it tapers off into a series of short beeps.

In a dream my memory always fails—it breaks into a million jagged shards when my consciousness falls into slumber from the dizzying heights of reality. It is from those shards that the sets and scripts of our dreams are put together.

I used to like sleeping when I was a child. The world of dreams seemed like a house to me. A very large and possibly infinite house. The house was crooked—terrible and beautiful at the same time. There were multiple ongoing construction projects within the house, undertaken by crews unaware of each other. Each built according to their own plans; some rooms seemed sturdy and reliable, while others crumbled at the touch. It was the world of cardboard and enamel. Some rooms were large enough to fit entire streets, the ski slopes of Dombai, or the Azov Sea. Others were so small they could barely fit the construction worker erecting them. But they were always rooms, and the low ceiling was always a ceiling, no matter how hard it pretended to be a sky.

The house was simultaneously overpopulated and abandoned. Its guests were akin to wind-up dolls, forced to act out strange scenes from ridiculous plays.

I learned to walk through walls. I broke windows and ripped wallpaper; I toppled the card houses of others' dreams and erected them anew. The dreams of adults were dreary and incomprehensible; they reminded me of spending time in the waiting room of a clinic. Children's dreams were a lot more fun. Kids my age resembled real people a lot more, in their dreams.

Everyone is born with the ability to remain self-aware in their own dreams, I think. But this ability is atavistic, akin to the Moro reflex in infants. And, like the Moro reflex, this ability fades with time.

Unfortunately, that's not what happened with me.

I don't open my eyes right away. With practiced patience I wait several minutes, so that the darkness from under my eyelids won't escape into the real world. A silly ritual.

The printed white elephants are awakened by dawn and hesitantly lumber across the red field of the curtains. Alya hung these curtains when she first moved in with me. Now they remind me of her, and of what happened when she left. That's why I don't take them down: they help me remember why I need the sleeping pills.

There is a moment's hesitation before I lower my feet to the floor. I want to jump away from the bed, before a tentacle or some other horror slithers from under it and grabs my leg. Instead I slowly put on my shoes. There's nothing under the bed.

Miha sleeps in the bathtub, wrapped in a camel-hair blanket. He washed out from the university half a year ago. Ever since then he's been bouncing around the dorms like a nomad, with his suitcase and his guitar. He pointedly ignores the bunk in my room that has remained empty ever since Alya left. Either he has an amazing sense of self-preservation, or weed has heightened his senses. He's always on his toes around me, as though he can see the darkness behind my back. The sleeping pills he procures for me from a nurse he knows are like an offering, a way to buy the reprieve from that darkness.

In the kitchen I sit on the wobbly stool that ended up there by some miracle. I stare at the gigantic palm print above the electric stove as I wait for the teapot to boil. It's merely the result of the explosion of condensed milk that Alya was cooking once, but the cracked brown crust looks very similar to blood. Someone traced a smiley face in the center of the palm. The steam from the teapot animates the face and turns it demonic; the palm detaches from the kitchen tiles and reaches toward me. This picture is harmoniously supplemented by the tapping sound from the teapot's lid.

The windows in the kitchen are taped over with newspaper pages. Miha taped them; he became quite a productive member of society after his discharge. My gaze wanders across newspaper columns seeking not sense but accidental forms, familiar patterns where none exist. This phenomenon is called pareidolia. But the letters have conspired against me and insist on forming words, and those words are on the offensive.

Best time in any young person's life . . . student A. jumped from a fifth-floor window . . . make a true specialist of the recently-graduated high-schooler and open doors . . . pursued by a fellow student . . . this opportunity, afforded to everyone in our country . . . will remain permanently disabled . . .

I can't read any paragraph in full—the lines jump and mix—but I can easily parse the meaning. Each article, each strip of paper taped to the window tells the story of my tragic love.

That's how it happened—but the newspapers hadn't covered it. The newspapers don't report on the dreams of regular students. They write about five-year plans and swine-breeding, of visits by friendly heads of state and satellite launches.

There are sounds of steps and voices coming from down the corridor and I shake in terror: they're about to read the truth about me and Alya. I try to rip the newspaper off the window but I can't; it's glued firmly to the glass and my fingernails slide off with an unpleasant squeak, snagging only a few small strips. Underneath the paper, instead of the glass and the dull cityscape, is the black abyss.

I'm still asleep. The premonition that loomed somewhere on the periphery becomes a certainty. I know the abyss waits for me beyond the window, grins at me via kitchen walls, dissects me with my own memories.

Morpheus.

I have to leave this kitchen and this dream. The steam, which fills all the space around me, thickens like jelly. The kitchen door smoothly recedes from me, or perhaps I recede from it, drawing ever closer to the darkness outside.

I check my watch. The time is never o'clock.

Knowing you're in a dream and being able to control that dream are different skill sets. I nearly forgot the latter; only the ritual with the watch allows me to somewhat attune to the right frequency. I may not become the puppet master, but at least I can sever the strings that connect to my extremities, and become a little less wooden.

I can't wake up, so I must run and hide. The window seems like the obvious exit. But now, having remembered Alya, I'm afraid. She jumped from this window. This exact one.

The remaining option is the free associations—the easiest way to move across dreamscape, and the least reliable. You never know where they'll lead you. I look at the newspaper column somewhat askew, so that the text becomes blurred and I can imagine TV listings in its place. Some innocuous children's programs from my youth.

The other children didn't like me when I was little. This dislike eventually blossomed within every social group I joined.

They didn't boycott me, and they almost never beat me, nothing like that. They just kept away from me.

I wasn't an angry child. I wanted to make friends. In reality and in dreams.

There are people who like to watch insects. Beetles, for example. They can flip the beetle on its back and watch in amusement as it helplessly waves its legs—a hypnotic spectacle. It's also possible to rip off its legs. Harness it into a paper chariot. Imprison it in a matchbox. Set it on fire. There are all sorts of possibilities.

My friendship in dreams was sometimes similar to those kinds of amusements.

Children are more finely attuned than the adults. They might forget the details of their dreams, but not the emotions. Children-beetles couldn't remember the dreams I participated in, but they could feel that I was dangerous.

At the age of eight I had no friends, but had a classmate who sat next to me: Seryoga, a neurotic and aggressive kid. That's about all I remember about him. I don't recall what he did to anger me. But that's how it always worked: anger, hatred, or rage built the bridge within the dream between the subject of my emotions and me. And then the game began. That time we played dinosaurs. I always wondered what would happen if the thing built from car tires on the kindergarten's playground would come to life. That's where I brought Seryoga.

By then I already began to figure things out. Morpheus was beginning to emerge. It was just a feeling at first, like when you're being watched. The attention of the unseen observer spread like the growth of mold and the smell of rot. It vibrated and it demanded. It whispered, wordlessly, like the white noise from the television tuned to a dead channel: *let me in.*

I searched for the source. I wandered across my domain—I thought of it as mine back then—hoping to find signs of monsters, or find the monsters themselves, hiding in the dark corners of the dream-house.

Morpheus revealed himself to me, in all his oppressive glory, the night Seryoga perished. I watched the beast made of car tires rip my classmate to pieces, and the mosaic came together, stone by stone. The rubber monster, the playground, bald dandelions, low sky, a rusty bike skeleton, a sandbox, trees and fallen leaves: every detail of my dream was part of a huge, insatiable monster. Even me.

Seryoga didn't come to school the next day. He never came back to school. He simply failed to wake up that morning. He fell into a coma.

That's how I learned that there were no monsters hiding in my dream-house. The house itself was a monster.

At eight years of age, I almost stopped sleeping. When I did manage to fall asleep, I found myself in the worst of nightmares. My ability to remain aware in the dream and to control the surrounding dream world lit me up like a beacon in the darkness. Every moment I felt the unkind attention of Morpheus upon me.

But I managed to forget. To unlearn. To turn down the intoxicating power. I think Morpheus allowed me to do that. He knew I'd be back.

If you gaze long enough into an abyss, the abyss will gaze back into you. Perhaps Nietzsche knew something of Morpheus.

Changing the plot of the dream through free association is somewhat like moving the layers of a Rubik's cube. At first glance it seems totally random, but there's logic and structure behind every move. Except a person is but a speck of dust on one of the edges of a huge cube being solved by Morpheus. It is not for the speck to understand the logic of the monster.

It isn't just memory that works under a different set of rules within a dream. Time also has unique properties here; it is circular, it forces you to replay certain episodes again and again, and then to forget them.

I recognize this place. To my right is the concrete fence topped with barbed wire. To my left, the factory wall. The space between them is overgrown with burdock, emmer wheat, and broadleaf plantain. Wild grape vines thread up the wall and the

fence. Green dominates the summer here, only somewhat diluted by scarlet in the fall. This is the perfect place for games, a
secret place that can only be reached via an inconspicuous hole
in a fence disguised by a currant bush. Beyond the corner the
space terminates in a concrete block that cuts across it. In reality,
the factory floor lies behind it; gray buildings with glass blocks
in place of normal windows, rows of containers, guard dogs. In
the dream everything is different: a shaded square in front of the
kindergarten, a playground under chestnut trees, a multicolored
dinosaur made of car tires rising all the way up to the sky.

You might not remember this dream when you wake up, but
you can't help but recognize it when it comes back. Seryoga is
about to say, "Last one across is a fool!" Then he'll climb the concrete block barring the way to the playground.

Maybe I'll want to stop him this time, or perhaps I'll prefer to
watch in silence as the dinosaur comes to life and rips him apart.
It won't be the real Seryoga either way. The dinosaur ate the real
Seryoga the first time around.

It's easy for me to tell the real people, the dreamers, apart
from the shadows, put together from the shards of my memories.
The shadows are vague; it's impossible to make out the details of
their faces or the tone of their voice, no matter how hard you try.
The shadows are functional and predictable. They're cardboard
cutouts. The living people on the other hand, are . . . alive.

"Damn, Egor, you're such a donkey," I hear. It's not Seryoga's
voice. Atop the concrete block that hides the chronicle of my first
encounter with Morpheus sits Miha. He smokes as he stares down
at me. He's real. Not a ghost made of the mix of papier-mâché and
memories, but the real, living Miha.

"What the hell?" I ask, confused. I come closer and look him
in the eye. His pupils are dilated.

"It's your dream, bro. So you tell me, why the hell did you
drag me here? Are you aware that there's a giant *thing* on the other
side of this block, and it's drooling as it waits for breakfast?"

I climb the block. It seemed almost insurmountable when I
was eight, but I'm not a kid anymore. I look at the car tire mon-

ster. It's just a slide on the playground, right?

"Relax, you're seeing things," I say. "How did you get here?"

"You dream too loudly." Miha shrugs. "Also, I have some pri-mo grass. Listen, man . . . I don't feel comfortable here."

Me neither. Benzodiazepine successfully blocks all the things it's supposed to block in my brain, which is why I can't manage to wake up. Sometimes it's not enough to just *want* to. Flying usually helps and I would take flight, but there's no sky here. Above us is an abyss. I don't want to go up there.

I'm tired. I don't understand how Morpheus managed to break through the wadding of the sleeping pills. I figure I should return to the very first dream with my Grandpa, hang out in the boat with him until I wake up. I figure I need to distract Morpheus.

"Fine," I say. "We'll jump down on the count of three." I point to the side where we should jump. The side of the tire monster. Miha gets up obediently.

I stare at the lawn below and imagine it isn't a lawn but a murky river. That seagulls are cawing in the distance.

"One . . . Two . . . Three!"

We jump. Time slows. I feel my feet hit the water and catch a glimpse of Miha's confused face. He hangs from the concrete block as though crucified. His wrists are chained to the concrete. It was easy to imagine such a thing—easier than imagining the river. Farewell, Miha. Forgive me.

I hear Morpheus rumble in approval. The tire creature pre-pares to jump.

The river waves close over my head.

I remember Alya. How she fell. How she screamed.

I shouldn't be thinking about her now.

She left me suddenly. There were no signs, no hints, no calls that kindly prepare a man for such drastic changes, allow him to regroup and get ready for the hit. One day we were making plans together; the next, she took her things and moved to an-other dorm.

Outwardly I was calm like a lamppost. Inwardly, I seethed. It was unbearable. We saw each other every day. I didn't pursue her, didn't try to talk it out, didn't write verses or cry in front of her door. Not because I didn't want to, but because I couldn't. From early childhood I got used to being—or at least pretending to be—indifferent. I avoided building emotional bridges. I avoided getting attached. But then, something broke within me.

For over ten years I'd lived in relative peace. I hid the knowledge about the nature of dreams on the furthest shelf of my memory; I learned to tiptoe around the dangerous thoughts and to avoid having dreams.

I fell off the wagon, crossing out ten years of abstinence. I decided that it would be easier to talk to her in a dream. Now I just had to remember how to do that.

When learning to play the guitar people scrape their fingers raw. Athletes exhaust their muscles as they prepare for competition. I trained my consciousness—until it was raw and bloody and exhausted—recalling how to control dreams, how to bend them to my will.

I came to her. Alya's dreams were gormless, but mostly nice. Nothing resembling a nightmare. I became her nightmare. There was no conversation, no attempt at an explanation—who was I kidding? I merely began reshaping her dreams. It was intoxicating. We were together on the other side of reality, and I didn't care who she loved when she woke up. Did I know how painful these dreams were for her—dreams where she came back to me night after night, gave herself to me, without understanding why she was doing it? Of course I knew. I believed that everything would change.

Everything changed the night Alya became aware during the dream, recognized herself, recognized me, and understood everything. Her gaze was terrifying.

She jumped out the window. Anything, to get away from me. Morpheus cackled behind my back.

*

The short beeps announcing the time emanate from a radio somewhere. I recognize their sound, even though the beeping in unceasing. Instead of six reliable points they draw an infinite dotted line across the surface of time.

I lie submerged in the bathtub filled with fetid water. I stare at the patchwork of cracks on the white ceiling above me. I surface. There's the sound of water gushing from the tap. The shower curtain with octopi and ships on it waves gently. This definitely isn't a river. Where am I?

I open the curtain. The bathtub stands in the middle of the living room and is surrounded by the labyrinth of junk. Stacks of books tower over armchairs filled with crumpled clothes. Dirty dishes and ashtrays filled with cigarette butts sail across the glass surfaces of coffee tables. The sound of running water is replaced with the sounds of the street. A huge floor-to-ceiling window is open wide.

In front of the window stands Alya. Her hair is long, like it was when we first met. She wears the dress with the flower pattern—my favorite.

I haven't seen her since the night when she . . . I never even visited her in the hospital. I was afraid of that gaze. The knowledge implied in it. The understanding.

I shouldn't have thought of Alya within a dream. And now I'm here. In her dream.

"By the way," Alya says, "you promised to take me to the theater."

She's holding a Rubik's cube. That's logical. She's the one who gave it to me. It was the real thing, made in Hungary, rather than a knockoff made based on the schematics published in *Young Technologist* magazine. I always fidgeted with the cube—solved it and broke it apart again. It became a habit, one that Alya found very annoying.

"Do you want to go right now?" I ask. I look around for the way out.

Alya laughs. Her laughter is pleasant. It sounds a bit naïve.

This appears to be a nice dream. Those occasionally happen. Perhaps here, in this dream, Alya doesn't remember us breaking up, doesn't remember the nightmares which featured me, doesn't recall that she no longer knows how to walk. Doctors said it was psychosomatic. There was no physical trauma, no brain damage. It was a self-suggestion.

"No, dear. First you must sort out the fish you and your grandfather caught. I know what you, fishermen, are like."

There's a large basin beside her filled with live pikes. Their tails are beating as they look at me and their eyes are filled with the abyss. *Morpheus.*

Morpheus is everywhere. I see that now. The cracks on ceiling and walls come alive. They dance and taunt me, and intertwine becoming ever wider. Tendrils of mold reach from the bathtub and follow my wet footprints across the floor. They reach for Alya, who doesn't notice them. Pikes look on in irony. I've led Morpheus straight to Alya.

No. I won't let him do this again. We'll both wake up. I look out the window—we're on the second floor. If I can't fly then it won't be a very long fall. Not a deadly fall. But somehow I'm convinced everything will work out. Perhaps because of Alya. She cleanses me with her light.

"Alya, do you trust me?"

"Of course." She looks at me in surprise. There's something familiar in her gaze. I don't immediately realize what it is. There's no time for contemplation.

I take her hand. We step out of the window.

We fly.

Without opening my eyes I listen to myself and the world around me. Me: My heart races, my right hand asleep, my mouth dry. The world around me: There's a cold breeze coming through the window; a door in the next dorm slams loudly; there's a patter of feet, laughter, a sharp smell of acetone—the walls in the corridor were painted yesterday.

I woke up.

Today is going to be a challenging day. It's the final practice run for the pathetic heresy that is the student concert. I've been roped in as the sound engineer for this travesty.

I can look forward to spending an hour on a bus filled to the brim with students and the proletariat, smelling of gasoline and overflowing with the sounds of everyone's morning complaints. Then at least an hour of waiting for everyone to show up. Three hours of listening to gossip, complaints, suggestions, and criticism. But then, if I survive all this, I can head over to Shurik and Kaban's place in the evening and play cards all night, because—oh miracle of miracles!—tomorrow is Saturday. So it's not all so bad.

I really don't want to get up. And then I realize that I can't get up even if I wanted to.

Yeah, I'm awake for sure. I see my room, the elephants on the drapes; I hear the sounds and sense the smells. But my eyes are won't fully open. I can't move. I wouldn't even be able to breathe if breathing depended upon my willpower.

I must not panic. This has happened before. It's the damned pills. My brain, infused with chemicals, is not ready to wake up and to unblock the mechanism that controls my muscles. Sleep paralysis: one part of the brain does not know what another part is doing. My amygdala, displeased with its inability to control my body, is about to fall into hysterics. Hallucinations will be borne of fear. It's not a dream anymore, but it's not reality, either. It would be easy to return to sleep from this condition, but—no, thanks. I try to calm myself and wait. Two to three minutes, and everything will return to normal.

There's a sound under my bed . . . No, there isn't. And the door into my room isn't squeaking. There isn't a sound of footsteps. No one is here to make that sound. No one is whispering into my ear: "Don't be afraid, dear, it's just me. No one else is here." It's not Alya. She couldn't be here.

But it *is* Alya, and she's lying. She didn't come alone.

I recall what I saw in her eyes: the longing and doom, just like I'd seen in the minnow's eyes.

Alya throws my blanket onto the floor. She gently traces something cold and sharp across my chest. She presses on it, lightly, seemingly without effort. But I feel the blade cut through not only skin and muscle but also the bone. It slides through easily as though my sternum is made of cake. She opens the sternum with both hands. Her hands are warm. She smiles and looks me in the eye, to see if I'm watching. I am. I watch through barely cracked eyelids. I see everything.

Alya opens her mouth and spews out the darkness. The darkness flows into me, fills my lungs, squeezes my heart in a cold grip; it flows through my veins.

A fishing string stretches along my spine, from the lungs to the head. There's a metallic taste in my mouth.

Morpheus smiles with my lips. He and I open our eyes.

COPY CAT

K.A.TERYNA & ALEX SHVARTSMAN

IMAGINE A RUSSIAN CAT. NOT JUST ANY RUSSIAN CAT, BUT A CAT from Leningrad.

Those who claim passing familiarity with Russian literature might imagine a cat straight off the pages of Pushkin or Bulgakov. An eloquent cat, dispensing folk wisdom while chained under an oak tree, or schmoozing the Moscow intelligentsia at parties, probably in a soothing baritone. But those are fictions, lofty lullabies from literary luminaries. In real life, cats don't recite fairy tales or ride the tram. In real life, cats don't talk.

This one is a typical cat from Leningrad. A mature cat, but not so old as to have one paw in the grave. He's lived his whole life with a prim old lady. You know, the born-and-bred-in-Leningrad sort of woman, one who could recognize tourists and recent transplants at a glance by the way they carry themselves, and smack them with her umbrella for the temerity to ask for directions. Now, this old lady has not one but both feet in the grave. Which is to say, she died.

The cat is at a loss for what to do. On one paw, the old lady deserves a proper sendoff. She deserves a funeral with a small band playing sad music, a priest waving a censer, that sort of thing. On the other paw, the cat realizes how that would play out. As soon as the word of her having kicked the bucket gets out, some thrice-removed relatives from the boondocks will descend upon the old lady's prime real estate—an apartment on Nevskiy Prospekt, no less. And they'll evict the shit out of the aging cat.

Not wanting to become a vagrant, the cat shakes off the indecision, comes up with a plan of action, and begins implementing said plan.

Back in the day, the old lady used to work as a radio announcer. Two of the three rooms of her apartment are packed with reels of magnetic Svema brand 6mm tape: hours upon hours of the archives of her broadcasts. *It's midnight in Petropavlovsk . . . In today's news We're taking your requests by phone . . . Broadcasting live across the Soviet Union . . . The first exercise in this morning's radio calisthenics is. . . .* An Aurora reel tape player occupies a place of honor in the living room.

The old lady used to listen to these recordings, at all hours and at high volume because her hearing wasn't so great. She would play the tapes and inflict the old Soviet broadcasts on her long-suffering neighbors. The neighbors became so indoctrinated by these obligatory concerts from the Soviet past that some had trouble falling asleep without them, and banged on pipes on especially quiet nights.

The cat, naturally, was part of the captive audience. He listened enough that he memorized many of the recordings, enough that he could've easily worked as a prompter for any radio announcer.

Given how sophisticated the old lady had been, it stood to reason that her cat wasn't a simpleton fur ball, either. He was a well-bred and intelligent cat, and he, too, would probably whack uncultured tourists and transplants with an umbrella. But the laws of physics trump breeding and intelligence, so he couldn't grasp an umbrella.

Little manicure scissors, on the other paw, those he could handle.

So the cat grabs hold of the scissors, the Svema tapes, and the concentrated vinegar, and gets to work.

The task is gargantuan to say the least. Think about it: the cat has to come up with a plan, sort through the tape reels, and do everything by memory because cat paws can't hold a pen or a pencil. Loading paper into the typewriter and hitting the carriage return after each line is frustrating to humans with opposable thumbs, let alone felines.

The cat's memory is excellent. He can name every dead relative of the old lady's from her photo albums, and recite the price of milk for every year starting in '63, even though he was born much later, in the year 2000. (Were he owned by a lesser human he might've been saddled with a terrible name like Millennium. But he got lucky; the old lady had way too much class to name him something like that.)

The cat starts out by sorting and organizing the many reels. The cat is a bit of a neat freak and feels both exhilarated and guilty to finally be in charge of the apartment. He wants to clean it up and live like a person—but to live like a person would take an inhuman (or infeline) amount of effort because those pesky laws of physics apply equally to cats. And so, the hellish marathon of work begins.

The cat loads tapes into the player one by one. He listens, selects excerpts, cuts the tapes with the manicure scissors and glues them together with vinegar. It would have been a difficult task, even for a human. But the cat perseveres. He is a Leningrad cat through and through, and not a bag of fur and bones from a lesser town. He manages to put together a decent-sounding montage by copying the excerpts together. It takes him just under two days.

The old lady's corpse is beginning to stink.

His next quest is to get the Aurora player and the telephone next to each other. The telephone hangs on the wall in the hallway, next to a dilapidated ballpoint pen on a string. The wall is covered in fading phone numbers with names next to them in all kinds of handwriting, from the flighty young girl script to the shaking scrawl of a grandmother. Numbers that have been long disconnected, and names that over the decades have migrated from phone directories onto tombstones at various local cemeteries.

The telephone isn't some modern plastic piece of junk but a rotary antique that weighs two to three times as much as the cat. So you can imagine the sort of effort it takes him to drag this hulking device all the way to the living room, looping the cable between the porcelain elephants, piles of books about the history of Soviet radio, and knitted doilies the old lady's aunt bought way back in the day, when she was a college student.

Finally, he reaches the player and sets everything up.

He calls a funeral home and leaves a message in the old lady's voice arranging everything. The message is a mix of instructions, threats, and an offer of a bribe—the cat estimates the old lady's savings are enough for a bribe.

Neither the Aurora player nor the cat's understanding of human nature fail him.

At night the undertakers come with a coffin. The front door is open, and the old lady is ready, dressed in her finest clothes. There's an envelope full of cash on the bedside table. The cat is hiding behind a wardrobe and scraping his claws unpleasantly against the parquet.

The undertakers pick up the body and leave. She gets a burial somewhere on the outskirts of town. There's no orchestra playing sad music or a priest with a censer, but it's still a decent burial with a nice headstone even if it bears a foreign-sounding stranger's name.

After having some time to think, the undertakers wonder if they should return and rifle through the empty apartment for valuables. But when they come back, the door is locked and the unpleasant scraping of claws against parquet emanates from the inside, followed by the stern sound of the old woman's voice, insinuating something about criminal prosecution. They beat a hasty retreat.

Left to his own devices, the cat cleans the apartment. He organizes the tapes, stacks books onto shelves, and dusts the porcelain elephants. He doesn't wash the floors though: there are limits to what a cat—even a Leningrad cat—can do.

For several months, the cat lives his best life. He listens to his favorite recordings each evening, eats as much cat food as he wants, and occasionally treats himself to a frozen sausage from the fridge or a saucer of a cognac-and-valerian-root cocktail. He's set for a long while. The old lady was a blockade survivor during the Siege of Leningrad, so every nook in the apartment that isn't occupied by tapes, books, and porcelain elephants, is packed with canned food, including cat food.

After all that effort, he gets burned by something really fucking stupid.

Over the course of months since the old lady's death, her mailbox gets filled with the sort of trash Remarque used to complain about from the World War I trenches in '17. And while they aren't advertisements for warm trench caps made from stinging-nettle, the flyers and letters inside are equally useless to old lady and cat alike. The mail carrier notices this. She sounds an alarm and summons the neighbors. Together, they keep ringing the doorbell.

The cat doesn't answer, obviously. He's trying to edit something appropriate from the tapes, but can't do it in so short a time. He plays some recording on the Aurora, but all the mail carrier and the neighbors hear in the old lady's muffled voice is a cry for help.

They call the police.

When the policeman arrives, he finds the door ajar. From inside he hears, "Come in, officer," in a cheerful voice.

So the policeman enters, and the neighbors try to follow, but the cat appears at the doorstep and hisses at them until they draw back.

The policeman enters the living room. The cat follows.

While the policeman looks around for the old lady, the cat jumps onto the table and begins operating the Aurora player. He loads various tapes and plays phrases arranged into a hastily prepared confession.

At first, the policeman isn't even listening. He pretty much loses his shit at the performance of the cat, who, over the period of months, has become so adept at controlling the player he could probably earn millions on YouTube.

The cat patiently rewinds the tapes and plays the confession again.

The policeman listens.

When the confession is done playing for the second time, the policeman coughs nervously, then speaks politely in a husky voice. He asks for a stiff drink and if he may please sit down, because his legs are trembling.

The cat nods toward the cognac, as in, "Go ahead. Make yourself at home." He'd have a drink himself, but he feels that may be too much for the policeman to handle just then.

After the policeman has had a few drinks, he recovers his wits somewhat. With shaking hands he lights a cigarette, and the cat brings him an ashtray.

The cat answers questions by playing recordings and occasionally cutting bits of tapes and arranging them into new ones, which would shock the policeman even more, if that were possible.

Two hours later, the policeman emerges from the apartment.

He tells the neighbors to disperse and chides the mail carrier about the latter's unhealthy interest in old ladies and how, while the postal worker is wasting her time, there are people out there anxiously awaiting their packages.

Ever since then, the policeman personally empties the mail box, once a month.

He visits the cat occasionally, bringing treats and cognac, because the cat is a very attentive listener, who only occasionally interjects with a clever comment in the old lady's voice, better than any psychotherapist. Sometimes the two of them get drunk and sing the old Soviet songs from the balcony.

The end.

*

You must be somewhat disappointed. As an expert on Russian literature and a connoisseur of Tolstoy and Dostoyevsky, you surely expected more from the Leningrad cat. You figured he'd wander the banks of the Moika River and recite poetry on the Anichkov Bridge—his own poems, but with references to Remarque, Rimbaud, and someone else whose name begins with an "R."

Perhaps you thought the cat might get a job as a conductor on a tram, then hijack the tram and drive it to Archangelsk, where he'd get hired on as a skipper for an expedition to the North Pole. When he eventually returned to Leningrad he'd discover that the city has changed too much for his tastes, and head for the Vnukovo Airport. He'd briefly become lost in the labyrinthine terminals and barely make it onto the flight to Paris by chasing after the plane on the runway and jumping onto the landing gear. He'd discover the plane is headed not for Paris but, let's say, Uryupinsk. He'd hijack the plane and fly it to Australia. . . .

But you must remind yourself that this isn't a fairy tale. It's a true story of a real cat. The cat isn't interested in a life of action and adventure that writers or readers might be tempted to imagine for him. He couldn't possibly give less of a shit about trams, expeditions, Australia, and—most especially—jumping onto the landing gear of a moving plane.

Instead, the cat curls up by the record player each night. He presses the Play button and closes his eyes, listening to the old lady's voice as she cheerfully announces which song had been requested by citizens calling in and is about to play next.

THE CHARTREUSE SKY
K.A.TERYNA & ALEXANDER BACHILO

I HAILED A SLED TO TAKE ME FROM PRESNYA TO KOLOMENSKY, plopped down into the seat, wrapped the beaver collar overcoat around my neck, and ordered the coachman to drive. The sooty red-brick factories were gradually replaced with gray apartment buildings and then white-stone aristocratic mansions, until the pointed towers of the Kremlin appeared on the horizon, as if pulled upward into the sky by golden eagles. All manner of pedestrians milled about on Hunters Row. Merchants called customers into their shops and tents, a colorful banner in the window of the Testov's Inn advertised burbot liver pies and bone marrow cooked in black butter.

At the edge of my hearing the phone rattled, its ringing growing ever louder and more insistent. This archaic and somber ringtone had cost me a pretty penny, its price calculated based on my solvency, as per usual. I must admit, I held my breath hoping that Nettie would change her mind. There were at least a dozen transport inspectors on duty, and I had other plans. Alas, this wasn't to be. The phone rattled with more and more insistency until I sighed woefully and snapped my fingers.

The trade booths of Hunters Row disappeared along with the sled, the coachman, the rump of a bay mare wagging its frosty tail, the greatcoat with its cozy beaver collar. Augmented reality channel Old Moscow does not support visual interfaces, which is one of the reasons I gladly pay its considerable monthly subscription fee. But, unfortunately, I need the visual connection for work, and so I got kicked onto the Moscow One channel with its eternally cloudless sky, mirrored skyscrapers, smiles plastered onto interactive billboards, and invasive news infographics. I sat in the cabin of the jet taxi and frowned at the idyllic world around me. "Almost like reality, but better" was once the slogan of the Moscow One channel. I'm old enough to remember that.

Toward the right edge of my field of vision, a bell pulsed in agony. An unbearable sight. I swiped the bell into the reading area where it unfolded into a priority message flashing red. A child was missing; a seven-year-old boy. An inspector was required to attend in person. That, again. Nettie could handle a search for a child far more efficiently, but mothers of missing troublemakers always insisted on getting a living person involved. If it were up to them, they'd flip the entire city upside down. I was sure the boy would be found by the time I got there, but there was nothing I could do. I flipped the message to the jet, which soared upward and rushed toward Arbat via a route Nettie calculated in a fraction of a second.

I don't like to fly. I'm afraid of heights, and the blue of the sky makes me think of the abyss. Moscow One is part of the free municipal channel bundle and isn't overly sensitive to the needs of its users. Even so, after a brief delay, it replaced the view of the sky with a wide track in my favorite color: green chartreuse (associations: spring, safety, health, and the French marshal Francois d'Estreth, may he rest in peace), This way I could imagine that I'm not flying, but rather riding along a picturesque and absolutely safe highway. It'd be nice to paint the sky chartreuse as well. I did so, on one of the art channels. It was quite pretty. But Moscow One isn't this flexible.

As it neared its destination, the jet suddenly fell through the phantom surface of the highway and dove sharply downward. My heart missed a beat; it nearly jumped out of my chest and remained behind in the blue abyss. For a second that felt more like an eternity I was convinced that my worst nightmares had come true. No more experiments for me. No more flights with unmanageable municipal augmentation.

I exited the jet onto Smolensky Boulevard. The channel directed me by marking my destination with a green box and lining the path toward it with a dashed line on the sidewalk. There, the mother of the missing child paced nervously by a park bench. She studied the face of each kid intently as they passed by.

During my short flight I didn't have the opportunity to get acquainted with the case—all my energy was spent fighting the terror of the blue sky that surrounded me—so I skimmed the files as I walked. Daniel Nechayev, age seven. His disappearance was recorded about an hour ago. He left home without his parents' permission. The photo showed a cute young prankster, but what good are photos these days? Augmentation changes a person's appearance to satisfy both their own needs and the wishes of others. Within the framework of current legislation, of course; I wish I never learned about the sort of underground channels my colleagues from the ethics department uncover on the regular basis.

The individual profile is far more important: the imprint everyone leaves in the system which Nettie can use to locate any given user in seconds. This imprint is, of course, private, and Nettie can only invade this privacy in exceptional cases. Cases like this one. But, contrary to my expectations, the boy had not yet been located.

"Greetings," I told the panicking mother (Eva Nechayeva, twenty-eight, homemaker) as I slid a temporary virtual key in her direction so that she could verify my identity.

Nechayeva accepted the key in an uncertain manner. Her movements were awkward and twitchy, as though she didn't fully understand what to do with the information packet she received. Initially I attributed that to some bug in the code of the Moscow One channel.

"What took you so long? So much time down the drain! He could be anywhere by now."

Nechayeva fidgeted with my key and occasionally stared at the sky with such purpose that I followed her gaze. The sky was its usual self, the same blue abyss.

"If you send me your son's key, I—"

She finally wrestled the info packet into submission but seemed not to care about verifying my authority. Nechayeva folded her hands, stared at me defiantly, and said, "There is no key, you see. That's the problem."

"Health issues?" I clarified, just in case, even though I already understood perfectly who I was dealing with. Her struggle with the augmentation interface made sense in retrospect.

"As if you don't know the risks of these implants."

"You have an implant," I said.

Fortunately, the explosion such a statement could have caused never happened.

"No one bothered to ask me," she said. "Did anyone ask you? Besides, I turn it on very rarely."

It is fortunate that I had activated the feature that hid my emotions.

I've developed a strong dislike for luddites after spending a month chasing the creator of the Devlet Giray and Napoleon viruses. Devlet Giray showed up first. Using vulnerabilities in the code of municipal channels, it forced users to believe a fire was raging around them in the most inopportune moments. It was done really well—even I bought into the illusion the first time around. The pieces of code we were able to snatch were written by a true virtuoso. The theory was that the terrified users would turn off augmentation and return to the real world, if only temporarily. But those users merely switched channels and flooded the Quality Control department with complaints. Napoleon was more cunning. It had smaller range, but its "fires" raged across the entire municipal grid. That really did make people escape into reality. It caused shock, psychoses, and crowded hospitals. And we never did catch the perpetrator.

Sometimes I think that our society is a little *too* tolerant. Judge for yourself; there are about a hundred free augmented reality channels in Moscow. There are countless paid channels, too. Nettie claims at least a dozen new channels are added to the catalog daily. Don't like modern-day Moscow? Here are seventeen thousand official futuristic modifications, and hundreds of thousands of historical ones. Some of them only differ from each other in such insignificant details as the ornament of the tiles on the facades of buildings. There are also jungles, infernal caves, alien sunrises, and post-apocalyptic sunsets. The options are boundless. If you don't like city noise, the augmentation will filter it out. If you don't like people, the augmentation will hide them from you and, if necessary, you from them. Personally, I like winter, calm, and the nineteenth century. Old Moscow is the right channel for me.

Even so, the dissatisfied have always existed, exist today, and will exist in the future. Roughly five percent of the residents don't use augmentation, or use it extremely rarely. I can't even imagine how they manage to survive with such bias in a world where practically all social life takes place in the confines of augmented reality. Still, that's a choice for each individual to make. But why cripple the children? Fine, forget the augmentation. Nettie has other tracking protocols.

"There has to be a key," I told her in the tone of a teacher trying to convince first-graders that the Earth is really round. "What about telemetry? Without it Nettie—that's the city AI—can't add a person to the city traffic map."

I didn't go as far as to remind her about the consequences of violating the law of universal telemetry accounting. She wouldn't listen to me, anyway. Nechayeva stared at the sky again, her face a mask of inhuman terror. I finally figured out that I should switch to the technical channel. The world around me became a cluster of multicolored info streams in the dark. It occurred to me that this was the mode I should use when I fly, far removed from anything human and natural.

The technical channel is the junction of two maximums. The maximum amount of information from Nettie that a human being is able to perceive, and the maximum of private information that is allowed to be collected, stored, and interpreted without additional conditions. Usage statistics for augmented reality in public spaces is within the Venn diagram of these two maximums. The technical channel painted Nechayeva in pale fuchsia. Above her head the help window displayed the name of her channel: Sakura: The Emotions That Govern the World.

Well, damn. In her field of vision the storm was raging, houses were crumbling, and trees were being uprooted and swept away by a hurricane. Sakura is an experimental channel, one that is surprisingly flexible and highly sensitive to the user's emotional state. I can't even imagine how it got into the municipal package, let alone as a default setting.

I have the authority and the ability to switch over the witness's channel. This is necessary; how can one question a person who's convinced you're a zombie chasing after their brain? I used my power, my teeth aching at the anticipation of the mountain of paperwork this action would later require.

I switched Nechayeva over to Moscow One and turned on Old Moscow for myself. The multi-colored silence of the technical channel was replaced by the susurrus of the marketplace. Rows of tents stretched across the Smolensky Square. The snow creaked loudly under the boots of idle buyers and freezing sellers.

"What the wife does when the husband is away!" shouted the bookseller as he danced briskly while balancing the tray on his belly. "Incredible adventures of the brave detective Nate Pinkerton! The question of sex, and the answer from Professor Freud!"

"Koti brand perfume! Persian bedbug powder!" A townswoman in a plush jacket and high-laced boots shouted over the bookseller. She seemed to have exited the warmth of her kerosene-heated shop only to escape immediately into the dark maw of the meat row.

"Tripe! Hot tripe!" The merchants' voices were like pipes of an organ and their immense skirts covered up steaming pots.

"Oranges! Good lemons!" echoed the falsetto of the greengrocers.

"Can't conduct much of interrogation in all this hubbab," cooed a gentle female voice into my ear. I turned around to find a young lady in round rimless glasses, wearing a fox-fur boa over a quilted coat tightly fitting over her fragile frame. Then someone did to me what I just did to Nechayeva—they forcibly switched over my channel.

The girl looked a lot more modern in the context of the Moscow One channel, though she still wore glasses, like some anachronistic fashion statement. With a graceful gesture she sent me a temporary key (Arina Lutskaya, eighteen, intern at the security detail of the Department of Architecture.) I responded in kind— an empty formality; Arina already know who I was.

Our relationship with the architects is akin to that between the King's Musketeers and the Cardinal's Guards. It would seem we're doing the same thing only in different layers of reality.

"Since when is the Department of Architecture interested in missing children?" I asked, failing to keep a hostile note out of my voice and hoping that my emotion blocker would filter it out. It didn't. I could see that in Arina's face. She wasn't even trying to hide her emotions.

"Don't worry, inspector. I'm not here to take away your kids." Her voice was filled with irony.

Ah, youngsters. When I was her age I, too, rebelled against the outdated courtesy standards, but then I realized that respect for elders was a useful thing. These neophytes will not come to the same realization. Augmentation has changed too much.

Meantime, Nettie confirmed that the architects' meddling was legitimate. They were conducting a special operation on Smolensky Boulevard, and any emergency within the five block radius fell within their zone of interest.

I felt briefly gruntled. Finally, the sixteen-story monstrosity next to the Institute of Forensic Medicine was being demolished. Nettie had already began the process of encapsulating the building and the area around it, cutting it from the virtual city maps and making it invisible to jets and users, redirecting routes, and leaving the architects and workers one-on-one with the monument from the Brezhnev era that was fated to disappear in a few hours. If we found the boy quickly, I'd have time to personally view this historic event. I was even prepared to turn off augmentation completely for the sake of such a spectacle.

I turned around, pretending to have lost interest in the affairs of architects.

"I apologize for the interruption," I said. "So, about the key—"

"She has no key," Arina interjected. "The boy has no telemetry built-in. I assume he was using an electronic bracelet. But today Danny-boy managed to ditch it. Am I right?"

Nechayeva nodded.

I couldn't help making a sarcastic comment. "What, do you still have a mechanical lock on your front door, too?"

Nechayeva looked down and I realized that I had guessed correctly.

Of course, Nettie isn't limited to tracking the digital footprint. There are also video recordings from the implants, an ideal piece of evidence for emergency investigations. There's no need to interview eyewitnesses; it's possible to see exactly what they saw. In theory that sounds great; in practice the information is so restricted, it isn't easy to gain access to it, especially when you need it from multiple sources. I dismissed this option; we'd spend hours waiting to gain permission. Traffic and public transport cameras are useful tools for investigating accidents, but aren't going to be much help in locating a pedestrian. That left stationary video cameras. There aren't many of those left, but that still gave us a chance . . .

"I already sent the request," said Arina, as though she could read my intentions in my face.

I grimaced. Arina seemed to catch that, too, but didn't comment on it. Instead she shared her visual feed with me. Logical. This way we wouldn't duplicate each other's actions. While Nettie collected video camera data, I resorted to the old-fashioned investigation methods.

"So," I asked Nechayeva, "Your Danny is cut off from all information resources?"

"How can you say that?" She was indignant. "He needs to be able to study. He has a smartphone. Except he left it at home today."

A smartphone? Wow. At least it wasn't one of those rotary phones.

"I need the parental access to his account."

Taught by bitter experience, I sent her a helper tool. After only three minutes I was rummaging through the boy's private virtual reality space. Study, web surfing, social networks, chats, chats, and more chats. The boy understood perfectly well what he was deprived of, and tried to compensate for his forced inadequacy by any available means.

Nettie reported that Danny hadn't been seen by any cameras. Arina, a stubborn girl, set out to manually check the recordings, one by one.

I wasn't surprised. The boy was clever beyond his age. At least from my ancient point of view. We're no match for today's children. Of course he knew how to avoid the cameras when he didn't want to be found.

The familiar ringtone sounded and the hysterical icon of a bell appeared again.

Arina and I received the notification simultaneously. A traffic accident, code yellow, no one hurt, logs require clarification. Seeing the address we exchanged glances. Only half a kilometer away, and some fifty meters from that condemned building.

We didn't bother with the jet and took a moving walkway instead, speeding it up to the maximum. I connected Nettie to Daniel's virtual logs and expanded the standard set of keywords. Was he interested in architecture? Perhaps he wanted to see the explosion with his own eyes?

Arina studied the accident details with a grim look. I admired her profile. An unruly black curl in an otherwise neat hairstyle fell over her eyes and she blew comically at it, not wanting to distract her hands from her work.

"That mother, eh?" I said.

People used to talk about the weather, but now the real weather is predictable, and everyone can set their own augmented weather. But talking about luddites was always en vogue.

"What?"

"She's damaging the child's psyche. Can you imagine what his school life must be like?"

"Yes, I can. I don't have an implant."

I didn't believe her. Who would? She may work for the DOA, but she was still a government inspector. How could we do our job without augmentation? I turned on the technical channel and confirmed that Arina wasn't lying. She was using an external device to access augmented reality—those rimless glasses. She was tuned to the base channel. No changes to the appearance of the world around her, just the ability to work with the virtual interface. Unbelievable.

The scene of the accident was cordoned off in all dimensions, so on the technical channel it looked like an air well in a sea of information flows. The system didn't bother to darken this well, so its impenetrable walls were crowded on all sides by jets filled with gawkers. I considered this to be a compliment: if a trifle like a stalled jet on the side of the road could arouse such curiosity among the citizens, this meant the Department of Transportation was performing its job well.

The jet involved in the accident wasn't municipal property; it belonged to the passenger. Private vehicles may be a relic of a bygone era, but a well-entrenched relic that's here to stay.

Having searched for and not found Danny among the gawkers, Arina took on the responsibility of interviewing the jet passenger. Meantime, I looked around. While Nettie may not have the right to remotely collect users' private data, at least I can see the basic information packet of each user in person. Kind of like the way the police used to be able to check people's IDs. While Nettie processed the data I collected, I tuned to a gallery of channels popular among the gathered. Images of fanciful variations on modern Moscow flashed before me, causing my head to spin. With a practiced motion of my right hand I slowed down the speed with which the channels were changing. The augmentation visualized the scene of the accident in a variety of ways.

A kids channel rendered a cartoonish car in trippy colors, surrounded by toy-soldier cops. The learning channel showed a fight between tyrannosaurs, for some reason. The most popular—as usual—was the zombie apocalypse; here Arina and the passenger were perched atop the jet, surrounded on all sides by dead things.

I noticed a gaggle of boys who were ignoring the accident. Instead they stared past it, across the street, at the doomed building. It was suspicious, but I didn't get the chance to do anything about it.

Several things happened at once.

First, the process of encapsulating the building was finalized. The building disappeared. The Moscow One channel almost immediately replaced it with a fence several meters tall, covered in posters featuring a mix of images of friendly builders in hard hats and of warning signs. When the boys saw this, they huddled, looked around, and then scattered.

Second, Nettie delivered the results of her analysis. She combed through Danny's entire private data cache, compared the information packets to those of his frequent chat interlocutors, and found the four boys. As they ran away, she carefully highlighted them in green frames.

Third, Arina returned, forcing her way through the crowd. Her visual feed already displayed the results of the interview with the jet passenger. Arina convinced him to grant access to the video stored in his implant and in his jet's memory. Danny Nechayev could be seen on the recordings. Fifteen minutes prior he had run across the highway and had strode purposefully toward the condemned building. Nettie hadn't seen him, but the jet's cameras had. That's what caused the paradox that required the presence of an inspector at the site of the accident: Nettie judged the private jet's autonomous decisions to be unjustified.

"Why did the perimeter let him pass?" I asked, surprised.

"The force field isn't active yet," said Arina.

Those damned penny pinchers.

Meantime, I transferred the info about the absconded boys

to Arina. Those kids were up to something. We finished reading their dossiers at the same time, and spoke simultaneously.

"Roof jockeys."

I dislike roof jockeys even more than I dislike luddites. They call themselves "rooftoppers" to claim affiliation with a century-old movement. Except rooftoppers of old only explored the rooftops. They didn't jump off. Roof jockeys are nothing more than adrenaline junkies. They should be out there climbing Mount Everest—and jumping off of that, too. Instead they make their way onto rooftops and jump down in order to experience the double thrills of free fall and then of the embrace of the force field which grabs hold of them and gently, via spiral trajectory, lowers them to the ground. Every time this happens, Nettie is forced to recalculate and redirect traffic patterns, but it's not as if the roof jockeys care.

"You think he's going to jump?" asked Arina.

"Looks like it."

"Little shit."

"You should understand him better than most," I remarked carefully. "Kid's tired of being an outsider and doesn't see any other way to fit in."

"There are better ways. Fight a couple of peers, punch their lights out, bingo—you're instantly one of the gang." Arina paused, gave me a scathing look, and changed the subject. "Teaching force fields new tricks is long overdue. But your department . . ."

I thought, yeah, right. You architects always want to rebuild, improve, and replace everything. But I stopped myself. The girl was right. The best way to combat the roof jockeys would be to deprive them of any pleasure they derive from their actions. No more smooth, waterslide-like landing. Instead, they should hang suspended a few meters above ground for hours, helplessly floundering in front of a laughing crowd. Arina was right: it was our department that was resisting the change. It would waste too much energy. But mostly, it might possibly interfere with the flow of traffic. And the traffic must flow above all.

None of that mattered now. The sixteen-story monstrosity

became invisible. Nettie erased it from its map, turned off all sensors, became deaf and blind. There was no one to react to the sudden appearance of a roof jockey. No one to turn on the force field. The boy will fall to his death.

Arina already rolled out her visual feed to three-sixty degrees and sorted through the data. She paused long enough to say, "What are you waiting for? Get to the roof. I'll try to cancel the encapsulation."

I glanced at her doubtfully. Everything happened a lot faster these days. Even so, big projects like this couldn't be reversed with a snap of the fingers. The chain of negotiations alone will take over an hour. This attempt would be akin to trying to stop a charging rhinoceros.

Arina correctly interpreted the look I gave her yet again.

"I won't be talking to people; I'll be talking to Nettie. I doubt we can restore full function, there isn't enough time or energy for that. But even at the very basic level, Nettie will react to your presence. Go!"

This was logical. The system operating at its lowest basic functions would ignore a boy without a digital footprint, but it would notice my presence for sure.

So I ran, periodically glancing at Arina's visual interface which was still shared with me. Her lines of code were each simple and practical, like lines of a sketch that combined into an elegant, even masterful picture which seemed somehow familiar.

I turned off augmentation without waiting to cross the line where Nettie would disconnect from me on her own. I didn't want my guess to turn into an accidental query. If I was right, I had good reason to think that Daniel and I were in good hands.

If all goes well, I thought, I'll ask her to have dinner with me. We can talk about the history of Moscow, about Devlet Girey, about Napoleon. Who among us weren't a hell raiser in their youth? It's just that some can raise hell at a much greater scale.

The world around me hadn't changed. Moscow One replicated the real look of the city almost exactly, except for the minor details. But those details were difficult to ignore. I almost forgot how many little details there were in the real world. Imperfections that were sometimes unpleasant, but stunning in their variety and scope. The leaves on trees were dull, partially yellowed as autumn approached. Tiny cracks in the sidewalk formed some abstract painting. Fresh and indecent graffiti were painted on the wall. There was a cacophony of sounds: laughter and shouting, the steady hum of the moving walkway and the disjointed squawking of birds, wind, rustling, creaking, whispers, crackling . . .

I never even noticed crossing the threshold.

No amount of augmentation could fix Brezhnev-era architecture. Especially on the inside. I usually avoid visiting such buildings; thankfully my job mostly keeps me outdoors, and I found an apartment in an old converted mansion with a tiny garden in the backyard, well-hidden from the bustle of the city in a vintage maze of old city side streets.

It was fortunate that Nettie had me respond to this call. It's not just the shock of switching from familiar augmentation to unpredictable reality, but also the means of interacting with one's surroundings. Because of my dislike for visual interfaces, I was better prepared to cope with reality than most. Better, but not perfectly.

I wasted precious seconds standing by the elevator and waiting for the lift to be automatically summoned before I finally figured out that I should press the button. According to Nettie, the elevators in this building hadn't been updated since 2020, sixty years ago. Realizing that I'm entrusting my life to such an ancient and morally outdated mechanism caused me to experience an acute episode of claustrophobia. This is despite the fact that the elevator functioned pretty well. It moved smoothly, if a bit slowly.

Honestly, I was hoping that a roof hatch would be locked. Then I hoped that the rooftop would be deserted, and then I hoped that I was seeing things . . .

But he was there. Danny-boy was standing at the roof's edge and staring with despair at the city that surrounded him. From the sixteen-story tall vantage point, the real unaugmented Moscow skyline looked majestic and solemn.

It was the kingdom of the color blue and the wind.

I walked toward him slowly, but not too slowly. Calm and casual steps, as though I too was a roof jockey.

In the real world it's impossible to mask one's appearance without a lot of foresight. I had taken my uniform jacket off back in the elevator and had rolled up the sleeves of my shirt, but when I came close, even a seven-year-old boy could tell I was in law enforcement.

"I didn't do anything!" he shouted.

"That's great," I said. "That means everything will be all right."

"Everything will be all right after I jump."

"If you jump, you'll fall. The system is turned off."

There was a flash of terror in his eyes, but then he stretched his trembling lips into an indulgent smile.

"Fairy tales for babies," he said. "I'd been warned."

Danny stared at the city beyond the edge of the roof, then back at me.

"I won't chicken out," he said. "I'm not chicken shit."

Augmentation would have undoubtedly corrected the phrase. In my preferred reality he would have probably said "I'm not afraid." But it was just the two of us on the edge of a real roof, without corrections and censors.

Danny closed his eyes and stepped off the roof.

The time slowed. I swear. Every time I read this phrase—I love to read, and always paper books, despite the futurists' constant predictions about the impending total victory of virtual technologies over print—I never believed it. But it really felt like the time slowed, individual moments strung like beads on its axis. I could examine each one of them in detail.

I thought that I had an easier time of it than Daniel. I had made my decision as soon as I saw him at the roof's edge. It was as though I could see the future; my words weren't meant to prevent it but merely to forestall it, to win some time, to get close to him so I would have a chance for when he finally took that step.

I thought Daniel had an easier time of it than me. He didn't believe that the system was turned off, that there was no one to catch him and to gently lower him to the ground. He didn't know that our only hope was young Arina, who had to stop a charging rhino all by herself.

I stepped forward, my hands trying to grab Danny but grasping nothing except cold air instead.

I screamed in terror. We all make a promise to ourselves to act in a dignified manner and to meet tribulations silently and head-on. One's true nature takes over when we face a trial in a real world and not an imaginary one.

There was the blinding blue of the sky, the infernal, terrifying, roaring blue. And the wind. And the certainty that we're not flying toward the earth but rather that it's the earth that jumped upward to catch us and to never let us go again.

For just a moment—and there's nothing I'm more certain of than the reality of that moment—the blue of the sky was replaced by the viscous and calm color of my repose. The chartreuse green.

Then a gentle force field enveloped both of us like the arms of some invisible giant.

THE JELLYFISH

A JELLYFISH SWAM SLOWLY RIGHT THROUGH THE DATAVENEER and hung at the center of the room, chaotically wiggling its tentacles. It was so dazzlingly multi-colored that it made Kalinka shut her eyes. She had already forgotten how bright colors could be.

Perhaps if those colors were sold separately, Kalinka might have saved up enough likes to buy a few—it would make the world that much more amusing, what with an orange ceiling and orange banner ads. And, of course, Kalinka would've painted the auras of all those foolish proactives with a delicate shade of fuchsia. And then she would've laughed inwardly in response to Mouser's arrogant remarks.

"How do you like my new aura, Kali? Oh, forgive me, of course you can't see, you poor thing. Should I spare you some likes?"

But the colors were sold only in a complete bundle, and the subscription cost half a dozen likes per cycle. It was an exorbitant luxury, considering Kalinka could barely afford a thin layer of dataveneer in lieu of walls. She was no pro, and didn't want to become one. She didn't earn likes through pointless content and flattering remarks, didn't hang around popular users, hoping to catch a few freebie bonuses along with the reflection of their fame. She was about to hit rock bottom with no prospects of ever climbing out. Without a room of her own, without walls and some semblance of privacy, hermits like Kalinka quickly turned into mere numbers; it only took a couple of cycles. They lost themselves along with their names, and there was no way back. At the moment, Kalinka was less than a step away from turning into a number. Half a step, even.

She didn't fully comprehend how this had come to be.

She'd carefully allotted the likes for the next twenty-four cycles. That and the strict austerity in everything was part of the plan. Kalinka didn't remember when and why she had come up with this plan, but she knew that she had to adhere to it.

Point one: Not to slip into becoming a number.

Point two: To get out of the Socium.

A very simple plan.

Except Kalinka hadn't the vaguest idea where to begin pursuing point two. She didn't even understand very well what it meant. Therefore, she focused on the first point.

Given: twenty likes. The goal: to maintain herself, and her dignity. How to avoid turning into a number if you only have twenty likes until the next bonus? And the next bonus is ten cycles away? No one could do that. Yet, Kalinka had managed.

Except the head office had lowered the coefficient without warning, and the little quiet hermits like Kalinka got the shaft.

The head office's actions were understandable.

The Socium must function.

Everyone in their place.

Users generated and processed content, numbers milled the byproducts into flour on enormous grindstones.

Proactive users—the pros—were to be encouraged; hermits like Kalinka were to be punished. Whoever didn't like it could go become a number.

Truth be told, Kalinka was sometimes envious of the numbers. All they had to do was walk in circles, push the wheel, and watch cheerfully as foolish comments, bad jokes, and ingratiating emojis were turned into a homogenous crunchy mass. But—point one. Do not slip into becoming a number. Obviously, there'd be no coming back from that.

Kalinka counted the pitiful seven likes she had been given instead of the expected seventy, over and over again. Never before had point one been so unachievable.

Even if, by some miracle, she morphed from a downtrodden hermit into a successful pro, became quotable and socially-useful, gained contacts and acclaim . . . The next round of bonuses would only be paid out in twenty-four cycles. She couldn't last that long on seven likes. The minuses were deducted from the karma immediately. That was Socium justice for you.

The jellyfish!

Kalinka opened her eyes, certain that the jellyfish had already swum away, or that she had hallucinated it. But it was still there. Blue, pink, lilac—the jellyfish shimmered and flickered, as though deliberately hypnotizing Kalinka. That was nonsense, of course. Jellyfish had no intentions. They had no minds. Probably.

Kalinka carefully and very slowly—as though attracted by an inexorable magnet—reached out with her hand toward the jellyfish. Who would have thought a jellyfish would have swum over, not to the arrogant Barker, not to the sugary-slick Beaverton, not to one of those vile, extrovert influencers, but to Kalinka. Kalinka the hermit. Kalinka the sociopath.

And—oh, faulty firewalls!—the jellyfish reached its tentacles toward her palm. Kalinka immediately felt its touch—cold, prickly, and a little bitter.

The jellyfish brimmed with data, so much so that, without any upgrades, Kalinka saw, heard, and felt things she shouldn't have been able to see, hear, or feel in her minimalistic configuration.

The jellyfish jerked and slid straight toward Kalinka's face. It froze. The fabric of reality rippled and vibrated around it. Kalinka felt a terrible, irresistible urge to open her mouth and swallow the jellyfish, which was beautiful and juicy, like a piece of candy.

Candy . . . What was that?

Grandma always brings candy. She walks along the path, so slow and sanguine. Julie runs toward her, joyfully anticipating the treats.

Kalinka recoiled. The vision was colorful, full-bodied, lively. Like a vid. A very expensive vid.

In the maelstrom of content, Kalinka had always kept far away from the central currents. Likes beget likes, content begets content. This is known. Pay a hundred likes to imbibe a data-rich vid, tell your friends, and you will recoup those likes four-fold. In theory, of course. One time, Kalinka had spent almost twenty likes on some stupid trash vid based on Mouser's life. Her review was reshared by one naïve hermitess, and liked by one newbie who hadn't yet acclimated to the Socium. And that was that.

Ever since, Kalinka had consumed only the public vids that were played for free for the hermits and the roomless. These vids were so hopelessly monotonous that it was as though they were compiled from freshly ground scraps of content, without any additional processing. But this gruel was enough to while away cycle after cycle without becoming a number. Enough to stick to point one of the plan.

Kalinka carefully peeked outside. Had anyone seen the jellyfish enter her room? There was no doubt this was a mistake. Everyone knew: jellyfish only swam to the worthy pros. Never to the hermits who barely had a pair of likes to rub together. But, over at the head office they ultimately didn't care who came to claim the reward. At least Kalinka really hoped so.

The gray world behind the datavencer hummed and boiled. Ads flashed, folding into headlines and emojis, trapping the unsuspecting hermits in their advertising nets. Ads rained down from the top levels like heavy snow. Down here, with merely seven likes to her name, it was only possible to hide from the ads inside her room. That was another advantage for the numbers: ads never reached them. Numbers possessed no likes, and were therefore of no interest to the pros.

Movement within the Socium was reminiscent of Brownian motion. Kalinka watched some hermit, purposefully rushing toward the showing of a public vid, run into a bunch of intrusive ads and become persuaded to exchange his likes for a stupid post by yet another influencer. A different user, who had been too short-sighted to invest in a quality firewall, was pounced upon by a news headline. He engaged in an unsuccessful struggle against it in a futile attempt to keep his savings. It was hopeless. The predatory headline, formulated by competent pros, sucked the likes out of the unfortunate hermit. He had no choice left but to repost and repost this headline in hopes of recouping a few likes, yet the lion's share of the earnings floated past him and toward the upper levels.

Indifferent auras flashed indifferently in this indifferent multi-level chaos, collided with each other, changed their opinions, reposted, cross-posted, parted with their likes and received new ones.

Fortunately, the Socium combined obsession and indifference in an ideal ratio. Nobody cared about Kalinka and her problems, as long as she wasn't planning to leave her precious likes under someone else's content—and she wasn't planning to do that.

Having dealt with the unlucky hermit, the headline spun around in search of its next victim, noticed Kalinka, and rushed toward her room, deftly maneuvering among the ads.

Kalinka immediately slammed the dataveneer shut. A handful of ads got in as usual, but that was a minor problem. In the confined space of the room, the ads died off quickly.

The jellyfish was still there. It shimmered, buzzed, beckoned.

She should have taken it to the head office immediately, without delay, and exchanged it for likes, before someone realized a mistake had been made and took the unexpected windfall away from Kalinka. But how would she travel across the whole of the Socium with the jellyfish and remain unnoticed? How to hide from prying eyes and greedy mouths, to avoid the maw of the headline? A predator would devour the jellyfish as easily as it feasted on the likes of imprudent hermits.

Kalinka thought about it. Seven likes. Just enough to subscribe to a basic firewall package for a quarter of a cycle. It was more expensive to buy piecemeal, of course, but there was nothing to be done about that. It would provide a safe path through the ocean of news. A solid firewall was too much for the little headlines to handle, and the big headlines were too clumsy and too lazy to chase a scrawny hermit like Kalinka.

That still left the problem of hiding the jellyfish. The solution appeared self-evident.

Kalinka opened her mouth and the jellyfish climbed inside as though it was waiting for the opportunity, its tentacles wiggling all funny.

It was a wondrous sensation, like holding a bit of living luck in one's mouth. Kalinka had never won the lottery before. At least she didn't think so. She couldn't be certain: her memory wasn't especially reliable on a diet of public vids, which was barely enough to remember the two points of the plan.

Point one and point two.

Not to slide into a number.

To get out.

Kalinka activated the upgrade interface, tossed the likes into the feeder, and confirmed her purchase. The firewall materialized immediately and wrapped Kalinka in protective flames.

There was no going back. Kalinka had spent all of her likes. The dataveneer of her room would dissipate into bytes in half a cycle's time, and then the only remaining path would be toward becoming a number.

That could not be permitted to happen. See point one.

Kalinka resolutely left the room, chose one of the vertical streams, stepped into it, and it carried her up past the envious glances of other hermits. The firewall looked fashionable and cool, and it was great fun to watch the ads burn in its flames.

Except the jellyfish didn't want to remain still in her mouth. Instead it fidgeted, burned with its tentacles, tried to get in deeper. It seemed to be losing its patience. Nonsense. Why would a jellyfish have patience? As if a lottery ticket could have a will and principles of its own.

The wind blows snow-white poplar fluffs toward her. The sur-

*rounding world is bright and blooming; reflections of the hot sum-
mer sun dance in her hair. Julia had just failed an exam, foolishly
relying on chance. In the past she had always spent the night before
the exam studying, and it had always been enough. But this night
. . . What a night! Kasimir, Kas, her dear, cheerful, warm beloved.
She had flunked the exam but she was happy—happy in a sweet,
full, endless way.*

The data hit sharply, abruptly. For a moment Kalinka was
there, in the warm happy place. She didn't truly understand those
pictures and sounds and thoughts—they were more complicated
than the vids made by Mouser and other top influencers. It was a
story out of a perpendicular world, one that was insane and unknowable. But this experience was the brightest Kalinka had ever
sampled within the Socium.

What is a jellyfish, anyway? Kalinka thought and became
frightened for some reason.

She only knew as much about the jellyfish as any other user.
Rumors. Many rumors about an unexpected stroke of luck—a
lottery ticket, bonus, gift from the Socium—showing up in the
form of a tiny jellyfish and jumping right into the hands of the
pros. The most proactive and energetic pros, of course; the most
well-meaning and socially dynamic. Certainly not into the hands
of passive hermits like Kalinka.

Collect one thousand likes and you'll earn a bonus jellyfish.

It's a peculiar idea, if you think about it: what do the pros
need a jellyfish for? They're already rolling in likes. Although Kalinka didn't actually know anyone who'd caught a jellyfish, not
even a tiny one. It was all just talk.

Talk was what pros were known for. Baby Angel's new aura,
Vito's reinforced shimmering dataveneer (a four-letter username
in itself a sign of an old-timer)—those were reality. Secret envy
and feigned friendliness, social activity for the sake of tiny per-
ception upgrades—those were reality.

Jellyfish were a fairy tale, like the ability to leave the Socium
or at least to climb to somewhere near the top of its pyramid.
To evolve from a consumer and regurgitator of content into a

true creator. To wit, a fairy tale.

Although, if one were to believe the persistent ads played during the commercial breaks in public vids, the likes paid in exchange for a jellyfish were real enough.

Ten thousand likes for a tiny one. Ten thousand! Enough to surround the room with firewalls. The colors . . . Forget colors, the music! Oh, the music. One time Kalinka had used a bonus to upgrade her hearing—just for one cycle, to try it out—to hear music just once. The music had been heavenly. Except, sharp hearing combined with cheap dataveneer turned that cycle into a true torture. But now, protected by the firewall from outside noise, she could have . . .

Kalinka choked on the wave of emotions—free and unaccounted for, like everything she felt in proximity to the jellyfish.

She would no longer have to chew on the gray public vids stuffed with ads. She wouldn't have to consume them at all.

With ten thousand likes she could easily afford to create content. To become a pro, or better. To record visuals and emotions into vids. To write music. To paint. She'd earn likes, so many likes!

Above her appeared the shape of an enormous rotund headline. The stream poured directly into the predator's maw, with several inattentive users already caught and stripped of their likes. Kalinka hurriedly switched to the parallel lane, again and again. Away from danger. She looked around. There were few hermits here. Envious glances were replaced by arrogant ones. Too bad. They wouldn't dare chase her off.

The jellyfish insistently tickled the top of her throat, as though the foolish thing wanted to be eaten. Each touch reverberated in a kaleidoscope of feelings and pictures within Kalinka.

A dusty office filled with old-fashioned bookcases featuring multicolored archaic book spines. The sheer curtain sways, obeying the light touch of the wind. The wind does nothing to dispel the humidity.

"My dear girl, you must understand, when signing a contract with them for even one year, you're practically selling yourself into slavery. The contract is renewed automatically, unless either of

the parties chooses otherwise. And they'll make certain you don't choose that. You won't even remember what to choose. They have their ways, you know." He's too old and too fat, but even in this heat he can't part with his uniform: a black three-piece suit with a striped shirt and a necktie. Adintsev keeps dabbing his sweaty forehead with a checkered handkerchief he keeps in his pocket.

"This is why I'm here, consulting with you instead of mindlessly signing those papers. You're a monster at this, Mr. Adintsev. Surely, you can think of something."

"Where did this ludicrous idea of entering the Socium come from?"

Julia is stubbornly silent. She retrieves a handkerchief of her own, only to crumple it over and over in her hands, preventing her nails from digging into her palms.

"You have a brilliant mind, my dear Julie. Why are you offering it to those vultures? To process accounting reports? To look for the next prime number, which nobody needs? To render a pink rabbit for some terrible movie? Stay, Julie. It was only by chance that you failed. Pfft. By next year you'll be the most brilliant student these walls have ever seen!"

How to make this old, fat man understand that she can't, she won't survive a year? Not with the terrible pain in her heart. Her heart, which didn't break overnight like a porcelain saucer, but is slowly crumbling under the pressure of a dark weight. It's becoming more difficult to breathe with each passing minute, knowing that her beloved, dear, red-headed Kasimir had betrayed her, betrayed everything they'd had together, for some stupid blonde in a striped dress. Who is she? Why is she there? Oh, god, Julia, what are you thinking about? Focus!

That had been oh-so-painful!

Kalinka had completely forgotten what pain was. Sometimes she purchased a little bit of cold and a little bit of warmth. The warmth by itself was three times cheaper, but without the cold it was not nearly as pleasurable. The cold was painful. The most painful thing she could remember. Until now.

There were those among the pros who consumed the feeling

of pain on a regular basis, and at a high cost.

Why did they need it? Kalinka hunched, cordoning off the pain that came with the vid. It was too dark, too deep. She would do anything never to feel such pain again. Anything!

The jellyfish tried to climb out, as though having read Kalinka's mind, but she didn't allow that. The jellyfish darted back and forth in her mouth, stinging Kalinka relentlessly. Her aura filled with data.

A large, white, shaggy dog named Bom runs across the grass, shaking off drops of dew. Julia runs after him. She feels her sneakers and socks getting soaked through.

Dad brought a real paper book—a huge one with black-and-white pictures and maybe a million letters. The letters don't dance and don't tell their own story at Julia's gesture. They stand still, lazy, arrogantly waiting for Julia to read them herself.

Mama, Mommy, where are you? Little Julie got lost in a huge department store, among automated forklifts and shelves filled with identical gray boxes.

Kalinka shook her head. The head office was within arm's reach. There were no headlines in her path. She only had to move. She only had to be patient. And everything would be fine.

"You could say hello," she heard a haughty voice nearby. Kalinka turned around cautiously. Mouser. A bore and a philanthropist, an unusual combination. It's easy for an influencer to be a philanthropist, he has plenty to give away, and it will come back to his karma tenfold, a hundredfold. It's just business, like everything in this world. It was Mouser who'd saved her each time she was a step from sliding down into becoming a number. Therefore, she should've at least smiled at him. But the stubborn jellyfish persisted in painfully stinging her, and Kalinka's smile looked more like a grimace.

"I'm serious, Kali." She could now hear a threat in Mouser's voice. And why not? Pros are very protective of their reputations, and the philanthropists especially so. What would happen to a philanthropist's reputation if some destitute hermitess failed to be aura-deep thankful to him?

Kalinka shook her head pitifully. She dared not open her mouth—the jellyfish might jump out, and all would be lost.

Mouser's aura darkened. The jellyfish shrank back. He never let offenses slide, and rancor was the key to his popularity. It was better to offer a like before Mouser suspected ingratitude. Let him say anything he wants to her, let him write a scathing post about her or even make her the antagonist of his new vid, an ugly roomless specimen languidly sliding into a number, anything but . . .

A minus from someone like Mouser weighed heavily and—like any minus—would count immediately. Kalinka glanced at his enormous karma. Ten dislikes, or more. Her own karma was at zero after purchasing the firewall. This meant that all of her property and real estate would go toward covering the minus. Including the firewall.

The most dangerous, agile, and ruthless headlines, used to hunting tough pros, waited for her above. They could even bite off a good chunk of likes from someone like Mouser. They would part a humble hermit like her from her jellyfish in seconds, if her firewall were to disappear.

No, Mouser, please, anything but the minus!

"Such ingratitude deserves a minus to your karma." Mouser was taking his time, as though he hadn't made a decision yet. He was toying with her.

Kalinka shook her head desperately. The jellyfish was kicking harder and harder, and Kalinka pressed her hand to her mouth so as not to accidentally spit it out.

Mouser interpreted the gesture in his own way.

"Wait . . . Did you trade away your ability to speak for the firewall? What a fool, how are you going to repost with this configuration?"

Kalinka nodded in relief. It was better to appear stupid than to earn a minus to her karma.

"Why didn't you *say so*?" Mouser laughed nastily at his own joke, and jumped into another stream without saying goodbye. He would go on to share the funny incident and it would earn him two hundred likes, easy.

But it didn't matter now. The stream brought her near the roof of the world and pushed her out onto the top level.

A dozen long headlines milled about the entrance to the head office, ready to attack anyone without sufficient protection. *I'm too much for them to handle*, Kalinka thought, watching as they scattered, burned by the flames of her firewall.

The jellyfish went nuts and it kept stinging, stinging, stinging. Kalinka was learning what true pain felt like.

"Julia Kalinskaya, our school's best graduate in a decade!" The director adjusts her triangular glasses.

Bom the dog is dying. Slowly. Painfully. He whines and jerks his paw. Why? Why?

"Did you know that the name Kasimir means 'stubborn' in Turkic?" He has red hair and funny freckles all over his face. He smiles like the sun. Laughs like the wind.

She deletes the traitor's letters from her inbox, one after another. They're too much! Awkward, laughable excuses. Does that stubborn man not realize that he only demeans her further by prolonging this spectacle?

"You'll be in a giant freezer, along with thousands of others like you. Having signed the contract you will cease to exist in this world, cease to belong to yourself. Your brain will become the property of Socium for the duration of the contract. It'll have to work, and believe me, this will be a strenuous labor. Of course, our experts will do everything they can to keep your personality in good shape. The basic configuration is provided free of charge. You will receive communication and an imitation of a social life, but no guarantees of safety. Everything is individualized." The Socium lawyer recites the familiar words somewhat mournfully, in the same tone employed by the beggars on the subway. He talks about guarantees, insurance, and guarantees again. About the money that will be paid to Mom. It's good that Mom won't find out about this until it's too late for her to stop it. Julia listens indifferently and nods thoughtlessly, crushed by her pain. Soon. Soon, she will forget all of it.

Kalinka thought she was about to explode. To blow up in colorful chunks of data, into little ads and lines of text. She squinted, trying to rein in the untenable stream, and when she opened them again—

—she lay in a cramped, cold space, and her eyes were still shut, and there was nothing except a solid tube in her mouth and a stinging liquid in her lungs. She tried to breathe in, choked on her pain, and once again fell into oblivion.

The entrance to the head office swung open and two specialists helped her in. Julia smiled at them gratefully.

"Attention!" the first specialist shouted. "We've got a JELLY-FISH!"

Those dandies could always see right through the users. It was no wonder: to have a full configuration in the world of the Socium was almost akin to being a god.

A specialist reached out his hand, in a soft but demanding manner.

"It's your lucky day, my dear. Not everyone gets such a windfall. My congratulations! The jellyfish, if you please."

The jellyfish refused to vacate her mouth. It hung on with its tentacles. It tickled, jumped, stung, stung, stung. It tried even more insistently do drill somewhere deeper. Seemingly, it really didn't want to return to the jellyfisharium, or wherever these things were held in between lottery drawings. Kalinka felt terrible for the jellyfish, but she felt even worse for herself.

Yes, her plan demanded some ruthlessness. Point one: not to backslide. Point two: to get out. If she left the head office and released the jellyfish now, instead of returning it to the specialists, both points would have to be crossed out as unachievable. She'd have nothing to look forward to but the trip all the way down, to the numbers and their mills.

That is why Kalinka opened her mouth and spat the jellyfish rudely out onto her palm. The specialist immediately and deftly grabbed it by the tentacles. Kalinka was horrified by how quickly the jellyfish turned gray and wilted in his hands. The specialist smiled, and in some imperceptible way came to resemble a predatory headline.

For a moment, Kalinka feared that he would chase her off

without any reward. But she almost immediately felt her karma filling with likes, becoming wider and heavier.

It had all worked out.

Her new life awaited her.

Adintsev sinks heavily into the opposite chair and dabs his forehead with a handkerchief. He frowns. He always frowns when he speaks about something important.

"*I found some guys. A small firm, you know, an underground one. Those guys are my students, so I trust them completely. At the right time, they will send a letter with a cast of your memory. You will receive the letter, I guarantee it. The rest, Julie, depends entirely on you. Best of luck to you, my dear. See you in a year.*"

He is a nice man, that Adintsev.

The hermit left, and the specialists exchanged meaningful looks.

The first one said, "We almost lost her this time. Semenych was about to signal an awakening."

"One user more, one user less," the second one replied philosophically.

"I wouldn't say that. If we lose a head such as Kalinskaya's, they'll take our heads for it, and they won't stop there."

The first one unloaded the jellyfish squeamishly into a container and reached for the disposal interface.

The second walked to a viewport. Beyond it buzzed the bright and restless imitation shell of the Socium.

"Don't let those things near her again, and we won't have a problem. As if you don't know how to do that."

"Oh, I'd love to, but this is a different matter. Adintsev himself wrote her contract. You know what sort of a man he was? My father studied under him. He wrote perfect contracts: point by point, unassailable!"

"But he died, that Adintsev of yours. Many years ago!"

"Adintsev may have died, but the contract is immortal."

"Whoever is sending the jellyfish will get tired of it. That person isn't immortal."

"That's something, at least. The bastard sure is stubborn,

though. What was it, the fourteenth jellyfish?"

"Either that, or the fifteenth."

"Hang on, it hasn't fried yet."

The first one retrieved the jellyfish from the disposal unit, deftly opened the package, and read theatrically:

"I'm still here, still waiting for you, still stubborn as a mule. You recall that Kasimir means 'stubborn'? I still love you. Come back, dearest."

"So, was it the fourteenth?"

"The fifteenth."

NO ONE EVER LEAVES PORT HENRI

I ENTER THE BAR AND ALL CONVERSATION CEASES, LIKE IN A trashy paperback novel. Patrons turn and stare at me. Francois must've already spread the news. Not that I was going to hide it—you can't hide something like this, tomorrow it'll be in the papers. But for now, I was unsettled.

What dragged me to Azure anyhow? I knew Francois couldn't keep a secret; his nickname—Loose Lips—was well-earned, after all. The thing is, when your mind is preoccupied with difficult problems, your feet carry you along the familiar path. Doc César calls this a "behavioral pattern."

Doc's here too—where else would he be? Hidden away in a dark corner so you can only see his eyes. Those eyes are filled with a devil's compassion. Others look at me with equal parts jealousy and genuine happiness for my fortune.

Their stares only serve to anger me. Especially César's. If not for his stories, I'd be the happiest man in Port Henri. But now?

Now I feel like a man at the edge of the abyss.

Not that I can explain this to any of them.

They aren't thinking of me, or of my son. They think of their own children who lost the most important lottery of their lives today. What future awaits them? They'll become fishermen and prospectors. Some, who are very lucky, might join the Cayman Guard. The not-so-lucky ones will become miners.

I've seen child miners. Grim, exhausted faces. Eyes that have absorbed the darkness of the mine shafts. It's as though they've seen things beneath the mountains that have changed them forever.

Any resident of Port Henri will tell you: the mountains are populated by demons who loathe parting with their treasure. They demand human souls in exchange. That's why children make the best miners: their souls are purer, tastier for the demons. A child carries such a demon back from the mine inside them, like an incurable disease, and the demon slowly devours the young soul, leaving nothing but a walking skeleton.

At first glance the people of Port Henri are like everyone else. Not better, not worse. At first glance you can't tell they carry the sorts of stories inside that make even my stomach turn.

"What are you standing over there for, Joe?" shouts Francois. "Buy a round for the good people, my friend. Surely you won't forget your old pals now that you're practically an Olympian?"

"That's Mr. Joseph Fellow to you, Loose Lips."

Francois grins a pocked smile at me.

They love nicknames in Port Henri. Seven years ago someone started calling me Convict. I had to break several noses to put an end to that.

I nod to the bartender. I've seen what's to come time and time again. Whenever fortune smiles upon some poor prospector he becomes an instant celebrity for a day. His meager handful of emeralds will barely cover a round for the barflies. And he'll spend it all, instead of buying a new dress for his wife, to bask in the smiles and approval of his buddies. That's how things are done in Port Henri.

I have no choice but to undergo this ordeal. Congratulations, friendly slaps on the shoulder. Everyone tries to shake my hand. The bartender asks for an autographed photo to put up on the wall. And why not—the Azure will become a celebrity hangout now. They might even rename Caipirinha into Joe Fellow in my honor.

The thought makes me sick. I down a shot of cachaça and ask for another.

The tropical nights sneak up on you, quiet and stealthy, like dexterous thieves. Perhaps the night *is* a thief, but what does it pilfer? And if it doesn't, then why does it sneak up on me so suddenly? Life taught me that every living thing has its agenda. But can the night be considered a living thing? When you think of it, even inanimate objects have a will of their own.

Take my grandfather's favorite fishing rod, which he used on the Little Tennessee River. When it didn't feel like working, the fish wouldn't bite for anything. I don't know what it whispered to the bass, but nearby fishermen reeled them in one after the other while Grandpa caught nothing but some peace and quiet.

I realize that last shot of cachaça was too much. My thoughts are tangled like the narrow Port Henri streets I'm traversing.

This won't do, Joe, I tell myself. You can't fall back on your usual solution of getting drunk instead of dealing with the problem. Not today. Sober up, convict. Sober up now.

Last time I got this drunk was five years ago. I was in my right, then. All fathers get drunk when their sons are born. The wives think of us as terrible egoists and weaklings for doing so.

The woman carries the child for nine months inside her. This miracle is a part of her, gradually becomes a part of her world. The same miracle catches the man by complete surprise. The new dimension opens in front of him, like a hole that leads into a parallel universe. Like a sunrise after a night that lasted a lifetime. As though he were falling into the abyss and realized, just above the ground, that he knew how to fly.

That's why a *real* man must get drunk as many times as he has children. But no more than that. Not even if his son's life is on the line. Especially not then.

I look around. The nights in Port Henri are murky and thick.

It's not easy to orient myself in the dark. But the sense of smell never fails me. I sniff at the air. Among the aromas of spices and the sea I smell the waft of typographer's ink.

The sounds confirm it. I hear the rattle of the printing press from the basement of the nearby building. The lights are on within the second floor. No doubt, these are the offices of the *Free Guanahani*. The newspapermen work best at night. I imagine the editor, his hair unkept, a cigarette dangling from the corner of his mouth. He stares grimly at his typewriter, dissolving his writer's block with strong rum.

I don't have to look over his shoulder to learn tomorrow's headline. I already know it.

"King Henri IX Chooses Heir" will be printed in huge letters across the top. A few lines about the poor young Henri IX will follow. They'll praise his bravery, the strength and grace with which the young king faces certain death. Underneath, it will say:

"His Majesty has finally reached the decision all of us have been waiting for with baited breath. He chose the five-year-old Nicholas Fellow as his heir. As per tradition, Nicholas will adopt the name Henri, and under that name will become the tenth king of Guanahani."

Next to that paragraph will be the photo of my son.

Then, in small print underneath, they might add:

"Keep in mind that all ports will be closed until Sunday night in celebration of the coronation."

I hear a shuffling of steps behind me. I recognize them without turning. Doc César.

The stubborn old man gets right to the point. "What are you going to do?"

"Go to hell, Doc."

"You won't solve your problems by drinking cachaça, Joe."

"Leave me alone. I don't want to talk to you right now."

"Don't be a fool, Joe. You have to do something. You can't—"

I shove him. Not too hard by my standards, but he falls onto the ground anyway. This damned town has changed me. I fight old men now.

"Sorry, Doc." I offer him my hand.

He gets up, dusts off his clothes, adjusts his glasses. He goes on as if nothing has happened. "You have to decide today, Joe. Tomorrow will be too late."

As if I didn't know this.

"When will they close the port?" I ask.

"They already closed it. They put up the celebratory flags."

"So there's no way to get the motor boat."

"No, no way."

I could take Francois's boat, but there's no point. It's a slow tub. Won't get far.

"No amount of money will rent you a motorboat," says Doc. As though I had the money. The lack of funds is the one constant in my life. "But it's possible to steal one."

Doc raises an eyebrow at me, as if to say: *You're a thief, Joe. You could easily do this.*

People in Port Henri are stubborn. Once they got it into their heads that Joe Fellow is a first-rate thief, it was impossible to dissuade them. They'll nod as they listen to how I ended up in prison as an innocent man. How the jurors were idiots, the judge was a scoundrel, and my attorney was a hack. And how I was the fool who was doing research for a book about the Parisian underclass and decided to collect some material in person. How I had nothing to do with the robbery and especially the murder of that old man—I only waited by the car and smoked a bunch of cigarettes. They'll nod and smile, and won't believe a single word. Joe Fellow is a first-rate thief, but he loves to spin a yarn, they'll say.

I tell Doc to get some sleep. Then I head to Madame Simone's. Her establishment is open all night.

Simone greets me personally, seats me in an armchair and brings me strong coffee. The old woman knows more about men than any other woman. More than we know about ourselves.

"Is Monty upstairs?" I ask.

She shrugs, as in: where else would he be?

I'll wait for him here. The important thing is not to fall asleep.

I stare at the faded figurine of the Virgin Mary in the corner for so long that Simone begins to make excuses: it's well overdue to be painted, but there's never enough time.

I don't hear her, just like I don't see the faded Virgin Mary.

I escaped Hell's Island, the most heavily guarded prison in French Guiana, where escape was said to be impossible. Surely I can find a way to leave the peaceful, quiet Guanahani.

I had almost choked on my rum when César came to me a week ago and told me that Nicki would be made king. The sun had been setting in the blue sea. It had been devilishly beautiful.

I never really came to like Port Henri. It's a shameful feeling, akin to hating one's own father. Or rather, a stepfather. Port Henri accepted me as one of its own. It forgave my sins. Gave me a wife, a son, friends. Fed me and kept me warm. But in seven years I never acclimated. Two things made the town tolerable: its sunsets, and my son.

When the sun had set and Doc began telling me about the Sek, I had to go get the second bottle of rum.

We'd known each other for seven years. You might say I owe him my life. That was the only reason I hadn't thrown him out and had politely listened to his nonsense instead.

I had listened and said, "Doc, this is nonsense."

"Have you never wondered why, seven years ago, none of your compatriots had survived?"

Of course I had wondered that. Although I tended to frame the question differently: why had I survived?

We had been practically corpses when we reached Port Henri. We spent two weeks on the open water in a dilapidated river boat which nearly sunk in the first storm. Sun and salt had wounded our skins. Dehydration had made me hallucinate. I had thought I was back in my cell on Hell's Island, and that all other prisoners were released due to amnesty but I had been forgotten in the dank, moldy basement. I had desperately knocked on the bottom of the boat, sending unrequited messages to an imaginary neighbor in the next cell. I had talked to dead people. They had shown up in the boat one by one, glaring at me silently from the next bench. I saw my grandfather, who died before the Great War. Saw my father and mother. Saw the German soldier whom I shot in the leg. The girl from Amiens whom I had once promised to marry. I was guilty of some slight toward all of them, and this guilt ate at my soul like salt that ate at my skin. I confessed and I prayed, but my only reply was silence.

When I had heard the cries of seagulls, I was certain it was another mirage.

Even the healthiest man might not recover from such a journey. I wasn't healthy to begin with. I was a pale scarecrow who had crawled into the sunlight after five months spent in dungeons of Hell's Island, where water flooded my cell up to my waist in high tide.

The three of us escaped together. Me, Antoine, and a kid whose name I never learned. None of us knew the ways of the mariner. It was a miracle our fragile vessel reached the shores of Guanahani.

Port Henri is the mecca for the convicts of French Guiana. It was the dream that gave me strength on Hell's Island. The oasis in the middle of the watery desert. There were many stories about it, but I only cared about one: unlike Trinidad, Curaçao, and Grenada, it didn't extradite runaway criminals.

When I regained consciousness in the Port Henri hospital, I learned that my compatriots were dead. I was the only one granted the miracle of survival.

Sometimes I wonder if perhaps I'm still there, on the boat, this life a fevered dream of a man dying of dehydration.

"I'll listen to your theories, Doc. But I can't promise to buy into them. You're not yourself today."

"These aren't theories, Joe. When you were brought to the hospital, the first thing they did was check your blood type. Of the three of you, you were the only match. When His Majesty learned of this, he dispatched his personal doctor."

"And who was this doctor?"

"Me, Joe. Me."

Such news after seven years of acquaintanceship, almost friendship. I never suspected Doc to be so complicated a man. Outwardly he seemed a typical old man from Port Henri—dark skinned and short. A regular at Azure. Someone who enjoyed a good drink, telling a good story, and listening to one. Unbelievable.

"Are you saying the others were left to die?"

"No, they were treated. But they weren't treated by me, so their chances weren't good."

"What's so special about my blood?"

It was a surprise that old king Henri VIII, grandfather of the current king, Henri IX, took personal interest in my fate. It was almost something to be proud of.

I've always been impressed with the fair structure of the Guanahani monarchy. When the king lacked direct descendants, he chose an heir among the children of regular citizens. In one hundred plus years Guanahani had seen ten different monarchs. Five of them were from the families of miners and fishermen.

It wasn't a big surprise. After all, the first King Henri had been a slave, bore the surname of his owner, and spent half his life roasting under the sun in the sugarcane fields, until the revolution of 1813. They say the rebels killed all the Europeans on the island. They had apologized later, but I suspect those apologies weren't especially sincere.

"You can't imagine, Joe, how important a thing blood is. Augusto Medina, my predecessor in the post of the royal doctor, once said that Henri planned on marrying one of the granddaughters of Queen Victoria. Believe me, had he made that decision, neither the Queen, nor the British parliament, nor the granddaughter herself would have been able to deny him. But Henri changed his mind when he learned that Victoria's descendants suffer from hemophilia."

"Which Henri was this? Fifth or sixth?"

"Joe, you haven't been listening. There had been no fifth or sixth. Just like there had been no second, third, etc. There has ever only been one Henri. One and only."

*

Heavy steps on the staircase. That must be Monty—Mr. Smith, the American consul.

The consul and I share a complicated relationship. Monty knows that it was I who taught everyone to call him by his first name. It annoys him, but there isn't much he can do. He'd be thrilled to extradite me back home, but he doesn't have the juice.

One thing I like about this portly gentleman: he knows how to keep a poker face. When he sees me, he only raises a single eyebrow.

Simone escorts us to a tiny room that serves as her office. Better than heading upstairs, to one of the bedrooms, I suppose.

I tell Monty Smith about the Sek, about the king, and about my son.

"Fellow, you aren't making any sense. How much have you had to drink?" he asks.

"Not that much. Practically nothing. Listen, Monty, you don't have to believe me. I'm offering you a once-in-a-lifetime deal."

"Why would I piss off King Henri?"

"Because you get *me*. You'll be a hero and finally get off this stupid island. Guanahani is a dead-end assignment for a diplomat. I can't even imagine how you must've screwed up to get this post. But I bet you'll be glad for the opportunity to fix things. To return to the civilized world where you'll be Mr. Smith again. Admit it, you hate when everyone in Port Henri calls you Monty."

"You suffer from delusions of grandeur, Fellow. Back on the mainland you're nothing, zero, an empty space. A deserter, a thief, and an escaped convict who once managed to write a mediocre novel. No one remembers your name."

"My name, dear Monty, is always on the mind of a certain senator who, I hear, stands an excellent chance of becoming the next president."

I seem to have nailed the target. I don't have a lot of skills, but I can read faces with the best of them.

"Why do you think your son will become king? I heard no such thing."

Monty is especially funny when he puffs his cheeks like this.

The American consulate in Port Henri is mostly fiction. Words on a sheet of paper. Smith has a grand total of three marines and two clerks on his staff. Most of his activity is focused here, in Madame Simone's establishment.

"Loose Lips—that is, Francois—and I finished early today. A wasted day, the fish weren't biting. The Cayman Guard were waiting for us on the pier, handed me the official notice. Do you think Caymans joke about such matters?"

Monty frowns. "Okay, Joe. I'll hear you out. But I warn you: I won't do anything that might be interpreted as interfering in the internal affairs of Port Henri."

That's something already. He's ready to discuss a plan, which is all I need. I have a good scheme, so long as Smith agrees to help.

"If you're right and everything I told you is nonsense, then nothing will happen. It would mean that it makes no difference to the king whom to select as his heir. Some other boy will be selected to become Henri X."

"Of course I'm right. Joe, you're a writer, an educated man, even if you're a criminal. How in the world did you come to believe this malarkey?"

I don't believe because of words, or because of Doc César. I won't say it out loud, but it's because of the nightmares.

I never remembered my dreams before. Not even on Hell's Island, in a cell, burning with fever. Not even then.

But now the nightmares come every night. The Port Henri of my nightmares is covered in gray spider silk. Its residents look like scarecrows with empty eyes and stitched mouths. All of their movements are controlled by the spider web—as though they're marionettes in the paws of a spider. The spider is always nearby. Hiding behind the corner. Looking at me through the irises of a passerby. Waving at me with the dead hand of a doll held by a scarecrow child. And then there's the screech. Barely audible but alarming, like whispers coming from the next room, when you're certain no one but you is in the house.

When I leave Simone's it's still dark. But I'm well-familiar with the cunning of Caribbean nights. I have to hurry. I go to visit Jose. Somewhere ahead, the network of his little ragamuffins passes along the news of my impending arrival.

Seven years ago, when I first arrived on the island, Jose courted me in hopes of recruiting a first-rate thief into his operation. To be honest, I was somewhat disappointed that I wasn't the man everyone took me for. I was curious to learn what sort of a heist required a professional thief on an island where no one locks their doors.

My refusal struck a blow to Jose's ego, and then I managed to do so again by stealing his girl. At least that's what Jose thinks. Truth is, Valerie chose me. This woman always gets what she wants.

I enter without knocking and head to the patio, where Jose is waiting for me. The bottle of cachaça and a plate of sliced limes are on the table. Knowing ahead of time about my visit and setting out my favorite drink is a special treat for Jose, a confirmation of his ephemeral power. The island has no organized crime in the usual sense of the word, but Jose is in charge of all the smugglers, unlicensed prospectors, and port beggars.

Jose's skin is dark like charcoal. He looks down on the natives like a crown prince upon his bastard half-brother. Jose's father walked on Africa's soil, breathed its air, and was never a slave. Over a glass or rum, Jose likes to brag that he carries a small part of Africa within him.

"I hear congratulations are in order, Fellow. You're no simple convict anymore. Now you're convict, father of a king."

One doesn't have to beat around the bush with Jose. Without preamble I tell him everything. I watch his obsidian face, hoping to understand his reaction. I'm sure of one thing: Jose isn't surprised.

This scares me more than my nightmares. What if they all know? Have always known, closed their eyes, hiding behind

bright-colored walls, picturesque flags, cocooned in their benev-
olence so that darkness of this knowledge doesn't disturb them?

But Jose says: "I've never heard a more foolish tale, Fellow.
You stole my woman and now you want to steal a king? It's no
wonder you ended up in prison."

He says more, but I can see past his sharp words: Jose will
help me. This man truly is made of stone, and his feelings are
etched into that stone. Several years are but a moment for stone.
He still loves Valerie.

By the time I return home, it's almost morning. I enter the bedroom. It always smells of cinnamon and lavender. Valerie is asleep.

Nicki is sleeping next to her.

I'm a bad person. Unlike most people, I recognize this fact
about myself. Some will say it's just pride talking, but to me, one
sin more or one sin less doesn't make much of a difference.

I was seventeen when I killed a man for the first time. It was
an honest fight. My opponent, should fortune have been on his
side, would have done the same without hesitation. The argument
was over a woman. I don't recall her face, her smell, or her voice.
Only her name. Agnes. She couldn't seem to choose between the
two of us, so she gave herself to both of us.

This other man was the son of a senator. Even then I didn't
put my faith in a trial by jury, so I didn't wait to be arrested. I
hired on to the first ship heading for Europe. Decided to become
a writer. But first, I had to experience more of life. In France I vol-
unteered for the war. I was no ideologue. I didn't care about the
Germans, the French, the English and all their politics. I wanted
to get to know war. One battle taught me everything I wanted
to know about the subject. I deserted. Headed to Paris, wrote a
stupid novel, which to my then surprise and current regret, was
published in a small print run. I was so proud of myself. After the
book came out I thought people would begin recognizing me in
the streets. They didn't. I bought my novel, reread it, and my disappointment was limitless. I decided to write another.

Instead, I got myself thrown in prison.

When Doc César nursed me back to life, I was certain that my time had come. Finally, I knew life and all the things I wanted to write about. I experienced adventure enough for ten men, first-hand. And, of course, I was very much inspired by Port Henri in those early days.

Port Henri is the sort of quiet place every writer dreams of. The writer tells themselves: one day I'll go to a nice tropical is-land, sit under the palms and listen to the cries of seagulls as I shape all the thoughts that have accumulated in my mind into beautiful sentences.

Lies.

No one has ever written anything of note in a place like Port Henri.

I'm a murderer, a deserter, a worthless writer, and an escaped convict. But I hadn't managed to commit my worst crime.

Seven years is a long time. Ever since I left Illinois at fifteen, I never spent more than three years in any once place. I intended to leave Guanahani several times. I had no qualms about leaving Valerie. When she told me she was pregnant, I decided I'd wait for her to give birth. I wanted to meet my son and leave with the memory of him.

But having held newborn Nicki in my hands I knew I would never leave him.

Valerie opens her eyes.

"Valerie, do you recall what Padre Anjel said when we got married?"

"Lots of things. Once Padre begins to talk, it's not easy to stop him."

Wrong opening. Padre Anjel isn't an authority for Valerie. The old man likes to drink but isn't any good at it. There's no bet-ter way to disappoint a woman.

"There was something from St. Peter," I say. If St. Peter isn't an authority for her, then my plans are ruined.

She stares at the ceiling, remembering.

"*Husbands ought to love their wives as their own bodies.* Do you love me, Joe Fellow?"

"I love you, Valerie." A familiar lie. Love is a word and words, as is well known, were invented by women. "What else? There was something about an obedient wife."

As the Church submits to Christ, so also wives should submit to their husbands in everything. Valerie frowns.

"Exactly. I've never demanded such obedience from you, and I won't now. But I'm going to beg. I beg you to be a good wife and ask no questions. Promise me."

She nods. Good.

"Get dressed. Pack Nicki's things."

"Something happened," she says. It's not a question.

"When you're ready, we'll go visit Mr. Monty Smith."

"He's disgusting."

"It's not for long. You and Nicki are going to take a boat to Florida."

"Without you?"

Clever girl.

"I have to stay behind for a day or two. I'll catch up." This lie comes almost effortlessly.

Valerie's eyes grow wide. I know what she's going to say. Two years ago I tried to leave Guanahani—along with Valerie and my son—and take an English ship to Wales, where they say there's no better reference than being convicted by the French. Valerie refused. She said no seafaring adventures until Nicki turned at least ten years old. Valerie knew what they do with children aboard ships.

Every ship has a special person whose job is to find homeless boys in port and recruit them by promising work, food, and a hammock. Hungry demons who live in the ocean demand tributes from every ship that dares a cross-continental journey. Small dark-skinned children are mercilessly thrown into the ocean while rich Europeans dance on the upper decks to the Caribbean music. The bodies of those children forever wander the ocean floor, searching for the way home. Worse yet, some of them find it.

I don't want to hear her agonize about that again. Such tales make me nauseous. So I rush to say, "Jose is going to escort you."

I pause, but there's no reaction. She's stone-faced. It seems she has realized that things are serious.

Port Henri is waking up early. In the morning it looks like a shiny toy or a bright picture in a children's book. One-story houses are painted in every bright color imaginable.

We walk past the barber where I get my hair cut each week. Raul waves his greetings. Old men sit on wooden stools outside the barbershop and discuss baseball as they wait their turn. In front of their houses, owners put out tables filled with merchandise. Everyone in Port Henri sells everything. Dried herbs, rocks of every shape, fruit, spices, painted clay figures of animals, jars and pots, bottles with lizards preserved in formaldehyde, stuffed birds, amulets for all occasions, home-rolled cigars, and home-distilled cachaça. During siesta the sellers rest on their patios, leaving the merchandise in the street.

Valerie stops in front of a friendly dark-skinned old woman, picks out a blue necklace and begins to haggle with her in earnest. I whisper in her ear that we're in a hurry.

Valerie tells me, *"Husbands ought to love their wives as their own bodies,"* and I pay for the necklace.

Nicki is enthralled by the wooden knives set out right on the ground by another seller. I buy him one. I figure he'll have something to remember me by.

We pass by an old mustached greengrocer. He pushes his cart slowly, deliberately, as though each step is measured in advance to help him last the entire day. A young man on a bicycle races past us. When he sees Valerie he begins to show off; he lets go off the handles and stretches, interlocking his hands behind his head. He nearly rides into a tree.

I ask for today's newspaper at the cigarette stand.

"They haven't come in yet," says the merchant. "Rumor is, the king has selected an heir. Something like this has to be written about using special words, so they're taking their time."

I look around. Could it be that no one is spying on us? They must be, otherwise this entire performance is for naught. I notice a dark-skinned sailor in a blue uniform who takes a suspiciously long time studying his reflection in a store window. He doesn't look away even when a gaggle of girls in airy, bright clothes showing a lot of skin pass him by. No sailor would resist staring at a sexy woman.

So they are spying on us, then. Good.

We turn toward the consulate, toward the old Spanish quarter which was built back in the days of Cortez, when the town was still called Santa Anna. The colors are less bright here, the lines more severe. Dark walls stare in opprobrium at neighboring streets.

Valerie and my son are on the patio, flipping through a world atlas. Every once in a while Valerie sighs theatrically. Smith and I are sitting in the study.

Smith tugs nervously at his mustache. He is sweating profusely.

"When will your man be here?"

"Soon."

When I asked him to send a marine to the underground tunnel that led to the southern piers from the basement of the consulate, Monty gasped in surprise.

"How do you know about the tunnel?"

"Please, Monty. The entire town knows about it."

Jose left in the morning to get the boat. I'm beginning to worry too, but I'm not letting it show.

An hour ago Doc César had joined us. Knowing that he was going to worry, I called him from the consulate. Doc brought a basket of food for Valerie and Nick. Idiot that I am, I hadn't even thought about packing food.

Finally, I hear steps in the kitchen. A marine who was sent to the pier comes in. Jose follows him.

Jose's shirt is soaked in blood.

"The guy didn't want to give up the boat," Jose explains. He sees the grimace on Smith's face. "Be calm, Yankee. Everything is all right. He's going to live."

While César tends to Jose's wound, I pull Smith aside.

"Send at least one marine along," I ask of him. "You can see Jose isn't doing great."

Smith doesn't budge.

"No marines, Fellow. It's one thing to host an American citizen in the consulate. It's another to assist in the kidnapping of the future king of Guanahani. Do you understand the difference?"

Damn politician. Of course, he won't let me go, either. The plan I proposed is too appealing to him.

Doc César says, "I'll go with them."

He's a saint of a man. Useless in a fight, but it still makes me feel better.

I say goodbye to them in the basement. I kiss Valerie and tell her everything will be all right. I hug Nick.

I tell Smith to lock the door and to order the marines not to let anyone in. Under any circumstances.

By nightfall Monty feels more confident.

"Drink?" he offers. "I'll have one. It seems all deadlines are past. No one is searching for you, except maybe a psychiatrist. What a story you made up, Fellow! I'm not upset. I have you, and an excellent anecdote to tell."

"Shut up," I tell him.

He shuts up. I think I can hear the sound of footsteps over broken glass.

Imagine you're having tea on the veranda with your favorite aunt when you realize there's a pack of velociraptors hiding in the back yard. There's no evidence of this other than a strange whistling noise, but that could be anything—perhaps a neighbor kid who snuck onto your property to pick apples. But no, you're absolutely sure: it's velociraptors. You look at your aunt and realize she feels the same thing. The world around you hasn't changed, the tea tastes the same, the air smells of autumn and fallen apples, but the velociraptors are about to charge from around the corner.

That's how I feel now. Nothing appears to have changed—the lights haven't gone out or even blinked. Birds are chirping in the palm trees. But I realize: it's beginning.

Smith plays the role of the aunt to perfection. His head shrinks into his shoulders and he shudders like a bird. He regains control of himself and moves toward the door.

"Don't you dare open it, Monty," I whisper.

"Nonsense," he says.

He opens the door wide and catches a bullet in his stomach.

The Cayman guards enter the study. Through the door frame behind them I see a marine on the ground, with a surprised expression and a cut throat.

The road leads uphill, which means I'm being taken to the citadel.

The citadel is the highest point of Guanahani. The fortress built by the first King Henri after the revolution. They say more slaves lie dead in the foundation of the citadel than perished in the war with the French. Even so, the residents of Port Henri are proud of their fortress.

In my dreams the citadel is the huge ink blot inside of which hides the spider.

In my seven years in Port Henri I've never quite seen the citadel. It's difficult to see it from the town below. Even on the brightest of days, the sky seems to find a few clouds to obscure it. On a rare day when there are no clouds, the citadel looks like one itself. Its walls are painted blinding white.

The truck shakes as it traverses the boulders on the road, but I don't care. I think about little Nick, and about Valerie. In a few hours they'll be in Key West.

The truck stops. Cayman guards roughly toss me outside, and I scrape my knees and palms on the rocks. It's nothing compared to what awaits me. Probably execution by firing squad. I'm surprised to realize that I'm not afraid at all.

I look around. Close up the fortress doesn't look all white. Its stones are covered with red moss. The walls are three times as tall as an average person. This wouldn't be an easy place to escape from. Good thing I don't plan on running.

A wooden cot is set against stone walls of my cell. The moss turns to dust and falls from the barest touch. A narrow window is situated just below the ceiling. If I stand on my toes I can just make out the shoes of the Cayman guards by the lights of their torches.

This isn't the worst dungeon I've ever been in. At least it's dry and devoid of woodlice.

The door creaks open behind my back. I don't turn around, preserving what's left of my dignity.

"Leave us. I wish to talk to him alone."

A woman's voice. That intrigues me. I turn around.

She's wearing a severe dark dress, closed to the neck. Something that's gone out of fashion two generations ago. A wooden cross dangles on a strap of leather over the dress. Her hands are gloved. She places a kerosene lamp on the cot. She looks like Valerie, but older by about fifteen years. Her light-brown skin, blue almond eyes, ink-black hair. The Port Henri women are very beautiful. Sun mixed with spices, sea salt, and clear sky. This island has collected the best of many different peoples and gifted it to its daughters.

There's only one woman for whom all doors of this fortress are opened. Camilla. Cami, as the locals call her. The daughter of old king Henri, who died six years ago. The mother of the current King Henri.

I sit down on the cot, breaking etiquette. It's a tiny, indulgent form of rebellion.

She's silent. I don't rush her. Perhaps she wants to see the man who voluntarily refused the throne for his son? Who knows what's in the woman's head?

"Do you know what the Sek is?"

The question catches me by surprise, but I don't let it show. I shrug. "César told me."

She frowns at the mention of his name. Is it anger? Contempt?

"You know the word, but the meaning escapes you."

"I don't believe in the afterlife."

"The Sek isn't an afterlife, Mr. Fellow. The Sek is like a sealed room where you relive the worst moments of your life, time after time."

What was the worst moment of my life? The cell filled with woodlice? The boat shared with dying men? The battle of Somme? The moment my blade entered the heart of a senator's son?

"If there's a hell, we'll all get there. I've never met a man who managed to remain innocent by the time he reached adulthood."

"My son was seven when old Henri decided it was time to begin a new life. How much do you think he had managed to sin?"

I don't know what to tell her. Now that Jose took Valerie and Nick away from here, all of this seems like an illusion. Even the memory of Consul Smith's death is uncertain. Perhaps I have gone mad.

"You're a fool to think your family is safe. No one ever leaves this town without Henri's knowledge. Everything happens according to his plan. Every time. If he has decided to steal your son's body, then he will. You won't be able to stop him. Your boy's soul will go to the Sek, following the souls of all the others. They'll wander there forever. Think about that, convict. Eternity is worse than death."

Damn, I think. Word for word, she's repeating what César had told me. What if they're in cahoots? Fed a bunch of lies to a trusting gringo. Is all of this about the throne? Perhaps she wants to become queen after her son dies? She could have convinced the Doc to spin some tales and set all this in motion.

I nearly slap my forehead. What a simple answer. Goddamned Occam's Razor. All of this adds up, even the delay in the morning papers. I drive away thoughts of nightmares and Monty Smith's death.

If this turns out to be a run-of-the-mill palace intrigue, I'll be quite relieved.

"Why have you come?" I ask, stressing frustration in my voice.

Cami looks at the door fearfully, as though she hears some distant sound. There's nothing there, woman. No one needs us. She comes closer and whispers: "I never loved my father. He's not easy to love. It's like loving this fortress, with its darkness and rot. But I was an obedient daughter. I had borne him an heir. If I knew then what he had planned I would have killed my son with my own hands. Do you believe me?"

She asks the question, but doesn't seem to expect an answer. She smells like Valerie, of vanilla and cinnamon.

"He told me everything after the coronation. Pride, Mr. Fellow. He sought a witness. Someone to appreciate his greatness. He's frustrated that everyone around him sees only a child. He needs fear. He came to me and told me in detail of everyone he had sent to the Sek. He told me that entering another's body is akin to rape. He said this in a voice of a seven-year-old child, looking up at me with the clear eyes of my son. Can you imagine?"

Fine, I'll play her game. "Why didn't you kill him? It's easy, especially now. His illness has done half the work for you."

"He forbade it," she says, a bitter smile on her lips. "His power is limitless. You'll murder your own mother, if he orders it."

"You could've told someone. Like you're telling me now."

"He forbade to talk about it outside the walls of the citadel. Left himself an opportunity to be amused. Because of me, three people have died. He forced a young Cayman, a god-fearing Catholic, to open his own veins. He forbade the second man to drink. He locked me in the room with him for several days, along with many jugs of water."

"What happened to the third man?"

Why do I ask this? I don't want to know. None of it can be true. Just ravings of an insane woman.

"He killed the third one by my hand."

Cami says this evenly, with no emotion in her voice.

She gingerly removes her cross.

"Don't move," she says. "Be still. He didn't forbid me from

coming here. Didn't forbid me from giving you a gift. Lower your head."

I obey. I've learned not to argue with the insane. Cami puts the string with the cross on my neck. The silk of her gloves tickles my ears.

She holds me by my wrists. Leans in. Whispers: "Don't touch this cross unless you want to die."

"Magic again?"

"No, foolish Yankee. It's poison. If it gets into the bloodstream, it'll kill in seconds. An adult or a child. Think about that, Mr. Fellow. Think hard. You can't kill Henri. But if you kill your son, Henri will be stuck in his current body. And then he'll die. If that happens, all of them will be free. Do you understand? All his victims, free. He'll go to the Sek in their place."

"Don't mess with me, woman. I'll never kill my son."

She stares into my eyes, as if trying to see the contents of my mind through them. I know this look. It's how I look at people.

Read me, woman. I have nothing to hide.

She lets go off my wrist. She says, regretfully: "No. You will not."

And then the door creaks and she's gone. The women of Port Henri are like the tropical nights. They arrive when you least expect them, and leave before you can come to understand them.

I shake my head. Was she ever here? I reach for the cross but stop myself from touching it.

I can tell time pretty well when I'm sober. I learned this on Hell's Island. Time can be measured in breaths, heartbeats, steps of the guards.

The door opens again an hour and a half after Cami leaves. The grim Cayman tells me to follow him.

We go through a maze of corridors, descending and ascending again via staircases. This fortress was built by a madman. Somehow I'm certain I'm about to meet the king. The newspapermen describe him as a kind child, very polite and considerate. I'm sure he'll gently inquire as to why I'd caused all this drama, kidnapping my own son. I have no idea what I'll tell him. I feel like an idiot, to be honest. Much worse than when the French policemen accused me of murdering that old man and I responded by mumbling something about seeking inspiration for writing a novel.

We arrive. The room doesn't look like a child's bedroom, and even less like a royal hall. A low-hanging lamp with a dozen candles barely illuminates the center of the room. The walls and ceiling drown in darkness. The room is empty. Our steps echo.

The Cayman pushes me so I enter the circle of light. He remains by the door.

A small silhouette moves toward me from the darkness. A boy in a wheelchair. King Henri IX.

The residents of Port Henri are in awe of their king. He was only seven when the old Henri died. His illness has turned him into a skeleton. His dark skin has acquired a greenish tint. His eyes are sunk deep. For a moment he looks more like an old man than a child.

"Thank you, Jorge. You may go."

His voice is low and weak. Very boyish. But in it I hear pure, unadulterated power.

After Jorge leaves and closes the door behind him, Henri says: "The Caymans are loyal to me, but they're like children. Never tell children the entire truth, Joe. Their souls are too fragile."

The axles of his wheelchair emit a barely audible screech. I recognize this sound. I've heard it in my nightmares.

He's right next to me. I realize that I'm lost.

I believe. I believe every word of what César had told me. Of what Cami had told me.

I could kill him right now. But Henri says, "Stay in place," and my legs refuse to move. They feel like lead.

Henri smiles winningly, like a child. His eyes are blue. Just like Valerie's. Just like my son's.

I don't want to look into these eyes, but I can't turn away. It's as though an enormous hand is holding me by the back of my head, forcing me to look. As if I'm falling into the abyss. No twelve-year-old boy can have eyes like these. Not even a hundred-year-old man could. I'm staring into the succession of centuries.

"You shouldn't have staged this circus with the consulate. Smith's death is on your conscience. Come to the window, Joe. Look outside."

I watch a pickup truck drive up to the gates. Valerie, César, and two Caymans climb out. One of them is holding my sleeping son.

"No one leaves Port Henri without me knowing, Joe."

All of this was for nothing.

"My plan worked, as it always does. You see, Joe, I don't need your son. I'm too tired of being a child. To be five again? No, thanks. Let him grow up a bit first. For now, I'm going to be you. The father of the king. That was the plan, Joe. All I needed from you was to believe. And Doctor César, a man of immense value in every sense of the word, has provided that for me."

The Caymans come in, followed by César. Valerie follows, holding the now awake Nick by his hand. She runs up to me, ignoring the king. She wants to hug me but I catch her by the shoulders and kiss her forehead.

"They killed Jose," she whispers. "He shot one of them in the leg, but there were too many of them. They cut his throat and threw him into the water, to the sharks. It was a bad death."

A bad man died a bad death for the woman who doesn't love him. If there really is an afterlife, I hope this will outweigh many of the other things he had done.

"I think," says Henri sweetly, "that your wife and son should rest after their journey. What do you say, Joe? You'll see each other again soon. All will be well."

"Go with the Caymans, Valerie." I take her hand into mine. "I love you. And I love Nick. I love you both."

Perhaps for the first time, I'm telling the truth.

"Belief is a funny thing," says Henri after they leave. "If you didn't believe in my powers, I wouldn't have been able to stop you from killing me. Have you heard about President Harding's death? It was quite painful. He made two mistakes. First, he wouldn't leave Guanahani alone. You Yankees love to appropriate others' belongings. You know this better than most, thief. Do you want to know what his second mistake was? He *believed*. He believed that his death was within my power, and it became true. Now I have no problems with America. Harding's successors remember what happens to disobedient presidents."

I don't give a damn about Harding. I stare at César, who is rummaging through his medicine bag. I'm trying to understand how he's so calm. Is he under Henri's power or is he helping him of his own volition?

"Listen carefully, Joe. This is an order," says Henri. "Come closer, and look at me."

My feet make several steps against my will. My head turns. I try to close my eyes, but I can't.

"Do you know why I showed you your wife and son, Joe? I wanted to be certain that you won't pull some sort of trick at the last moment. I want to make sure that you let me in, voluntarily. I can't order this. You have to let me in yourself. I hate it when they try to resist. Fools. I can't be stopped. I'll break past any door if I have to. Have you ever had to break a door, Joe? It's somewhat painful, but worse, there's this feeling like you're not respected. Like they didn't prepare for your arrival. Didn't tidy up. They twitch and scream. Then I have to clean up myself. Wash off the blood. Repair the door. That isn't nice, Joe. You can't treat guests that way. That's why I like children. They're so nice, so trusting. It's easy to fool them. But I'll be honest with you, Joe. Our dear doctor is going to finish the necessary procedures and you're going to be a good boy. You'll open the door, let me in, and head into the Sek. The doctor told you about the Sek, yes? I won't lie, you won't like it there. Just think about your wife and son. It could be much worse for them here. Do you understand me, Joe? Nod if you understand."

I nod.

César picks up a curved knife and approaches the king. Henri tilts his head forward. The doctor makes a cut along the nape, just under the hairline. Then he retrieves a syringe and quickly draws blood from Henri's vein.

He walks toward me, blood dripping from the syringe across the floor. I let César make a shallow cut on my neck.

I wonder, what will happen with the body of the child in the wheelchair when the spirit of Henri leaves it to occupy mine?

It's as though Henri can read my mind.

"Don't worry," he says. "He'll last until the coronation. Just like Consul Smith, by the way. Have you heard of chickens who seem alive even after you cut off their heads? They run. They worry. You wouldn't guess that they're dead. People aren't much different from chickens. So long as you know a few tricks. César, leave us."

César backs up toward the door.

"That's it," says Henri. "Wait for me, Joe. I'll be there soon."

His eyes gloss over. His head falls onto his chest, and then the boy's entire body falls forward until he's lying on the floor, unconscious.

Then nothing happens.

Except for the spider which climbs from the cut in Henri's nape. This is impossible. Spiders don't live in human heads. Yet here it is, in front of me. It descends to the stone floor and runs toward me along the path of blood left for him by the doctor. If I could only take a few steps, the spider would never find me. But Henri forbade me from walking away.

That's okay. I have another plan.

The spider jumps onto the hem of my trousers and climbs up my back. I feel its cold legs on my nape.

It's time.

Once I feel the spider inside me, binding, I grab hold of the cross gifted to me by Queen Cami.

I hope, my dear, that your poison is truly strong.

Of all the deaths, I chose the most ridiculous.

I could've died from the knife wound to the heart.

I could've caught a German bullet in the battle of Somme.

Could've perished in the cell of Hell's Island.

Could've drowned in the vast expanse of the Atlantic Ocean.

My last thought is: who knows? Perhaps that's what happened. Perhaps I died a long, long time ago.

MADAME FÉLIDÉ ELOPES
TRANSLATED BY ANATOLY BELILOVSKY

1. MADAME FÉLIDÉ AND THE SMILE MERCHANTS

On Friday Madame Félidé bought all the smiles the local merchants had for sale. Merry and sad, shy and modest, childlike and old, tender, happy, polite, ugly, warm, soft, villainous, ironic, open, timid, grudging, obsequious—every single one. Shopkeepers dug through their deepest cellars to find silly grins that rarely sold and usually gathered dust amid bits of obsolete gossip and jokes peeled off the floor after they had fallen flat. She emptied the display cases of fleeting smiles and gullible smiles and especially made sure to acquire every single sincere smile in the entire town. She also bought two ounces of contagious laughter and half a pound of good cheer. For change, the sales clerk gave her a tulle sachet full of pointed double entendres.

Dancing, skipping, and humming a silly little song about a cat, Madame Félidé hurried home. What a stir she would cause in the town when everyone realized they'd have to spend holidays with serious faces! Some may have smiles squirrelled away for a rainy day, some may have to rifle through keepsake boxes for antique smiles inherited from their grandmothers. How funny they will look wearing grins a century out of date, and mothball-scented at that! But the rest will skulk along the boulevard, avoiding their friends. What if someone makes a clever joke? Does one respond with cheap tasteless laughter scraped up with pocket lint? Or with a silent nod, betraying shortsighted stinginess?

On the way home Madame Félidé encountered prim Anglian women who walked their well-schooled children and well-bred dogs—or was it the other way around? All of them—women, children, and dogs—cast great quantities of disapproving looks her way, opprobrium being an inexpensive commodity often shared generously with strangers. In return, Madame Félidé took a brand new mysterious smile from her reticule and tried it on right there in the middle of the street. She walked on, warmed by the sounds of Anglians' horrified whispers as they gossiped about her odd spendthrift profligacy.

Avion waited in her garden, squeaking his wheels nervously; his high-strung personality kept him awake instead of sleeping quietly in the hangar. A family of siskins perched on Avion's prow-like nose chittering happily to each other as she approached.

2. MADAME FÉLIDÉ VISITS THE SEA SHORE

Madame Félidé did not like painting. That is why she painted dozens of landscapes and portraits which now gathered dust in her attic. She did not hang her work in rooms she actually used, believing (correctly, as it turned out) that the bright colors of her paintings would ruin the delicately tasteful Anglian style of the interior which was a source of justifiable pride for her House. Madame Félidé was a softhearted woman who often showed more consideration for her friends than for her own comforts.

Only one picture, painted the day before, remained in the living room, and even so she placed it in a dark corner and covered it carefully in black cloth. House frowned, its walls curling in disapproval around the easel on which the painting rested, but did no more than that: he was too well brought up to express his pique openly.

Madame Félidé took her purchases from her reticule and tossed them carelessly onto the table. She waved at the painting, and at her gesture the black cloth crawled down to the floor, revealing a huge—half a wall in size—canvas on which a raging ocean clawed for the sky. Sea spray filled the room, Madame Félidé smelled and tasted salt on her lips, and a gust of wind blew a bundle of frivolous smiles off the table.

In the painting, the rocky shore appeared deserted except for a bright spot where someone's discarded clothes lay near the water's edge. Madame Félidé peered into the waves hoping to make out the person who went for a swim in such inclement weather. She did not succeed, and so picked up the cup of tea that her House had made for her and left the room.

Avion had already rolled to the airstrip and huffed impatiently, hurrying her to board. Madame Félidé eased into her seat, careful not to spill her tea, and Avion took off.

House looked wistfully toward them, regretting not being able to go for a walk to Enger Street and back. He thought it unseemly for a well-bred Anglian home to dream of travel and adventure, but still a small bit of longing entered his heart, bringing back the memory of his childhood when as a tiny brick he had made the long and dangerous journey from Chester to Warrington to receive his education in Socratic discourses with a cat.

At first Avion flew low and slow, like an elderly pigeon. Madame Félidé marveled at the familiar landscape, taking it in as unhurriedly as she drank her tea. For perhaps the first time in her life she wanted to cut the flight short and to return home immediately. Therefore she directed Avion to fly toward the sea.

Having finished her tea, she threw her teacup overboard. Knowing that Anglians consider shattered porcelain a favorable omen, she tried as often as possible to brighten the lives of her neighbors. It was also a good way to rid herself of tea sets which a distant aunt of hers, with clock-like regularity and bovine perseverance, sent her as gifts for every imaginable holiday. The cup whistled through the air under the very nose of an elderly gentleman and shattered on the pavement. Immediately Avion rose through the clouds into bright sunshine and clear blue sky.

A half-hour later the sea appeared on the horizon. It rolled its slow waves toward the shore and debated with the sky about the clarity of their colors. The sea was tranquility itself and looked not at all like the tempestuous force of nature that had hidden under the cloth cover in Madame Félidé's House.

Having returned home, Madame Félidé hurried to the living room, pulled the curtain off her painting, and recoiled at the darkness revealed before her. Her heart skipped, but then she saw the stars and heard the distant surf, and her heart returned to beating. The man of her dreams slept in her easy chair. A few sheets of paper lay scattered on the table. For a minute Madame Félidé listened to his calm slow breath, then carefully covered the painting again and tiptoed out of the room.

That night her sleep was filled with visions of tiny silver fish, purple sky, warm rain, and the man of her dreams.

3. MADAME FÉLIDÉ AND UNWELCOME GUESTS

Madame Félidé could not stand having guests, so each Saturday at eleven in the morning she put on tea. When no one came, which happened often, she retrieved from her reticule a vial with sighs of relief and happily released one of them. Each sigh cost her practically nothing, especially compared against incessant chatter of her Anglian acquaintances whose tongues unfurled rather quickly in her presence.

There was a knock on the door at the same time as the clock struck. Madame Félidé donned her most joyous smile and hurried to answer it.

Anna Meadows and Bess Thompson were the two of greatest of all misfortunes that could befall one on Saturday morning. Tall, ungainly Anna Meadows usually glared such powerful distaste toward all that surrounded her that Madame Félidé often wondered where she's bought it. Anna Meadows was also extremely stingy, her dresses, her gossip, and her jokes apparently purchased at garage sales. She wore a wide childish smile as she came in, and exuded a faint odor of mildew, having apparently extracted the smile from her deepest cellar simply to annoy Madame Félidé.

Bess Thompson, blessed with the intelligence of three goats, had on an everyday smile of the kind they sold at last year's farmers fair. Bess's stupidity was entirely natural and did not at all go with her clothes, or with her position as Women's Auxiliary Council Chair for the town in which they lived.

The tea party went far better than Madame Félidé expected. Bess talked incessantly of suffragettes and of the Queen's impending visit while Anna Meadows shared last year's gossip about the college rector's wife. Madame Félidé stayed out of the conversation, only nodding occasionally and in all the wrong places, and glancing nervously at the picture that stood covered in the corner about which House's features twisted in disapproval.

After the blueberry pie was eaten to the last morsel, tea drunk to the last drop, smiles worn off and gossip chewed and spat out, it was time to go home. The guests hurried to get ready when Anne's wandering gaze fell into the curve of the far corner of the room.

"How cute," she said and pursed her lips, the smile she had nursed through two hours of tea having finally disappeared.

Madame Félidé watched in silence as her guest headed toward the painting. The words "If you don't mind, my dear?" had barely enough time to escape Anne's lips as she raised the edge of the cover.

Had Anne thought to lay down a supply of high-quality shrieks, she would have used it up that instant. Lacking not only that but even the cheaper generic exclamations, she stepped back, pulling the cloth with her, and froze in an incongruous pose before dropping everything and running from the room.

In the picture, bright noonday sun shone on a rocky sea shore. A man who had only just stepped out of the water hurriedly pulled dry pants on over wet underwear.

4. MADAME FÉLIDÉ'S DEPARTURE FROM ANGELIA

On Thursday Madame Félidé wanted to listen to music, so she went downstairs to the living room and practiced painting rabbits. The rabbits came out looking far too frightened, and Madame Félidé painted over them, accidentally painting the man of her dreams in process. His eyes were full of sorrow and understanding, as if the man of her dreams had waited all his life for her to paint him.

"Stand still," said Madame Félidé, "I will paint you a smile."

The man of her dreams stood motionless; only his lips moved a little as he whispered: "I love you."

"Such nonsense," said Madame Félidé sharply and picked up her brush.

None of her attempts to put more brush strokes on the canvas succeeded. She tried all her paints—in vain. The painting lived its own life, refusing to obey its creator. Madame Félidé found herself at a loss: how can the painting be without a smile? It cannot. She covered the painting and went to bed.

Her sleep that night was haunted by visions of surf, acacia trees, cinnamon, a boat house, and the man of her dreams.

That is precisely why Madame Félidé went smile shopping on Friday, and not because she was a frivolous kind of a person. She only needed one smile—but which one? It was a good thing that her intuition told her to buy the lot.

And now, having shepherded Bess Thompson out of her home, Madame Félidé set herself to the task of attaching the smiles to the canvas. She tried paper glue, shampoo, jam, milk, treacle, ink, and even oatmeal. Beset with anxiety, she accidentally ate several of the smiles which turned out to be delicious, especially when smeared with raspberry jam.

Madame Félidé felt chagrin at having drawn such a sad man. How silly for a person to lack a smile! Like a cat without whiskers. And Madame Félidé picked up a length of silk yarn and threaded it through the eye of her needle.

"Now I will sew a smile to your face, the sincerest smile of all," she said. "Just don't be afraid, and don't move. You wouldn't like to smile with your nose or your ears, would you?"

"I am terribly ticklish, you know," said the man of her dreams. "Don't sew anything. Why not just marry me instead?"

And he smiled—tenderly, courageously, merrily and a bit ironically.

This was an unexpected development, and, caught by surprise, Madame Félidé agreed without a second thought.

"Wait a minute," she said, "while I get my toothbrush. But as soon as I return you simply must tell me where you found such a magnificent smile!"

Madame Félidé was not a sentimental woman and so she walked out of her House to say farewell to Avion. She kissed him on the propeller hub and turned away to sweep an uninvited tear off her face.

Avion thought for a moment about trying on a bit of sadness but changed his mind. Instead he rolled slowly in the direction of the sea, the ungreased left gear wheel whistling a merry tune. Avion knew that on the road he would undoubtedly meet a little girl who dreams about the sky.

Madame Félidé returned to House and ran her hand over his rough brick wall. House did not answer; only the faucet in the seldom-used guest bathroom sprung a tiny leak, dripping water that, were anyone to taste it, would have proved unusually salty.

Madame Félidé donned a wide-brimmed hat, tied a silk bow at her collar, and for no apparent reason retrieved her black umbrella from the hall closet. Returning to her painting, she closed her eyes (thinking herself a terrible coward) and stepped through the canvas.

5. MADAME FÉLIDÉ CATCHES UP ON HER READING

After Madame Félidé learned to smile, sigh, and cry on her own, as well as many other important things, after her elder son went to school and the younger said his first word, "Boo!" and shook his soup spoon at the cat—in short, many years later Madame Félidé decided to sort old papers that gathered dust in the attic. There, among old theatre playbills, yellow newspapers, post-cards from Aunt Fannie, and expired stagecoach tickets, she found a few pages covered in her husband's impatient handwriting.

She put away the file with important documents, perched comfortably near the attic window from which a beautiful view of the rocky sea coast could be seen, and began to read:

"On Friday Madame Félidé bought all the smiles the local merchants had for sale. Merry and sad, shy and modest, childlike and old, tender, happy, polite, ugly, warm, soft, tender, villainous, ironic, open, shy, grudging, obsequious—every single one."

THE TIN PILOT

THE INVITATION STATED THAT THE GOLEM HUNT WOULD TAKE place on Friday. In the seven years since the Machine was created, Noah had never participated in the hunt. Still, he received the invitations regularly; the Brotherhood chancellery remembered everyone. Usually Noah tossed away those gray notes with mild irritation and promptly forgot about them. But this was a special event, as the secretary indicated by underscoring a line of text twice. This was the last golem. The Premier himself—Friar Yakov—was going to attend.

Noah began feeling unease on Monday morning. It happens like this: you get into the shower, or brush your teeth, or brew coffee. A stray, unwelcome thought zigzags across your sleepy consciousness and you freeze as though you had been stung. You drop the loofah, stare in confusion at your toothbrush, or pour milk past your cup and right onto the cat.

In that very moment, a single foolish thought changes you. You don't realize it yet, but there's no going back.

Noah watched his cat pretending to be upset while he actually was quite pleased, licking his milk-soaked tail. Noah didn't see the cat, didn't see the kitchen. Somewhere in the darkness inside his head, between the eyes and the nape, between the left and right ears, in that spot where we hear our inner voice and see images from the past, the slippery and repugnant stray thought had taken up residence and grown roots.

What if—all the bad things in this world begin with those words. To be fair, some of the good things do, too.

Villain the Cat, whose temperament matched his name perfectly, finished licking his tail and began to scream. One couldn't call those sounds meowing: more, more, more. Unable to think of anything but the hypnotic *what if*, Noah poured the rest of the milk into Villain's saucer.

Masha entered the kitchen, wrapped in her favorite blue towel. Masha's skin was pale with faded freckles. Her hair was also pale—somewhere between ashen and colorless. Her eyes were gray. That's why Noah called her Masha the Mouse. But never out loud.

"What are you doing?" Masha threw up her hands. She gave the cat a stern look. Upon her arrival, he redoubled the speed with which he was lapping up the milk, as he had good reason to suspect that the implacable Masha would confiscate it. Villain was lactose intolerant. "I'm the one who will have to clean this up!"

She took away the nearly empty saucer.

Noah shook his head, chasing off the daze and banishing the ludicrous thought. He automatically kissed Masha, drank the coffee in one gulp—it was nasty without milk or sugar—and went to the bedroom to get dressed. Masha picked up the cat and followed.

"You're an emotional deviant," she informed him. She said this without anger, but rather tenderly and with affection. The way a ruffian's loving mother might speak about her son: *my little troublemaker.*

Masha stood in the door, cradling the cat with her right hand and holding up the sliding towel with her left. Noah admired her. Masha looked perfect.

"Put Villain down," said Noah.

"What for?" Masha asked indignantly.

"Put down the cat."

Villain cooperated by escaping from Masha's grip. He went back into the kitchen to check the sink for traces of milk.

Noah didn't even notice how he and Masha ended up in bed. They intertwined, merged, fell apart. All thoughts disappeared, exited the dark room known as human conscience, and politely closed the door behind them.

A single unwanted thought lingered right behind the door, near the keyhole, and quietly buzzed its annoying melody.

What if I am the last golem?

Such a simple little thought.

At first, Noah had been envious of the golems. He'd been seventeen when the war had ended and he had missed all the interesting stuff, which had bothered him terribly. For the past couple of years he had tried to enlist, demanding that he be made a pilot and sent right into the heart of battle. Of course, he was turned away, politely but firmly. Of course, he'd tried again. He was certain he'd make a fine pilot and return as a war hero.

It never occurred to Noah that he might not come back; might remain up in the sky, in space, among the lunar craters, like all our men had. The golems had finished the war in their place. And the golems had returned, with medals and songs and terrible memories of war. The world we inherited was wounded and worthless. But we were alive, even if, like our world, we were wounded and worthless, too. Our women, poisoned by radiation, lost their ability to bear children, and to live their lives. Our best men perished in the war. Rebuilding was up to those who were not as good, and to those who were not old enough to fight.

Noah didn't want to rebuild, he wanted to be a hero. He wanted to walk down the street wearing a uniform filled with medals and smile at girls, like in the old movies. He wanted to visit his father's grave and drink a shot to honor the man's memory in dignified silence. (This Noah would've done even without a uniform, but his father was buried alongside thousands of other infantrymen under the regolith dust of the inaccessible, permanently dead Moon.)

Noah had only seen golems in the documentaries and the recording of the victory parade: slender men and women in military uniforms whose faces were concealed behind the face-plates of helmets. Our heroes. Noah's orphanage was located in an industrial suburb where the radiation counter never ceased to crackle in warning, and where the sky never turned gray, but remained pitch-black even in daytime, due to the smoke from factory chimneys. It was no place for heroes.

One time Noah had had the gall to visit a bar hidden in the basement of a dilapidated, yellow, two-story building that had seemed like the setting for secrets and adventures. It was populated with grim old men in their forties who frowned as they drank shot after shot of their vodka. Noah had rejoiced, as he'd first mistaken them for golems. He'd found a few pennies in his pockets, ordered a mineral water, and nursed it as long as possible under the opprobrious gaze of the elderly female bartender. He'd stared at the old men, hoping to recognize traces of their artificial origins and military past in their occasional utterings and calm, manly mannerisms. He was soon disappointed: from the overheard conversation it became clear that these were factory workers. They may have been foremen, but still, ordinary people. They were no heroes, having spent the entire war on the factory floor. In those days Noah had condemned anyone who could've served and didn't in a typical angry-young-man fashion.

A vagabond of an indeterminate age had entered the bar. He was dirty, but he hadn't yet hit rock bottom: he'd still smelled like a man and not like a mongrel. His thin beard had been unkempt, his nose sharp, his long coat patched in many places. The vagabond had looked around, noticed the bristling bartender who was prepared to throw him out at the first opportunity. He'd flashed her a bitter toothless smile and asked, "Won't you stand a drink for a veteran of the Moon wars?"

The factory workers had fallen silent. Slowly, heads turned

toward the bar counter. The vagabond had been visibly embold-
ened by the attention.

"Yes," he'd said with a challenge. "Yes, I'm a golem. What, I
don't look like much, eh?"

There'd been no answer, but Noah had felt the silence turn
thick and suffocating. The vagabond had carried on, as though he
hadn't known how to stop, as though a tight coil had unwound
deep within him.

"I effing fought! I spilled my golem blood for you. For you,
and you, and you." Noah had been among those the vagabond
had pointed to with his dirty finger, and the gesture had made his
heart ache. If he'd had even a penny left, he would've given it up.

The bitter speech had elicited a different reaction from the
factory workers.

The foremen had gotten up in silence, surrounded the vagabond, and proceeded to beat him without a word. They'd hit
him without anger, without emotion, as though performing some
annoying but necessary chore. For some reason the vagabond
hadn't struggled and had also been silent. In that silence there
was some sort of mutual understanding, something akin to an
agreement. Then they'd tossed him into the street.

Back then Noah hadn't known anything about the Amnesiac
Amendment.

What if I am the last golem?

On Thursday Noah woke up exhausted. He couldn't recall his
nightmare, but he knew it was something ruthless and terrifying.
Perhaps it was about the Moon, Noah thought hazily, as he found
himself in the bathroom. He stared intently into the mirror, as
though seeking the divine spark in his blue eyes.

Reality caught up with Noah in bursts. This used to happen
to him during the university years, when he would avoid sleeping
for several nights in a row. It was classes in the morning, work on
a cleanup crew in the afternoons: daily volunteer sessions trying
to mend the dead city, filled with songs and youthful vigor. In the

evening it was drinking alcohol by the fire and more songs. After days of this regimen, the hallucinations came, the world spinning in dangerous and unpredictable ways. That's how it felt now. One moment Noah was in the shower, lathering his scalp, the next he's in the kitchen, naked, perched on a stool and staring at the wound on his left palm. He'd made a shallow cut with a knife and it hurt. Blood pooled at the edge of the cut and trickled toward his wrist. It was ordinary human blood; Noah had never seen anything different. If golems could be identified so easily, the last one would've been killed seven years ago.

And yet. Yet.

Masha materialized next to him with a first aid kit in another burst. Without a word she sprayed peroxide onto his palm, spent half a minute skeptically observing as the clear liquid bubbled, mixing with blood, then deftly bandaged the wound. Who was an emotional deviant now?

Noah listened to the silence and to the pain in his cut palm. He recalled that Masha no longer looked him in the eyes.

A fearsome, playful Villain the Cat tumbled past him. He pushed a small, light object with his paws like a hockey player. The object seemed very familiar.

Noah found Villain in the kitchen. The cat settled under the stool and gnawed at his toy, ignoring everything around him. He gave Noah the sort of look that said, "I won't give it back." Instead of insisting, Noah poured milk into Villain's saucer. The cat immediately ceded the battlefield, leaving its victim to the mercy of the victor.

It was a tin soldier.

Noah had had that soldier for as long as he could remember. His father had gifted him this toy before he went to the Moon. Father had gotten the soldier from grandfather, who got it from his father in turn. It was a pilot. The color of the once-green figure had long since faded, and its flat face had acquired indentations that made him seem surprisingly real and almost alive.

When he thought about golems, Noah always imagined their faces to look like that.

*

How did they allow this to happen to them? The newspapers had said something about freedom of choice. Noah didn't buy it.

At times he tried to imagine: here they were, back from the war. There was ash in their eyes and fires burning in their dreams. No mothers had met them upon their return, because golems had never had mothers. By then, almost no one had living mothers anyway. Moon radiation was especially cruel to women and older people.

It's doubtful that anyone had told them the truth. Who would voluntarily allow for their hand to be cut off? And memory was dearer than a hand. It's not merely a lizard tail that can be cut off and left to rot under a rock. Memory is the self.

There was probably something like a post-war medical examination declared. They chatted in the corridors as they awaited their turn. They flirted with the nurses, smoked out of windows, laughed while flashing white teeth, grew somber as they recalled their fallen comrades.

The Amnesiac Amendment was universally praised at first.

We were crippled, then. Men who'd hidden from the war, boys who hadn't grown up quickly enough to become soldiers, women who'd become old before they turned forty, girls who would never become mothers: mutilated humanity that had barely survived. We became accustomed to the difficulty and hopelessness of war. The early post-war years, once we were rid of this difficulty and hopelessness, were soaked in this special blend of ease and happiness. The world was tough, but it was honest and right. The Amnesiac Amendment had seemed that way, too.

We wanted to be strong and forgiving. We imagined how they'd appear among us: almost but not quite like humans. Without memories. Without the past. Without knowing how to live.

Come on then, come, bring out our heroes we said, when the newspapers first wrote about golem conversions using cautious, oblique words. We'll take care of them. We'll become their elder siblings. And maybe that will make us feel whole.

We got our answer: all is well. They're already among you.

A week ago Noah had remembered this. He'd still remembered on Sunday night. After that, his memory, suppressed by insomnia, began to fail.

As he ascended the staircase, smelling fresh paint and wondering at the unfamiliar fresh color of the walls and lack of cigarette butts in the corners, Noah recalled what today was, and why he should've already been at the lab an hour ago.

When he reached his floor, Noah carefully glanced from the staircase into the corridor, trying to figure out where the Premier might be. There was emptiness to his left, and silence to his right. Perhaps the enemy was holed up in one of the biochemical labs on the floor above. Noah moved down the corridor, calm and steady. It wouldn't do if he were discovered here rushing about with a guilty expression on his face. Noah was aware of his surroundings: lab 301 was empty, its door locked. 302 was potentially dangerous, but, no, it was quiet. A door creaked in 305. Ah, his colleague Ian was waiting and peeking out, which meant the Premier wasn't on this floor yet.

Noah nodded to Ian and ducked into his lab—307—then calmed down right away. Here, he was safe.

The Premier's visit to the institute had been scheduled nearly three months ago. At the moment, Friar Yakov was being shown laboratories that appeared outwardly promising and effective. Labs with buzzing centrifuges, picturesque bacteria growing in petri dishes, and servers blinking with multicolored lights.

There was nothing for the Premier to see in Noah's quiet, empty, and meticulously clean room.

Noah looked around and frowned. Now the lab seemed too clean to him. Suspiciously clean. Noah put his toy pilot down on the table to dilute the frightening sterility. In a world where the past had been erased by war, this tin soldier was his most valuable possession. It was proof that Noah was real. That his memory wasn't a fabrication.

And yet. Yet.

Golems dissipated among us, mixed in the crowd: alive, soft, warm, real. This proved the truth better than any propaganda: they were the same as us. It was impossible to find a golem in this last, half-dead city, where loners had gathered from all over after the war. Those with no past, no relatives or friends. It was impossible to tell them apart. And why? The golems may not have been entirely human, the blood flowing in their veins may have been artificial, but hadn't they earned the right to live on this scorched earth? If they hadn't earned it, we certainly didn't deserve it, either.

Whenever he heard such talk, Noah was surprised: if everything were so simple and obvious, then why did it bear repeating over and over again?

He was eighteen when he'd moved to the capital, passed the university entrance exams, and joined the Brotherhood—it was an informal youth organization back then. At eighteen one couldn't do without outrage and protest. Noah had been indifferent toward music and too shy for promiscuity. That left only politics.

The Amnestic Amendment had just been passed. Its nuances and the golems themselves were being discussed by all sides. Golems were still considered heroes then, albeit anonymous and invisible heroes. But now some special, elusive intonation was mixed in with the people's love. Noah heard it, measured it with his youthful barometer—precise and sensitive—but he didn't yet know how to analyze it.

Friar Yakov, a very wise and experienced man, helped with that.

Golems, he said, are our children. We made them to win the war. But the war is over, the war is in the past. And they remain. They were born to die in the war, to disintegrate. Instead they came back to our world, which was not ready for them. Sooner or later the seeds of war would awaken within them, grow through their crippled memory, and we will be surrounded by the thousands of broken heroes, who are not suited for the new, clean world. We must help them. Save them from themselves.

Back then, Noah didn't quite understand what such help would entail.

Noah woke from a strange nightmare: he had dreamt that there was no air left and he'd have to learn to live without it. He opened his eyes and realized he'd been sleeping at his desk. The Premier stood next to him. Somehow, Noah immediately realized it was him, even without turning his head. Friar Yakov smelled of the past in a unique way. He picked up Noah's pilot from the desk and studied it with a smile.

"This is how we slept during the war, right by the machines in the factory," Friar Yakov said good-naturedly, and placed the toy back on the table.

The Premier's entourage was also there. Noah imagined how they must've come in, carefully, on tippy-toes, so as not to wake him. That was Friar Yakov's nature. He liked a good joke, and knew how to appeal.

He was over forty—a rare and demonstrative age these days. Yakov's contemporaries had perished in lunar craters or rotted in the factories. Legend had it that the Premier had spent the entire war working on the production line, making ammunition for the Matryoshkas. That was a lie, of course. Friar Yakov looked like an old man, but he was alive and well. Anyone who had anything to do with the Matryoshka innards had died off from radiation exposure ten years ago.

As if to compensate for his embarrassingly advanced age, Friar Yakov surrounded himself with young, smiling faces. His assistants were youthful and productive. One of them—a tall raven-haired man—looked at Noah with a special understanding. This was Friar Pavel. Seven years ago, soon after the Night of Unmasking, he had gone straight from the university auditorium to a private office next door to Friar Yakov's. That same Friar Pavel who'd invented the Machine and, using formulas, graphs, and tables, had convincingly proved its value to the Premier.

Friar Yakov made more jokes and everyone laughed in unison. Noah felt a new wave of doubt cresting. Why had Friar Yakov come here, to this quiet, dark, and insignificant room? The man did nothing without a reason. Seven years ago he'd paid with hundreds, even thousands of golem lives to reach his political apex.

Could it be—Noah thought when his visitors had left—that he came only to see the last living golem for himself?

Seven years ago, during the Night of Unmasking, Noah had lived in a dormitory. He'd had a room to himself. His friend Peter had grown disillusioned with the new world, dropped out of the university and headed for the coast, to study the frozen ocean.

During that night Noah had listened to the sound of footsteps, and the screaming. He'd peeked out into the street, brightly illuminated by the friars' carbide lamps. In that moment he deeply regretted not heading for the ocean alongside Peter. He couldn't believe his eyes, even though he had been expecting this to happen ever since he'd understood the motion vector of Friar Yakov's thought process.

Noah had long since quit attending Brotherhood meetings, as had many of his friends. Those who remained were the ones marching in the streets with carbide lamps and radiation counters. They searched for golems, expecting to easily recognize them by the traces of lunar radiation.

It was after midnight that a man had emerged from the epicenter of footsteps and shouting. The man had climbed in through the window. He wasn't anyone Noah recognized and looked nothing like a golem—he was emaciated, awkward, lanky. He moved as though he was made of nothing but knees and elbows, which knocked against everything in his path, introducing ruin and chaos to any sort of order. The man whispered and cried, smearing dirt across his face. He was pitiful. He couldn't have been a soldier; he was hardly human. He appeared to be an underground dweller, someone who'd waited out the war in some cave, subsisting on worms and moss. Noah asked about this, expecting a firm denial, but the man only nodded rapidly, and went on whispering details, spittle spraying from his mouth. He talked about the long-abandoned subway tunnels, where the radiation may have been higher than on the Moon. About incredible monsters—three-headed rats and centipedes large as dogs. About how it was only yesterday, incredulous about the war having ended, this man and his fellow underground dwellers had crawled cautiously out into the city, ready to retreat to their caves at a moment's notice. Of course they were soaked with radiation and any counter would click like a machine gun in their presence.

There was an insistent knock at the door, and the man had immediately pressed himself to the floor. Noah winced in opprobrium and pointed him toward the closet.

He'd gone into the corridor, his chin held high and his shoulders spread wide. He'd counted the seconds, and his heart had felt so large that it had filled his entire self with its thunderous beating. The visitors at the door were Brotherhood, and Noah had recognized some of them: they weren't students, but people a little older. Inexperienced Noah had once confused them for workers, before he'd recognized their gangster mannerisms. He thought back to his childhood, the time not so long ago, spent in an industrial suburb where he'd absorbed his fill of radiation. He said: you're raving lunatics, and so is Friar Yakov, so go ahead and shoot. The air tasted nectarous and thick after those words, and for a brief while—fifteen seconds or so—Noah had felt truly alive. Later he'd tried to recall this feeling and to replicate it, but couldn't.

The raving lunatics had waved their radiation counters, which had emitted only a handful of clicks, had glanced inside the room, and had gone away.

In the morning, Noah had kicked the underground dweller out, and then ripped up his Brotherhood membership card.

Friar Yakov had delivered a speech—a convincing and clear speech, unlike the then-Premier's recycled words—letting everyone know that it was the golems responsible for the pogroms and the murders. Golems, whose artificial minds had rebelled and thirsted for war and blood. That it was the golems who'd walked around with carbide lamps in hand and killed innocent people. His words had been confirmed by multiple eyewitnesses. Noah was surprised to recognize the underground dweller he had saved among them.

The people had trusted Friar Yakov's words. He was impossible not to believe. He'd rapidly risen from the leader of a little-known society to the leader of our small remnant of humanity. Golems had become enemies overnight, and we'd accepted that. For some, it had been easier to accept the manufacturing flaw in artificial people than the possibility of existing in complete and definitive equality with them. Others—Noah among them—had simply kept quiet, stunned by the absurdity of what was happening around them but unable or unwilling to try to change anything. That is when Noah had realized it was a good thing that he'd never got to go to war, that there was no place in war for a coward like him. He wasn't worthy.

On Friday, pain woke Noah up. He squeezed the tin pilot in his bandaged hand. Blood had soaked through the bandage, turning the pilot red.

He felt Masha the Mouse's gaze on his back. She wasn't sleeping, either.

He turned toward her. Masha lay on her side, her hair crumpled by the pillow, her eyes puffy. Noah gently traced his finger across her milky-white stomach. Masha seemed to be pleased by this gesture; she pressed Noah's hand tight with her small, warm palm.

What would happen to her if Noah turns out to be a golem? He didn't want to think about it. Not now.

In recent days Masha became distant, cold, alien. But now, lying silently next to her and looking into her gray eyes, Noah felt happy.

*

Some days, one can feel like they can do anything.

On Friday morning Noah was certain he was heading to work, until he found himself on a winding street in the eastern suburb, not far from the orphanage where he had spent his childhood.

The weather was nice. Fresh snow had fallen, and Noah's boots crunched pleasantly against the prickly black coating on the ground. Noah hadn't been here in a decade. He often saw this area in his dreams, but in a dream it was filled with nonexistent details, scents, and sounds.

These real streets were more gray and bland than how Noah remembered them. Moreover, they were totally empty. Like all manufacturing towns serving the war effort, this neighborhood was dying a slow and lonely death, covered in black snow and permeated with radiation.

Still, his trip was a lot like his dreams. Noah felt the same unjustified high, the same ease and self-confidence. The same thoughts raced through his mind as those in the dreams about his childhood.

The orphanage was around the corner. The once-red brick walls had turned black over time. This was no dream. In the dream, everything remained the same. Staring at this hopeless darkness, Noah realized that he, too, had irrevocably changed over the years, and not for the better. At twenty-eight he was an old man from the point of view of the youngster who'd sought adventures and secrets in the basement bar. As useless as those factory workers who had beaten up the poor vagrant who'd made the mistake of pretending to be a golem. Those workers had long perished from radiation and other hazards they'd been exposed to in the factories. Their lives at least had had meaning. Perhaps not as much as that of Noah's father, but they'd spent their lives in the service of our victory.

What had Noah done with his life? Wasted years at the university and his embarrassing time as a member of the Brotherhood? A routine job he barely understood at the lab, the point of which was known only to the scientific director—assuming it wasn't just busywork the director had invented in the first place?

Midlife crisis struck Noah with its merciless hammer. He had stood in this very spot aged seventeen, filled with hope, and the great path he had embarked upon had turned out to be pointless. If he had to look his seventeen-year-old self in the eye now, Noah would die of embarrassment.

And yet. Yet.

He had seen the sun once—a few rays, for all of five minutes. They said this was the result of the work his lab was doing, among others. Which meant one of those rays belonged to Noah.

He had experienced love, such that the past infatuations seemed little more to him than playing with toy soldiers reminded real soldiers of an actual war.

He'd never become a hero, never become a pilot, but he was a person. He remembered his gray, worthless, empty life, which was more than any golem could boast.

Noah climbed over the fence and found himself on the concrete grounds that surrounded the black orphanage building.

The windows were boarded up, the door handles wrapped in thick lengths of chain. Noah remembered that he had seen all of this in his dreams. There, he easily ripped the chains and walked in like he owned the place. Noah carefully tried the door, heard something reply with a dull echo from behind it.

He walked around the building. To the left of the back door there was a special window, which Noah had often used to climb outside in his dreams.

The window was there, sloppily boarded up crosswise. Noah ripped off the boards and kicked in the glass. The window was too small for an adult, but Noah made it through, scratching his arms and leaving strips of cloth on the frames. His palm was bleeding again.

Noah clicked a lighter and discovered that the basement hardly resembled the one he had recalled, the one from his dreams. As though it had experienced its own small, ruthless private war. The bare concrete walls had been burned, the floor was covered in splinters and rubbish, the rusted boiler in the corner was split in two by a crack. Dust was everywhere. How had the dust gotten in? Noah hadn't seen it in years. The dust seemed to have disappeared, finally and irrevocably, after the war.

Noah walked down the dark, dead corridor, trying to recall the times he had walked here as a teenager, the times he'd greeted his friends and planned an upcoming prank or exchanged treasures found beyond the fence.

He couldn't recall anything like that. Memory served up only the familiar pictures, but those pictures didn't match with what he was seeing in real life. It was as though pieces of several different jigsaw puzzles were mixed in a single box.

The dust finally caused Noah to sneeze. A floorboard squeaked underfoot, and this familiar, sharp squeak scraped against his memory like a knife against glass.

A flare to his left. And Noah saw number nine, who'd lost his entire arm on the Moon. The new arm hung limp and irritated number nine terribly. And there he is, trying to learn to hold a cigarette with it.

Number twenty-two is walking toward him, an invalid's cane in hand. His leg drags—a foreign, disobedient leg. He must walk, move, so that the dead artificial leg can become living and real. Number thirteen, the captain, smokes by the window. His sad eyes stare at the factory smoke outside, as though they see something no one else does.

They're all young, seventeen at most. They're all old men, veterans returned from the war they went to fight two years ago as children. Even if they were tin children and not real ones.

The next door leads to his hospital room. There should be a handwritten sign above the bed made in a crooked, wounded handwriting. The sign reads, "We'll return home." It's still there.

It was here—under this bed, under the sign—Noah, who had been called number seven then, found the little tin toy soldier, a pilot, left there by another veteran. By a real person.

*

The Brotherhood meeting traditionally took place in the Chinese Room of the art museum. The museum had been almost completely destroyed during the war, but this room had miraculously survived. Noah has been here a couple of times—nearly a decade ago. Chinese art remained the same: dead and beautiful. Calligraphy sang absolutes to him from the walls. Sometimes Noah thought that if only he would learn Chinese, the multifaceted and all-embracing meaning of life would reveal itself to him.

Noah came here because he had no choice. Having left the hospital he'd spent a decade thinking of as an orphanage, Noah scooped some black snow into his wounded palm and watched snowflakes melt in his blood. He pictured himself appearing in this museum room, looking everyone in the eye, only to see fear. The man Noah had been that morning could've run. To the dead ocean, to the underground subway labyrinths. The man could run, but not the golem.

After the Night of Unmasking friars had stormed the scientific archive where they'd hoped to find the personal dossiers of the golems and their names. They'd found nothing. Noah often wondered: how would all of this end if Friar Pavel hadn't appeared with the blueprints for the Machine—the unholy device that, according to its creator, could differentiate between human and golem? What went through the head of the still-young man when he invented this insidious device? What must pass through a person's head for them to invent the hunt? This was probably beyond a golem's ability to comprehend.

Noah had heard a lot about the hunt. Snippets of conversations, rumors, and fabrications. But also one reliable account: an enthusiastic story by his colleague Naum, a dedicated member of the Brotherhood. Naum himself eventually turned out to be a golem and became yet another victim of the Machine.

Naum had said that playing cards would be dealt. So it was; Noah received a ten of clubs. It looked like nothing special, but today this was the Most Important Card. Why a ten? Why clubs? Even on an evening like this he was denied the chance to be a king.

Then, Naum had told him, grab some wine, engage in conversation with intelligent people, enjoy life. Be sure to sample the spinach-filled tartlets. The tartlets were served, but Noah declined to try them. He was a wound-up spring, an electron that required movement. He found it impossible to chew, to drink, to stand still. He walked and walked across the room, searching people's faces. He was looking for unpleasant traits, for a reason to hate them.

These were ordinary faces, sometimes even familiar ones. Open, clear, simple faces. Devoid of villainy and fear. Most, like Noah, had come here for the first time, or hadn't been here in a while. They looked around, hoping to catch a glimpse of the Machine.

Noah looked around as well. Was it hidden under the floor or in the adjacent room? They said the Machine was as inconvenient to use as the idea of equality between people and golems was inconvenient to hear. It was too large to be mobile. Too delicate to work with a large crowd. Too sensitive not to become overwhelmed by extreme emotions.

That's why the Premier found Friar Pavel's idea so clever: to make the golems come to it. And yes, they came. Each one certain that someone else would turn out to be a golem. Noah understood this certainty: that very morning his memory was human, was real and indisputable. But he couldn't understand their desire to watch a living being perish inside a trap, even if it was only a golem. Friar Yakov understood this. He may not have known science, but he was an expert on human nature.

How did the Machine work? What did it measure? Rumors had it the Machine could detect the presence of a soul. A soul that each human would have and each golem obviously would not. Friar Pavel, the creator of the Machine, neither confirmed nor denied such rumors.

Friar Yakov approached the podium. The curtain was pulled back and revealed an alcove where the Machine stood, enormous and grandiose like a pipe organ.

Noah took a step back when he saw it. He felt ill. He kept waiting for the feeling he had experienced during the Night of

Unmasking to return. Waited for the air to become nectarous and thick, so he could inhale deeply of it before he died. Instead, he felt only nausea and heat.

Not knowing what to do with his hands, Noah shoved them into his pockets. He felt for his tin pilot with the face of a golem in the left pocket. He retrieved it and squeezed it in his fist.

Friar Yakov waved, calling for silence.

"Let us begin, my friends. This is a special evening. It marks the beginning of our future. The future of true humanity. The future without golems. You, the last golem, hear me." Friar Yakov paused, looking around the room. For nearly a second, he looked straight at Noah. "You don't yet know your fate, and I pity you. But you must die, so that we can finally be rid of our past. Be rid of war. Be rid of pain. Be strong and hold your head up high, soldier."

A low, barely audible whistle, emanated from the walls. The Machine behind Friar Yakov crackled to life.

Noah thought that, upon hearing the whistling sound, the friars stepped aside, as though to clear the path between Noah and the Machine. But this wasn't the case. Everyone froze in their place.

The whistling ended as abruptly as it had begun. The Machine clinked as it spat a playing card through a small slot in its wooden frame. Friar Yakov collected the card without looking at it. He has done this many times before and, yes, he derived pleasure from the experience.

Friar Yakov grinned slyly, dragging out the pause like a host from some old show. Finally, he flipped the card over, and frowned. He retrieved his glasses and put them on, deliberately slow.

This irritated Noah terribly. The damned old man was making some sort of spectacle out of his impending death. Noah was ready to step forward and end the show, when two junior friars approached Yakov. One of them collected the card from Friar Yakov's hand and another copy of the same card from his jacket pocket. It was the king of spades.

Two identical cards. This meant the Machine had declared the Premier to be the last golem. Impossible. Nonsense. He was the only one present, perhaps the only one in the entire town, who couldn't possibly be a golem. He was too old, and too human.

"This is some sort of a mistake," said Friar Yakov. He forced a smile. "Where's Pavel? Summon him."

Immediately, Friar Pavel appeared. The omnipresent, deft, raven-haired Pavel.

"There's no mistake," he said in the same respectful tone he always used when speaking to the Premier. "The Machine doesn't make mistakes."

The Premier looked around, seeking his assistants. They were there, but looked up indifferently and didn't move.

"What are you saying? How could I be a golem? I was never even at the front."

"Everyone says that. Absolutely everyone. Hold your head up high, Premier."

"Arrest him! I'm putting an end to this farce!"

No one listened to the Premier. They twisted his arms, shook him roughly, crumpled his jacket, took him away. Friar Pavel threw up his hands, as if to announce that the show was over. The room was filled with noise, but that noise was almost devoid of bewilderment, as if everyone had expected such an outcome.

Friar Pavel's gaze met Noah's and he nodded, smiling in a warm and friendly manner. And Noah's crippled memory suddenly responded to this smile: Noah recognized him. Friar Pavel was the captain of his flight squad. Number thirteen was older now, his brow wrinkled, his black hair showing touches of gray. But his gaze was the same: as though he saw something no one else did.

Without yet understanding anything himself, Noah smiled back. He drew in a deep breath. The air was nectarous and thick.

Noah thought about Masha the Mouse. He'd refused to permit himself to think about her when he'd come here, but now everything was different. His mind, free from the shackles of false memories, finally sorted out an uncomplicated mosaic. How Masha had changed lately, how she had become distant and uncertain. She wasn't the first. Noah had heard about such cases, even if those were only rumors. A friend of a colleague of his ex-roommate; a wife of a young worker someone from accounting department knew personally; some other women—nameless and strange, but surely beautiful in their unexpected fortune.

Let it be a boy, thought Noah. I'll give him the tin pilot so that one day he can give it to his own son.

LAJOS AND HIS BEES

THIS HAPPENED IN VANAHEIMR, IN THE MOUNTAIN VILLAGE OF Medven; not so long ago, but not yesterday, either. Prior to either of the Mähren Wars, if you must know.

There was a whisperer there by the name of Lajos who disliked people. There was no hatred within him of the sort common men suspect all whisperers to be guilty of. Lajos didn't wish ill on anyone, but he felt no kinship with other members of the human species, either. As a boy, he didn't join in any children's games and preferred solitude to all amusements—he ran off to the mountains at every opportunity. At first, his father would follow him, but he quickly realized that returning Lajos home was a senseless and even harmful task. It was better for him in the mountains. Soon, his mother resigned herself to this as well.

They say wild clematis, which so enjoys grasping the foot of a careless traveler, never touched Lajos. The spruce branches never whipped him unless he wanted them to. The birds in his path fell silent or began to sing on command at his mere gesture. Mountain cats came to warm him during cold nights.

Lajos was a respectful son. While his parents were alive, he would regularly appear in Medven—a sullen, hirsute fellow, but never malicious.

Mother sat Lajos on the porch and brushed his hair for a long time. She combed weeds, branches, dried flowers, and a multitude of dead bees out of his mane. Live bees always hovered around Lajos. He didn't chase them away, and his parents eventually grew used to them.

One after the other, Lajos's parents passed away. His visits to the village became far less frequent after he had buried them. He abandoned the house and didn't look after the graves. At first, the villages condemned him, but only behind his back as his formidable appearance inspired respect and fear. Ever since his mother died, there had been no one to groom his beard and mane, and soon Lajos came to resemble a tree giant (he was nearly four alns tall). One couldn't tell with certainty that birds hadn't built their nests in his hair. And the number of bees was increasing by the day. These bees were far more fearsome than Lajos himself. Always vigilant. Should one wave their hand recklessly they'd immediately appear: Where are you looking? What have you planned? But there was never an instance where they'd harass someone without a reason.

Lajos came to the village whenever he needed things he couldn't procure or make on his own. Barrels for honey, steel, and occasionally clothes. Sometimes he yearned for banitsa, a layered pastry dish his mother used to make when he was little. He was unsocial, but also honest and generous. Lajos took what he wanted without asking, but always paid a good price for anything he took. He paid with carved wooden trifles, and honey. The trifles were strange; a mockery of nature, perverted hybrids of species. A hare with the body of a snake. A dog with the head of a fish and a lobster tail. A redshank bird on spider legs. Lajos never repeated himself, and each new creation was seemingly uglier, more unnatural than the rest. Moreover, these curios were crafted skillfully; were it not for the feeling of disgust, one could endlessly admire such work. Children cried when they saw these trifles. Adults were wary of touching them as they felt each one possessed a soul. The villagers weren't thrilled about such payment, but they accepted it; one could profitably sell these wondrous creations in Olmutz. Rumor had it, if you were to place one of these curios under your pillow, its ugly visage would repel nightmares.

Honey was another matter. Lajos's honey was marvelous. One could follow its aroma beyond the edge of the world, leaving one's earthly troubles, forgetting one's mother, father, wife, and children. Its smell ended arguments and its gentle bittersweet taste caused some to experience magical visions: alien lands that could've been Midgard and even Troy; landscapes never before seen by the human eye, lands of ice and fire, and sometimes a dark abyss. Perhaps that was Ginnungagap itself, the void in which the world was created. Others yet thought they could understand the language of birds, or learn the secrets of their ancestors from touching their grandparents' belongings. It was as though the honey turned each person into a whisperer for a brief time.

They said Lajos possessed two souls. He imbued his dark soul into the trifles, which was what made them so ugly. He mixed his light soul into the honey. And along with it, bits of whisperer dreams.

The honey was famous far and wide. At the market in Olmutz it was even more popular than Lajos's wooden freaks. They recall the honey to this day, although the last drop was eaten nearly forty years ago. There's even a proverb: Fine as Medven honey. Perhaps you've heard it?

Lajos's domain was difficult to reach, but not impossibly so. Still, the Medven villagers never ventured there. Why, you ask? Everyone asks that. Townsfolk can't fathom the soul of a mountain dweller. It is well known that there are no secrets in small villages. Mountain people are a curious lot, and they tend to stick their noses into their neighbors' business if it's even remotely interesting. Still, they didn't trouble Lajos. It was because the villagers didn't think of Lajos as merely a neighbor, as their equal. Condemnation had long since given way to quiet respect. The sort of respect afforded to a bear or a mountain spirit, who won't harm a human so long as that person doesn't break his simple rules.

On occasion, a shepherd would wander near the border of Lajos's land. Those borders were marked with stones similar to commonplace waystones, except Lajos didn't know runes and wasn't literate at all. Instead, he etched rough approximations of bees drawn as several rhombuses. These markings had no magical power but they warned all who saw them to stay away. Anyone who saw such a sign would give Lajos's domain a wide berth.

One little shepherd—still a boy—had a lamb go missing in the night. This lamb was especially precious to him, perhaps because of its exotic black coloration. The boy left the herd to be tended by his loyal dog and went out in search of the lamb. He didn't find it, and forgot about the lamb altogether once he realized he'd wandered onto Lajos's land. The little shepherd returned to Medven in shock, his eyes big as saucers, hair standing on end. He came back alone without his herd. He earned a beating for this, but everyone—even the kmet, the village elder himself—listened to his story about the wondrous home of Lajos.

In Lajos's domain, the boy told them, there were bells hanging everywhere, woven into marvelous contraptions made of branches, stems, and scraps of leather. These bells ought to ring from the slightest gust of wind, but instead they rang whimsically, as though obeying the will of an invisible musician. One fell silent while another picked up the melody; some rang together but with discord. They led you, beckoned you with their sound. And then they quieted down sleepily and it felt as if you were left alone, completely alone. Not a rustle was heard for many alns. The boy followed the sound of these bells across unfamiliar terrain as though it were a thread, marveling at the land's untamed splendor. These mountains were magnificent even without the work of whisperers, but the place where the little shepherd ended up was gorgeous, with a wild, ruthless beauty. This beauty slapped at the unwelcome guest. He bent down, writhed, growled in pain, but kept moving in spite of this. Against his will, which demanded he turn around and leave this forsaken place.

He followed forest trails, past the cave where Lajos most likely dwelled, past the beehives, empty and silent, until he reached the edge of a clearing carpeted with soft grass and moss, finer than a priceless rug. He stopped there. The bells fell silent and he could've turned around and run away, but what he saw in the clearing had mesmerized him.

Lajos was there. And so were the bees. An enormous swarm that obeyed the same power as the bells in the trees, the same power as the little shepherd. The power of Lajos.

Lajos was whispering. He did so inaudibly, silently. His lips barely moved. Even so, the little shepherd had no doubt: Lajos's words were gentle and affectionate. Lajos whispered, and the swarm listened. The swarm encircled him, sometimes hanging nearby, sometimes covering Lajos in waves, separating and re-uniting to form bizarre silhouettes that were reminiscent of the trifles Lajos carved from wood. Except these figures were enormous, large enough to cover half the sky. So said the boy.

And then—the boy swore to this by everything he held dear—the bees formed into a figure of a girl, and Lajos began to dance across the clearing with this form as though it were a real woman. The little shepherd told them what happened later, but it is uncouth to repeat this and besides, you can probably guess for yourself.

The shepherd boy watched all this, not believing what he saw, wanting to turn away but never moving; wanting to shut his eyes but never blinking. He looked on in horror and delight, and he recalled the taste of Lajos's honey with absolute clarity.

He would have gone on watching forever, not daring to move until he turned to stone, became covered in moss, until centuries later nothing remained but his bones, except he felt the gaze of someone watching him back.

This wasn't Lajos's gaze. The whisperer appeared out of it, bathed in the unconscious bliss which is known to anyone who has already become a man.

It was the gaze of the bees. The entire swarm, like one being, looking at him. A dark, alien, piercing gaze. The entire swarm became this gaze, and the boy thought that the swarm would at any moment re-form into a new figure—that of an enormous eye belonging to neither insect nor human.

That's when the little shepherd turned and ran away as fast as he could.

This tale didn't alter the relationship between the residents of Medven and Lajos. It was exactly the sort of existence—albeit without such sensual details—they had imagined for Lajos, since they thought of him as a mountain spirit. As for Lajos, he behaved as though nothing out of the ordinary had happened.

Only the shepherd boy could no longer venture into the mountains. It wasn't Lajos he feared—it was the bees. Their gaze. Less than a year later, the boy ran away from home and traveled to Olmutz, where he fell in with the wrong crowd. His life would subsequently become both interesting and difficult, as the first Mähren War loomed, and the second wasn't far behind.

But this story isn't about the shepherd boy.

Even before he ran away, the little shepherd's adventures became a yarn that flowed across the region along with Medven honey until it reached Olmutz itself. The townsfolk, unlike the mountain dwellers, didn't believe such fairy tales; the townsfolk believed their own eyes, and the town whisperers behaved like regular people who didn't engage in unnatural relations with the bees. The yarn was considered to be a clever invention, meant to enhance the already sky-high popularity of Medven honey.

Only one man became curious about the origins of the yarn. This man was a circus master; strange creatures were his bread and butter, and he spent his entire life searching for talent in order to chain it with contracts and force it to reveal its soul for the amusement of crowds, wherever the Veneti circus caravans would travel. His own talent was his ability to sniff out anything wondrous, and he could very clearly sense Lajos and his bees.

The people of Medven refused to lead the stranger to Lajos's domain, but he was a stubborn man and set out without a guide. He came back a week later, stung, swollen, and barely alive. He threatened to report the entire village to the authorities, but never followed up on this threat. They say he spent the rest of his life deathly afraid of bees, and that he saw them everywhere. They also say the problem wasn't the circus man's vivid imagination, but rather that at least one bee would always hover near him. And it would always be watching.

But this is not the story of a greedy circus master.

One time, Lajos fell in love. This didn't seem to suit his grim and lonely nature, but facts are facts. Perhaps what he felt didn't contain the sublime shades which we customarily use to decorate the description of love. Perhaps it was merely lust. So spoke the evil tongues, and the way he chose to get what he was looking for corresponds with their version of events.

Matchmaking among the mountain people was associated with many rituals, the observance of which was closely monitored by the elders. Lajos, of course, wasn't familiar with any of those rituals. He didn't waste any time on courtship. One day, the kmet discovered that his daughter Radka had disappeared. In her stead, five barrels of honey—an entire fortune—was left at the kmet's doorstep. They also discovered a multitude of carvings in Radka's room: snails with cat faces, a grasshopper-horse, and other ugly trifles.

As her mother was in hysterics and the women tried to calm her down, while also whispering the shepherd boy's story to one another, the kmet gathered the men to go to the mountains. They brought gifts with them, everything that Lajos valued: the best knives, embroidered linen shirts, the banitsa pastry hastily baked by one of the old women, and several pairs of boots. There were also two barrels of anise mastic from the kmet's personal reserves. The kmet dusted off his old, rusty saber.

They reached Lajos's domain by evening. Lajos, as though he knew to expect guests, met them by the border stone. He was wearing a clean shirt, his hair brushed, his beard braided. There were no bees with him, which was unusual. Without them, Lajos suddenly looked defenseless and small, despite his four alns of height. The kmet's hand rested on the hilt of his saber.

They stood by the border stone and stared at each other in silence. Lajos was always silent, while the kmet would have said something if only he could find the right words. The men at his back were unusually quiet; they didn't crack jokes, or groan, or even breathe. Everything—even the air—was still. If a stray spark had found its way there at that moment, it would have ignited a black flame.

That's when Radka appeared. She was small in stature—a fidgety, feisty girl. She showed up and broke the silence with her irrepressible chatter, laughter, and wild gesticulations. She apologized for leaving without permission, threw up her hands asking how her mother was doing, hugged her father and kissed his palms, and talked, always talked. There was no happiness for her without Lajos, how nice he was, what a fine husband he'd make, how they'd have many children.

She flatly refused to return home.

She meticulously studied her father's gifts, resolutely returned the alcohol, and accepted the rest.

She said her good-byes warmly.

The kmet resigned himself to the loss of his daughter (he had two more ready for marriage) and calmed his wife, then mentally calculated his profits. A beekeeper son-in-law was much better than random offerings from a mountain spirit that the Medvenians had become accustomed to. There was potential for a large-scale operation.

Three days later, Lajos came to the village.

It was a clear morning, but the fog followed Lajos and descended from the mountains. The fog wrapped a cloak around its mighty shoulders and spread it further along the ground, extending its tentacles in all directions. Lajos was filthy. He bent low to the ground. It wasn't from the load he carried in his arms—Radka had been tiny even in life, and in death she seemed to have lost half her mass—but from the weight on his soul.

He laid her down on the ground—gently. As though she were sleeping rather than dead. Radka was unrecognizable—black and swollen. There was an investigation later, the bailiff came from Olmutz and brought a medical examiner with him, who was a fuss and a bore. The examiner counted one thousand three hundred and seventeen stings on Radka's body. The bees. That's what he said. He added some more fancy words, but no one was listening. The bees, all of Medven rumbled. The bees.

In that moment when Lajos placed Radka's body near the well, no one thought about the bees. They weren't even around—for a time.

Lajos walked away a few steps. He got down on his knees, lowered his head, and waited silently.

They say it was the kmet's wife who threw the first rock. They say everyone in Medven threw rocks, from young children to ancient hags. This is not true. No villager threw a single stone.

The kmet's wife lay next to her dead daughter, hugged her, and whispered a lullaby in her ear. She lay there for a long time, not letting go. It took four men to pull her away. The other Medvenians stood still, not yet able to comprehend, to understand what had happened. People stood and watched, even the kmet, who was barefoot and wearing only a nightshirt. They stood there as Lajos waited. He would have told them what he was waiting for, but he had long since forgotten how to speak.

The stones flew on their own. Ripped by an inhuman will from under the feet of the villagers, they flew true, striking Lajos in his chest, his back, his temple. And still, Lajos would not fall. He wouldn't fall until there were no stones left. Until there was no life left in him.

When the whistling and rumble had ceased and the dust settled, nothing remained of the giant that Lajos had been in life. Not a single bone. But, they say, all the stones in Medven have been red ever since.

That's when the bees appeared. A swarm. A terrifying, formless cloud covered the sky, and darkness fell.

Nobody ran. They stood as one, mesmerized by the chaotic flicker of the swarm.

They waited for death, but death wouldn't come.

There was a gust of wind—mighty and cold like Nidhogg's breath—and the bees disappeared.

When the bailiff and soldiers traveled to Lajos's domain, they found nothing out of the ordinary there. Regular mountains, regular forest. Bells in the tree branches obediently sang along with the wind. Only the clearing near Lajos's cave held scraps of beehives, which looked as if they had been exploded from inside by miniature rune bombs. The bailiff, who had already learned the story from the villagers, studied the splinters, the chips, and the corpses of bees that were abundant across the apiary; he walked around, measured something with his steps, muttered under his breath.

The bees, he reported, had been locked in their beehives, but they struggled so mightily to free themselves that they had smashed the hives from the inside. Strange things happen in the world, the bailiff said, but didn't write this observation down in his report.

They say that even today one might encounter the bee swarm in the Olmutz Mountains. It moves about restlessly, taking outlandish forms—an eye in the empty sky, a frog with owl wings, but more often a girl who dances and dances with her invisible partner.

They also say that when Lajos died, so did his carved trifles. They didn't turn to ash, as happens in fairy tales about whisperers and their treasure. They didn't disappear, and their outward appearance didn't change. But everyone they had protected from nightmares now sleeps with their eyes open, so terrifying have their dreams become.

THE FARCTORY

I: HERE

THE SHADOW

It started when the vending machine which dispensed senses broke down. It was the last such machine on the block. Its screen, once sparkling and bright, collapsed into a pile of white noise that felt prickly to the touch. Squeamishly, I shoved my hand into the hissing mess, twisted the levers at random, feeling the upset electrons hop like fleas across my palm. Nothing changed.

I used a knife to poke at the opening under the speaker. The speaker emitted a puff of smoke and its cover creaked open, releasing a small gray russle, which chittered at me indignantly. I wasn't surprised: the russles were everywhere these days. The rodent cut its fiery squeak short, deftly jumped onto the pavement, and skittered away. Immediately thereafter, rusty gears tumbled from the machine, followed by zigzags of celluloid punch tape. The machine's screen blinked for the last time and trickled down the drain into a sewer grate. I was left standing alone in the middle of an empty street.

Unless you count Hare, who was clumsily trying to hide around the corner—the boy huffed like Grandma Bach's teakettle. I pretended not to notice him. Mauk probably wouldn't have done` likewise. But I had no other alternative.

That's when the shadow appeared. I turned around as soon as I sensed its chilly smell.

The shadow was sickly, flat, and transparent. In other words, it looked like any other shadow.

Frankly, I hadn't been able to stand shadows since childhood. They were cold. They made the most unpleasant rustling noises. Nowadays, there was no reason for their existence at all: the Farctory was closed, the color mines had been shuttered.

For as long as I could remember, shadows had snuck into the city from the dungeons under the Farctory. They burrowed their way up with their cold curious noses. The repair crews couldn't keep up. The shadows were more keenly motivated, hence the unfortunate statistic: three new wormholes dug for every one patched up with a harsh thread of reality.

Feral shadows were a source of chaos and destruction. Taming a shadow was like taming an abyss. It would stare with hungry eyes from every corner of your home. It would spew its nonsense. And it would wait for the right moment.

You might call this selfishness. I say, it's the love of order. Tenderness toward meaning.

The shadows had always been attracted to me, as if by an invisible magnet. I sometimes wondered if I should attempt to dislike girls with a similar passion, so as to obtain their infinite, warm attentions. Frankly, however, I scared off the girls without trying. At first because I was with Barbara, and then because Barbara was gone.

The shadow blinked. Instead of walking away, for some reason I looked it in the eyes. The shadow's eyes were poorly drawn and wrinkled. A raspy draft blew out from them. I didn't know if that was the norm for all shadows.

The shadow held out its hand to me. A small pile of senses wiggled on its palm, dying. They squeaked plaintively as they dissolved in the shadow's flat shading.

It appeared the broken vending machine was the shadow's fault.

Some among your acquaintances were surely shadow sympathizers. This was a common thing. Here and there, people spoke out in defense of these mindless creatures.

One of my friends, Eyck, fed shadows a little salt on occasion, and wrote down their ravings while concentrating so hard that his tongue stuck out. What else is there to say?

I wasn't like that.

The shadow said, "Stepped candareen in the miniature bedstead. Yes."

This sounded almost meaningful compared to the usual shadow drivel. Its voice was entirely devoid of color, quiet and mournful.

I began to walk away.

The damned shadow didn't give up. It overtook me and stopped. It blinked its eyes and flashed a pathetic single-line smile.

What bad timing! Mauk was already waiting for me at the Dichotomy, and I couldn't arrive late.

And so I took out a revolver and shot the shadow right in the face.

Habitually, I wondered what Barbara would say when I found her. She'd say, what have you become, Bach?

Worst of all, I hardly believed anymore that I'd find her at all.

COLOASTERS

The walls of the Dichotomy were decorated with the most unusual objects, which comprised the past of the bar's owner, old man Ulle. There was an ash bow loaded with the world's slowest arrows. An arrow fired from it appeared suspended in the air, as though it wasn't moving at all. There was also a huge tortoise shell which, according to Ulle, once housed an entire brood of feral vowels. There were photos—mostly smudged and out of focus— that nevertheless attested to the photographer's eventful and adventurous life. Only one photo impressed with the amazing clar-

ity and sharpness of its lines—a portrait of an unknown woman.
I could make out every little detail in it: broken tree branches,
the attendant bird in the sky, the self-assured striped meowler on
the table. But the visage of the stranger herself slipped away and
crumbled whenever I tried to focus on it.

I liked Ulle—he was a tough old man who'd tasted of both
reason and chaos. A retired, lonely hunter, he generously poured
memories for anyone. At one point, I could have become like
him, had Barbara not entered my life.

Dichotomy was one of the last places where they still served
colors. No matter how often I asked, that scoundrel Ulle wouldn't
admit where he got them. The answer to that was almost certainly Mauk.

I went here every evening for nearly a month. I sat on the
same unremarkable stool at the bar, and remained there until
midnight. After two weeks of this, the regulars began calling that
stool "Bach's spot" and would chase random patrons off it upon
my arrival.

The bar-going public are a straightforward lot. It's easy to gain
their trust.

I ordered a glass of Ulle's finest blue every time, which gained
me his favor. The glass came with a thick cardboard coloaster
shaped like a tortoise. From the first evening, I repeated the same
exact trick: I drank exactly half of the blue color, set aside the glass,
and proceeded to cut open the latest tortoise with my pocket butterfly knife. It must be said: neither the butterfly, nor the tortoises,
nor the assorted patrons, nor the bartender were pleased by this
procedure. I understood them very well. You would, too. If you
were to encounter a teenager who keeps thoughtfully scraping
a rusty nail on glass, you would probably smack him upside the
head, and he would deserve it.

I dutifully played the role of such a teenager for nineteen evenings, until my finely tuned sense of timing went off. Something
inside me knew it was time to wrap up. I didn't care for the opin-
ion of the butterfly knife or the tortoises, as they couldn't reach
my head, let alone smack it. Ulle and his customers, on the other

hand, were on the verge of exhausting their collective patience. Everyone was ready for an endgame, and this endgame plunged the audience into a state of true ecstasy.

The story I told them as I dissected one of the first tortoises was simple and naïve like a newborn meowler. I claimed that one in every one hundred coloasters had a sense prize inserted into it at the Farctory, back when the Farctory was still open. It was impossible to prove or disprove this claim. It would seem one could ask the first Farctory engineer they met, and the truth would crawl into the light. Except, first, a layman is thoroughly convinced that every engineer is completely and irrevocably mad. Second, ever since the Farctory closed, not a single person had admitted to having had anything to do with it. All engineers I knew disappeared that day, leaving behind nothing but a damp smell of solvent in their empty apartments. And these were tough guys, who worked with undiluted colors daily!

My audience watched with unhealthy fascination as I destroyed the round cardboard tortoises one by one, committing crimes against common sense. Their faith faded with every dissected coloaster, just as their frustration and desire to smack me upside the head flourished.

Finally, on the nineteenth evening, I deftly swapped out the latest tortoise coloaster for a different one that looked the same. I'd prepared the fake in advance by carefully cutting the tortoise in two layers and inserting a little ordinary sense in-between. Then I painstakingly glued it back together.

Imagine: I downed half a glass of blue in two gulps. (I felt a buzz and warmth in my head, and I momentarily lost my balance, as though cradled by soft ocean waves; it smelled of salt and sand.) I set the glass aside. The audience held their collective breath. They were on the edge. They didn't need to glance at each other: the air was filled with the invisible weight of their judgment. It was very clear, I was about to be beaten up. As soon as I dragged the rusty nail across a pane of glass again, scratched their nerves with yet another senseless destruction of a coloaster, they would, quietly and efficiently (and in some cases with poorly concealed enthusiasm), proceed to smack me upside the head. To put it mildly.

I retrieved my butterfly and flipped the blade open in a practiced motion. *Slice.* I made the cut. Silence. Anticipation. Eager readiness. I carefully separated the two halves of the coloaster. The tension reached its apogee. The dim light of the bar lamp wasn't enough for the audience to see the sense yet. I slowly finished my glass of blue. (Cries of seagulls, transparent lightness, and wind in my face.) I hooked the sense with the tip of my knife and victoriously raised it above my head. The sense had nearly choked in its cardboard coloaster prison, but it was alive. It shimmered in the light. Aaand . . .

Explosion. There was a roar of voices and a thunder of applause. The audience rejoiced.

Warmed by their inexpensive colors, they were as genuinely happy for me as they had genuinely been prepared to rough me up. They clapped me on the back so energetically that it might have been easier to suffer their fists.

I handed my prize over to Ulle: an ordinary sense was enough to treat everyone present to a glass of a strong red.

Via this simple trick I became "good ol' Bach." Fritz excitedly told me about the latest accomplishments of his youngest, Max complained about the ladies, young Eyck offered me the best-friend discount as he tried to sell me his handwritten manuscript, its rustling pages languidly playing a non-existent melody. In short, I was now part of the pack.

Also, after that evening, all tortoise coloasters disappeared from the bar counter. They were replaced by the expensive cork coasters, which Ulle typically reserved for special occasions.

THE RIGHT PERSON

I knew very little about Mauk, but I knew the important thing: he was the right person.

Mauk was a grim, bearded man with a hooked nose, unhurried and thorough. Only his eyes contradicted his thoroughness, and they argued loudly and incessantly. His eyes were shifty, full of mischief, and very curious—like those of young russles. Mauk's eyes appeared to live an independent life and looked out of place on his serious face. Occasionally they would freeze and turn dim, like the shell of a dead snail. There was no doubt that in those moments the eyes looked within Mauk himself, stunned by a sudden idea or conclusion that visited his large, elongated head.

We sat down at a separate table, located underneath the tortoise shell covered in scratched-in autographs.

"What are you drinking? My treat."

"Don't worry about it, Bach. Bach, is it? Did I recall that right? Good, good." Mauk retrieved a crumpled plastic cup and a dark, flat metal flask from the inside pocket of his coat. "Thank you, but I exclusively imbibe my own."

The liquid he poured into the glass was undoubtedly a color, but I couldn't tell which one.

Ulle brought me a glass of blue. Before returning to the bar, he glanced unkindly toward Mauk and his flask, but said nothing.

"Would you mind if I smoke?"

What incredible luck! I wasn't sure whether Mauk was a smoker and was trying to come up with some awkward excuse for performing my little trick. "Not at all."

Suddenly there was a match box in my hand, and then I was leaning over the table, offering Mauk a light. Everything was going swimmingly.

"Let's talk frankly. I don't know you. But Eyck insists that you're a great guy."

I had ended up buying Eyck's damned manuscript and made the rash decision of bringing it home. Everything in my room: the drapes, the carpet, and even the stove became drenched with the smell of its nonexistent melody. It was decidedly impossible to be there now: anyone entering the room fell into a semblance of a cataleptic state as they painfully tried to recall the familiar-seeming notes that stubbornly refused to form into anything meaningful. I had to hope that my sacrifice wasn't in vain.

After all, Eyck had connected me with Mauk, and that meant a lot. Assuming Mauk was the right person.

"Eyck wouldn't lie," I replied, also lighting up.

I took a deep drag, then exhaled calmly. Everything inside me roiled and boiled, but outwardly I resembled a sleepy sphinx. Puffs of smoke formed into a triangle. Mauk grunted, impressed. I'd practiced this trick for far longer than the one with the matches.

"Tell me about your problem, Bach. Friends of Eyck are like relatives to me."

That's right. Mauk was a problem solver. Except no one ever heard of people like him having relatives. People close to them were the kind of problem someone like Mauk got rid of first.

I held back my answer, even though I knew exactly what I needed. I had known it a month ago, when I first set foot in this bar.

Mauk poured more color from the flask into his cup, and drank before I had time to examine it. But I could tell from the smell: his color was stronger than the strongest blue or red I'd ever tasted. This was fortunate, for two reasons.

First, it was confirmation that Mauk really was the right person. A color this rich could only come from the Farctory.

Second, the sharp concentrated taste would hide the bitterness of the powder I'd used to spike his drink when I offered Mauk the light.

I held back my response because I wanted to stall until the powder took its effect. Don't think it was anything untoward. Just some light spices, a mix of mint and time. When combined with a thick color, it would make Mauk a little more frivolous and agreeable.

Otherwise he'd deny me without hesitation.

"I won't rush you," Mauk said softly. "But do keep in mind that anything you say will remain between us. Pretend like I'm your kindly grandmother."

"I better not," I replied. "Grandma Bach was an especially insidious creature."

It seemed Mauk was used to dealing with indecisive clients. The smoke from his cigarette crept across the Dichotomy, its fins twitching lazily; Mauk's calm was that of a great wise fish. A fish that hid its teeth for the time being.

I took a sip of the blue and felt the sea flowing through my veins.

"Do you prefer the blue?"

I nodded.

"Believe me, a single sip of the real, undiluted color, and you will never appreciate the cheap facsimile they serve in this bar again. Would you like some?"

He reached for his flask.

To be honest, I was tempted to sip a tiny little bit of his mysterious color. If Mauk wasn't lying, it should be something incredible . . . But no, I had to remain sober that day. I replied with an ill-fitting cliché. "Silence is the best color."

"You're cautious. And yet, you sought me out. This characterizes you as a man with a complex inner world."

He was wrong about that. Ever since Barbara disappeared, my inner world had become empty, dusty, and simple. No more complex than a button, and equally filled with holes.

Mauk gulped down his color and immediately poured another portion. I knew that the moment had come.

Dichotomy was the perfect venue for such conversations. Cigarette smoke reliably absorbed and chewed-up sounds, making it seem as though we were surrounded with a thick layer of pressed cotton. Still, I looked around, making sure that no one was curious about our cozy chat. Only then did I notice that the place was unusually empty. There was Ulle behind the bar counter, me and Mauk under the tortoise shell, and Eyck scribbling something in his old notebook in the far corner.

I took off my hat and ran a hand through my hair (the gel hissed as it tickled my palm). I leaned forward and looked Mauk right in the eye as I said: "I need to get inside the Farctory."

Mauk slowly extinguished his cigarette in the filthy ashtray. He studied me from behind his stern eyebrows.

"Are you sure you want to go there? Take your time, Bach, think about it. Once I grant your wish, there's no going back."

I nodded. "I'm absolutely sure."

"Now?"

"Now."

"In that case, I suggest we don't dawdle."

As though Mauk led people into the Farctory every day.

He got up, put on his captain's cap, which paradoxically made his head appear even more oblong, buttoned his duffle coat, and headed for the exit. I dropped a small sense onto the table, under an empty glass so it wouldn't escape.

Mauk paused by the door, and asked. "What's that smell? Tangerines?"

I didn't respond.

As we left the bar, a shadow hissed and slid inside the gap in the Dichotomy's slightly open door.

RUSSLES UNDERFOOT

People used to disappear before. Here's what I mean by *disappear*. You leave your home wearing checkered slippers, carrying a shot glass in the left hand and a fishing rod in the right. You plan to milk a little bit of sense out of the nearest vending machine, and possibly catch a couple of pikes. A week later, you return with a bucket filled with sense, and a matchbox filled with fish. I don't know about you, but I refuse to call that a disappearance. When you return home and discover that your wife isn't there, now that's a different story. At first you wait patiently, the way she'd waited for you, then you imperceptibly switch from drinking the light green to the strong blue. Then you notice that the bald guy on the third floor isn't rattling his castanets anymore, and the old lady downstairs has ceased reciting poetry in the voice of a striped meowler stuck inside the radio. You come to understand that you're alone in the building. Perhaps you're alone in the entire block.

You go to the nearest bar and, while sipping a mug of considerably diluted green, you learn that the Farctory has shut down. That people are disappearing irrevocably, leaving behind nothing but the echo of yesterday's footsteps.

I planned to put a stop to this.

It was really late, or perhaps a little too early. We walked along a dark street, russles skittering underfoot. Mauk walked evenly, with calm dignity, as though there were no russles about, as though no russles ever existed.

I thought that Barbara would've probably found Mauk interesting. Barbara collected people; she liked them. She gathered them like stray meowlers and warmed them by the fireplace.

And not only people.

Barbara found something in common with everyone, and electrons ceased biting, and senses multiplied on their own in her presence.

Even I was alive, while she was by my side.

I think Barbara could've loved even the russles.

It's possible that russles appeared even back when the Farctory was still operational. Perhaps I'd even noticed them. I'd seen them with my eyes, but didn't recognize them with my mind. I was in love then, and everyone knows that love captures a man whole, leaving not even a single square centimeter of attention for some tailed rodents.

Then the sense vending machines began melting one by one, and russles became the least of my problems. But, you know this. Everyone has their own story like that. You look around and realize, it's too late. The wife has disappeared, the world rumbles as it rolls toward chaos, and russles are skittering underfoot.

Hare stalked us. He did this awkwardly and loudly, and it took a considerable effort for me not to stop and chide him right there and then. It would've been a curious scene, considering that Hare's presence was supposed to remain concealed from Mauk.

Therefore, I endeavored to walk as loudly as possible, pounding the soles of my shoes against the pavement. Mauk seemingly didn't notice my trick, lost in his own thoughts.

You might rush to judgment, thinking me some sort of a grifter or a thief. But Hare was only my insurance. Frankly, a good-for-nothing insurance.

It wouldn't matter, if Mauk didn't plan to cheat me. But who could know that in advance? I continued to strike the pavement like a proper tap dancer.

But, when we approached the Farctory, Mauk said, "Let your boy come out. He can carry the lamp."

THE FARCTORY

All roads led here. A quiet whisper at the next table, where instead of the disappeared people, rumors shyly bristled their mustaches. Mysterious signs on the walls of empty houses and arrows on the pavement. Everything pointed toward the Farctory.

This used to be a good neighborhood: old buildings, bricks in conversation with tiles, cirrus clouds tickling the ears of meowlers, gloomy sycamores sprinkling the ground with thorns.

And at the center of it all—the Farctory. A squat building— three or four stories total. The walls and the windows were covered in cracks, but still remained unbreakable.

It was quiet and empty there at night. The smell of decay wandered the streets; the wind surreptitiously licked the pavement.

In reality, the Farctory occupied a city-sized space underground. Perhaps even larger—I didn't remember for certain.

Over the course of the past month, I had circumnavigated the Farctory seventeen times, looking for a way in. I had come here with an axe, matches, a hacksaw. It was no use: the walls and windows of the Farctory were indestructible.

This is why I was so curious to see what trick Mauk would pull to get us inside. I imagined a secret passage from an apartment in an adjacent building: grim wallpaper, a suspicious old woman in a greasy dressing gown and an untidy cap; her husband leading us into the damp basement past a purring meowler. Or maybe a rooftop run: brick dust disturbed by our boots filling the air, clogging our eyes, noses, ears; crows scattering from the chimneys.

Instead Mauk led us straight to the central gate and casually unlocked a small door at one of its sides.

Before entering, he pulled out his flask and took a sip of color. He offered it to me. I shook my head, declining.

"Drink," Mauk insisted. His voice sounded enchanting and smooth like silk.

I resolutely turned aside his hand holding the flask. Mauk shrugged.

We entered. Mauk gave Hare a cast-iron kerosene lamp that seemed heavier than the boy himself. Hare obediently accepted it and lifted it as high as he could.

A frightened echo stomped across the enormous workshop shrouded in darkness. There was a sharp smell of engine oil and color. Mauk walked in the lead, followed by Hare, and finally me.

Clack, clack, clack, the darkness whispered. I imagined enormous machines looming over us with their condescending sleepy smiles.

The light from the kerosene lamp snatched glimpses of this incredible structure from the darkness: pipes, enormous turbines, staircases. The main assembly line. And finally, the circuit breaker. Huge, impressive, promising, it shone invitingly in the dim light of the lamp.

I reached into my pocket and felt for a bundle, wrapped in rough tangerine peel. This bundle, hidden for the time being, contained my distracting maneuver.

Suddenly Mauk stopped, turned around. The lamp in Hare's hands lit his face from underneath.

"Why do you smell like tangerines?" he asked sternly. Fire danced in his restless eyes.

I had to give it to him, Mauk was insightful and he asked the right question. But it was too late. Obedient to the touch of my hand, the tangerine peel crumpled, releasing the manuscript— the same manuscript sold to me by Eyck. Carefully at first, but gaining confidence with each instant, the rustling melody flowed across the dark space—languid and intrusive like the morning trill of the attendant bird. I'd long since grown used to this melody. I no longer became lost in its dusty labyrinth. But for the unprepared, it was a real trap.

Mauk's face turned unnaturally focused; he froze, as though wrapped in invisible threads. The same thing happened to Hare.

I left the circle of light in two steps.

You see, I was certain that the Farctory was behind everything. The sense shortage, the missing people, chaos and chamomile tea—the reasons behind all of that were in this dying, abandoned, and impregnable building. If my troubles began when the Farctory was shut down, then everything could only be fixed by returning the Farctory to life.

To be honest, I only had a vague idea as to how to approach this problem. I drove the cowardly idea of sharing my plan with Mauk deep into the far recesses of my hole-riddled consciousness. Saving the world couldn't be trusted to a man who seemingly profited from that world's death throes.

And so my plan was simple: to reactivate the conveyor belt. That would be enough, for now.

Tasks should be completed gradually, one at a time. That way there's a chance that the tasks will show initiative, pick up the baton, complete one another. That's how our world works. The circuit breaker that starts the conveyor belt sat at one end of the electric labyrinth. At the other end—a wife and an apple pie. Simple, really.

Thinking that, I resolutely pulled the switch upward.

After that, everything happened on its own.

Slowly, one after another, the lamps lit up, filling the air with the smell of warm dust. I saw hulking silhouettes of machines, their roots deep in the cement floor, their tops reaching toward the roof far above.

It was a titanic sight. A huge automated line for pouring color. I imagined how the senses had rang, gnashed, popped, and celebrated here back when the Farctory was alive.

The multilevel conveyor occupied all the visible space on the floor and above; its lines weaved a complicated web among giant, dusty flasks, rusty boilers, and darkened pipes. I noticed a movement. Several russles quickly poured thick yellow color from a huge tank into a dirty canister. Directly above me, on an engineering platform with a trellised floor, a russle was counting dark unlabeled bottles. Russles scurried along the pipes and stairs in the most businesslike fashion. One sat atop a lamp and selflessly nibbled on the long cord that secured that lamp to the ceiling.

Although the conveyor belt was still, life at the Farctory hadn't ceased when it stopped.

Mauk and Hare remained at the center of the workshop, locked in the trap of the melody. Mauk's face was a mask of concentration. Hare's still eyes stared at me in mute opprobrium. I hadn't warned him about my trick and now I felt a light pang of guilt.

The russles weren't too scared by the light being turned on; they appeared used to it. But then one of them noticed me, squeaked something, and immediately all work in the entire workshop ceased. I felt thousands of intense gazes upon me. The canister rolled down the stairs, the bottles clanked. The pipes rumbled loudly. The russles abandoned their pursuits: they had a new focus.

Never before had I had cause to view the little gray inconspicuous russles as a threat. I must admit, this time they made quite an impression on me. Perhaps I should have recruited a dozen meowlers as my co-conspirators instead of one Hare; the russles were wary of meowlers.

DOWN

I retreated step by step, hoping to come up with a clever plan on the fly. The gray wave of russles blanketed the floor as they approached me. I took another step and felt the massive conveyor at my back. Without thinking, I jumped up onto the conveyor belt.

The belt came alive. This seemed like the logical and proper ending to my heist: the belt would take me higher and higher along the multilayer conveyor, up to the roof of the world, or at least the roof of the Farctory. Perhaps Barbara was already waiting for me there. I looked up: the first rays of dawn streamed through the gaps in the ceiling.

Except the belt was moving in the wrong direction. It was carrying me away from the light, down, toward the dark dungeons of the shadows.

I reacted in the most foolish manner: I ran along the belt in the opposite direction. This was a pointless waste of effort: the belt moved faster and faster.

"Don't resist," I heard Mauk's calm voice. "It will only make things worse."

Impossibly, he had managed to untangle himself from my trap in so short a time. He stood in front of the switch I had used to reanimate the Farctory. His eyes glistened coldly. In those eyes I saw the truth in all its frightening simplicity: I had lost.

From the very beginning everything had gone according to another's plan. All my traps and tricks, my clever subterfuges were nothing more than child's play. The insidious Mauk had observed all of them through the lively russles of his eyes. He predicted my every step, and each step had led me into the web he had spun.

"You should have drunk the color when I offered it."

Instead of listening to him, I pulled a revolver from its holster. I fired, then fired again.

The bullets were well-trained. They needed no help in choosing their trajectories. They went hunting, leaving behind the predatory path of sparkling air. I realized my mistake before the bullets reached their target. Color is a highly explosive substance, too dangerous to discharge a weapon in a place where color permeates the air.

The brightest flash instantly gave way to total darkness. I was blind.

As if no light ever existed. As if there was ever only darkness. I was falling.

II: THERE

THE CARDBOARD CITY

My first thought is: I'm alive. I landed on my feet like some lucky meowler.

I search my feelings: darkness, nothing hurts, a bit of an eclipse in my mind, a confusion in my memory. But that's nothing.

I focus and begin to remember. The Farctory, me discharging a weapon. The flash. Mauk.

I get up and walk.

I hope to reach the wall by my hundredth step, at most. I find it on my three-thousand-six–hundred-and-seventy-fourth step. Plus or minus two steps: I may have lost count twice.

Dead stone masonry at about the height of my waist. It's wet; a cold fog rises from somewhere below. The darkness turns gray as it freezes: I see that my palms are pressing against the fence that surrounds a bridge. Somewhere in the damp, toy-like, papier-mâ-ché or painted fog, a steamboat cries plaintively.

Cracks snake lazily under my palms. So it seems to me at first. When I look closely, I see that they don't snake at all. Dead cracks on dead stone. Someone might call their sluggish multi-year journey a life—but not me.

My heart pumps like a crazed meowler. This makes absolutely no sense. *Sense.* Is all of this about the broken vending machine? I try to recall something important, but my memory fails me.

"Bach!" I hear an echo of a vaguely familiar voice. "Are you here?"

For some reason, I'm afraid to turn around.

Very afraid.

I turn.

A translucent figure rises over the bridge. It's difficult to make it out in the uncertain shading of the fog.

The shadow. Half drawn, half roughly fashioned from card-board. My hand reaches for the revolver of its own volition, but the revolver isn't there.

I mentally order myself to remain in place. Still, I run away in the most cowardly fashion. I cross the bridge. Twelve steps. I stare into the darkness in the foolish hope of finding a door which I could use to get out of here.

With my every step, the shading of the fog thins out, recedes. Everything is even worse than I could imagine. To be honest, I have no clue what I could've imagined. But definitely not this.

To my left and right is the black stillness of inanimate water.

Ahead of me, ridiculous in their geometric simplicity, as if drawn by charcoal on rough paper, walls reach up toward where the sky should be. There is no sky. Instead, there's a low-hanging lilac-gray ceiling. It swirls slowly, with a sense of belonging, over my head, and rumbles curses in its cardboard tongue. The street frightens me with its merciless straightness. It's too predictable and unchanging to be real.

I step carefully as I walk on dead pavement alongside dead walls with dead window displays.

Imagine a city built of cardboard pop-ups on the pages of a children's book. You flip the pages, and one street replaces another. A voluminous world filled with finest details and amazing depth is borne of a flat pane.

But if you were to close the book, this world would disappear. Houses, trees, streets, and people would become flat, turn into dead cardboard.

I walk across such a page.

There's no doubt: I'm in the dungeon of the shadows.

"Cut out these games, Bach!"

The shadow catches up to me and rests its hand on my shoulder.

There's a glimpse of hope: I'm about to see Barbara.

But, no. I won't.

THE CLUB OF DARING MEOWLERS

The basement belongs to Schultz—a short bald man who doesn't know how to bluff. Schultz wrinkles his forehead, pretending to think, but his red ears and twitching eye thoroughly betray him. He's holding a nice fat flush, or better.

Somewhere upstairs, wearing curlers and a plush robe, shadow Natasha, Schultz's Russian girlfriend, is zealously crushing garlic: there will be real Ukrainian ajoblanco soup served for dinner. It sounds as though the ceiling is about to collapse onto our heads.

Don't frown, Schultz, it'll make your ears fall off, says the Canadian. He has sharp teeth, red hair, and no name. The Canadian is certain he's from Montreal, that sooner or later a girl named Rose will fall for him, and that his hand of three fours is good enough to beat Schultz.

Obviously, he's wrong on all counts.

Gret is silent. Gret is always silent. Cardboard crumbles are stuck in his beard, his sad eyes tear up from the dust of the cartoon city. Gret believes that he was born in the middle of a huge traffic jam, and that the Black woman taxi driver who delivered him told his mother: keep this child safe, kiddo—he's been kissed by Jesus; the grateful mother named her son after that woman. In this one thing Gret is definitely right: he has a woman's name.

The cats yowl in the yard. Cats are very similar to meowlers, except they're more daring and not all of them meow.

I'm like that, too. I'm almost real, except I live in a cardboard city. Among my cardboard friends.

I study the drawn faces. Why don't they remember?

Shultz doesn't recall his huge trawler, doesn't remember that the largest, most extraordinary and nuanced senses have been caught in his nets.

The Canadian doesn't recall that his name is Asmus, that any deck becomes magical in his hands, and that he can beat anyone at cards.

Gret doesn't recall that he was born with a gun in his hand, doesn't remember how he used to shoot attendant birds in flight from atop the Tobacco Tower. Doesn't remember how he traded a narwhal skull in exchange for the remnants of a giant sense.

When I tell them about these things, they smile in embarrassment.

They say: isn't it time for you to see the doctor, Bach?

THE DOCTOR

The doctor is a dull old man with a stern gaze. He never argues with me. He listens attentively and marks up his notebook. He asks, why are you smiling, Bach?

Is it possible not to smile when a cartoon little man is trying to cure you of a non-existent disease?

How do you sleep, asks the doctor. I sleep well, I reply. I sleep very well.

The shadows sleep, you see. They lie down on their lush cardboard mattresses, close their eyes, and attentively view their so-called dreams.

They demand that I do the same.

Tell me about your dreams, the doctor says.

I make stuff up. I tell him how, in a dream, Gret dealt me four aces and I won a real bus. How I vacationed by the sea, and met a nice girl there. How I found myself naked in the middle of a street filled with strangers.

The doctor nods and writes it all down. He says, tell me about Barbara.

I reply, trying to slow the traitorous beating of my heart: Barbara is dead.

I hate this lie, but in this cardboard world, I'm forced to lie often.

GRANDMA BACH

I have come to like this old shadow more than I used to like Grandma Bach back there, up above.

That one was looming, harsh, and very active. No one dared contradict her. Grandma Bach of the shadow world is a dry woman with defenseless eyes behind the thick lenses of her glasses.

In this world everyone thinks the old woman has long since lost her mind. To me, she's the most sane of all the residents of cardboard city. If some amount of sense from the real world is allotted to the dungeon shadows, then the lion's share of it is here, in Grandma Bach's room.

The nurse pours me some cartoon tea into a cardboard mug and exits the room, leaving the door ajar. She's definitely spying on us. This is a useless task. Grandma Bach and I understand each other without words.

Grandma supports her wrinkled chin with her small fist and watches as I take small sips of terrible tea. The creaks and hisses of the gramophone dilute the melody of the Neverending Canon.

Grandma considers this to be the ideal tune, and gets very upset that I can never memorize the composer's name.

This music gives me hope. I'm convinced I've heard it before.

Grandma asks: You still aren't sleeping?

I shake my head. Can't fool her.

I honestly try to sleep. I toss and turn, count the boring cracks in the ceiling, imagine meowlers leading a round dance on a poppy field, smoke cardboard chips that pass for tobacco here. But instead of sleep I fall backward, into my real, infinitely beautiful world, where I so dream of returning.

Call it a nightmare, if you like.

Still looking?—she continues her interrogation.

I nod.

I'm looking. Nights. Days. In the most paradoxical of places. Seeing a door makes me turn into a madman. Refrigerators, cabinets, wardrobes—I search for an exit everywhere. Often I ascend into attics, but sometimes I go down to the cellars—out of sheer contradiction.

I climb ridiculous towers wrapped in cardboard wires. Ascend onto the roofs of skyscrapers. I try to reach the sky and pierce it with scissors.

And then I come here and drink tea.

It's time for me to go. I kiss Grandma Bach goodbye on her cartoon forehead. I read the truth in her sad eyes: we will never see each other again.

MY DREAM

If I manage to defeat this cardboard reality, if an accidental observer thinks that, having closed my eyes, I fell asleep, then on the inner side of my eyelids I see the following: a dark corridor I spent an eternity traversing terminates in an impossible, incredibly beautiful sunset of my world. I step forward and find myself in the middle of an empty street, next to the sense vending machine inside of which—I hear this clearly—the russles are fumbling. The machine is dead inside. I rush toward it, hoping to shake out the remnants of a sense that might somehow help me grasp on to this world, to stay in it. But there's no life within me, my hands are transparent. I'm a shadow. I'm powerless.

It's impossible to be a man and a shadow at the same time. Question: when did I stop being a man? When I fell from the darkness near the bridge? When I lied to the doctor about my dreams and drank cartoon tea? Or is it now, in my sleep, up the rabbit hole where I climb out under the gloomy sky and open my eyes, translucent, easily blown away by the wind?

I should run, hide. Try to change something. But the events of this nightmare aren't dependent upon my will. I can only observe.

A man named Bach approaches the vending machine. This is me—the way I used to be. Living, real, corporeal. He shoves his hand into the hiss of the broken machine, twists the levers, frowns.

I approach. Honestly, I shouldn't do this. But I'm incapable of stopping. I must warn him.

I approach and begin to speak.

The real Bach looks at me coldly, indifferently. He walks away. I follow.

Listen, I say, listen to me this once—

He shoots me in the face.

It's hellishly painful.

This is why I prefer not to sleep at all.

THE DEALER

The dealer is waiting for me under the canopy of an inconspicuous building entrance. His hat is pulled down to his eyes. The collar of his cloak is raised. He studies the street behind me with a tenacious gaze. Then he walks by me indifferently, casually shoving me with his shoulder.

I feel my pocket has been emptied. The space previously occupied by a stack of stupid gray pieces of paper with gloomy portraits on them is now taken up by an almost weightless bundle.

The sound of the dealer's footsteps reverberates through the cardboard walls with a dull echo as he walks away. There's something vaguely familiar about his gait.

I go home. It's silly to call the geometric construct with empty walls a home—it contains no memories, not a bit of warmth. I endeavor to spend as little time here as possible, but now I need the solitude.

BARBARA

For the man who has tasted of life, there's no sin that would justify the punishment of rotting under the cardboard sky of the dungeon, amid the musty aromas of yesterday, in the dust and soot of an artificial world.

But I would forgive this world everything—for my Barbara.

Her eyes would be blue. The real, deep, penetrating blue. The color of surf and salty waves. In that old life, I'd never tasted so rich a color. In this new life, the color of her eyes would be my salvation.

Here a color can be seen, heard, and even spoken. But it's impossible to drink it and feel it spread within you. (I'd tried gouache and watercolors.)

Sometimes I dream of oblivion. To become a shadow. To learn to read books instead of hearing or breathing them. Sometimes I wish to believe that this life is the only one given to a person. To collect immobile stamps and to never be surprised by the predictability of time and weather. To pay with nonsensical gray pieces of paper at the bar.

To sleep, like everyone else.

To dream.

Sometimes I think: somewhere behind the cardboard walls hides another Farctory. Inside it there is a third, a fourth, a fifth . . .

Sometimes I think: everyone but me drank from the river of oblivion as they crossed over. I recall the dark figure of Mauk, his duffle coat and captain's cap. I recall how persistently he offered me a sip from his flask.

How many did Mauk bring here? I look around and answer my own question: everyone.

Everyone, except my Barbara.

I check twice to make sure I locked the door. I boil water. I prepare the strainer and the tea.

I take out the bundle the dealer had left in my pocket. I unwrap the crumpled newspaper page.

III: NOWHERE

THE TRIP

This time the black tunnel was very short. One step—and I thought I had become God. I heard the world (my real, living, knowable world) pass through me; I drank its color. The whistling whisper of wind, the loud trajectory of an attendant bird, the melodies of books, the sleepy teakettles, clocks with a checkered *tick-tock* sound, senses arranged in descending order. My home greeted me.

Then I saw the pavement through my hands and realized that everything had repeated itself; I came home a shadow. I looked around. The set pieces were the same: dusk, empty street, broken vending machine, which the real Bach was about to approach.

But something had changed. I no longer felt the insistent need to repeat my learned motions. I didn't feel the heavy will of sleep. I could breathe sweet air and live. Even if it was life as a shadow—a sketch portrait of my real self with dots for eyes.

As a hero of a cardboard western.

A good guy, hoodwinked by the villain in a duffle coat, having overcome the savannah, the scorpions, the blonde's bed, and the noose, returns to an empty, raided town. He comes out onto the main street. His hand shakes nervously as it hovers over his revolver.

Except I didn't have a revolver anymore; shadows aren't allowed revolvers.

I took a step back, toward the warm brick wall.

Right after that, another shadow burrowed its way out of a new hole. This was me, of course—from one of my nightmares. A marionette, unable to resist someone else's script. I must admit, I looked pathetic as a shadow. The real Bach was another matter—the hat, the trench coat, the revolvers on my belt. Shoulders wide, chin up, arrogant gaze. The shadow approached him, and I rushed to turn away, remembering what happens next.

Hare came from around the corner. He looked to the real Bach with fear and admiration. I knew this look; I once granted it to the heroes of my childhood. Poor boy. The real Bach won't even think about you when he turns the Farctory into a torch.

There was the sound of a gunshot. Hare shuddered and closed his eyes, but quickly got hold of himself. Bach left, and the boy followed.

I followed them as well.

DICHOTOMY

The city was dying. There wasn't a single meowler, nor a single person left. There weren't even any shadows, other than me.

Something had gone terminally wrong here. The world twisted, cracked, and crumbled before my eyes. The bored wind dragged a tumbleweed across the cracked pavement. The dry shutters whispered in alarm. Black fractal growths made themselves at home on building walls, where they sprouted, and occasionally enveloped entire buildings.

The lack of sense could be felt sharply.

Through a small window designed to resemble a tortoise I watched the real Bach in Dichotomy play out his naïve con, thinking he was cleverly misleading Mauk.

Hare stood guard by the door. He looked at me sullenly, silently. He wasn't overly talkative with other people, let alone some shadow. The night poured a generous sprinkling of cold over the street. Hare, not dressed for the weather, was trembling. But his stern face showed he was prepared to endure any adversity for the sake of the important task entrusted to him by his idol.

Why did I drag him into this story? What assistance did I expect from this frozen sparrow?

The door creaked, and Mauk exited. I pressed against the wall, hiding from his tenacious gaze. I burned with furious desire to kill Mauk immediately, to erase him from reality with a single well-placed shot. It was a good thing I was only a shadow.

Because I couldn't afford to kill Mauk, at least not until he an-
swered my questions. And to ask them, I'd have to learn to speak
coherently again.

Bach emerged, and the two of them headed toward the Farctory in silence.

I slid through the door of the Dichotomy which was left
slightly ajar.

"Ulle! Ulle, it's me, Bach," I said.

Ulle looked at me sternly and without recognition. He didn't
like shadows. But deep within the Dichotomy I saw Eyck and
darted toward him before Ulle reached for his formidable weapon—the broom.

Eyck was a good guy. The thirst for adventure hadn't yet completely uprooted him from the warm embrace of normal life, but
one could see in this youngster's gaze that he was prepared to
jump head-first into the whirlpool of mad adventure. I was just
like him, before I met Barbara.

I sat across from Eyck with some difficulty. My current body,
translucent and flat, kept trying to fall through the oak bench and
onto the floor. I somehow managed to settle in.

"Hi, buddy," I said.

Eyck tilted his head in thought, and I was glad I wasn't in his
shoes. Only a handful of my acquaintances would bother with
the shadows. Usually they'd fire without warning: everyone knew
this old, proven method of returning the escapee directly back to
the dungeon.

Ulle approached. His unkind gaze cut sharply into my back,
between the poorly defined shoulder blades.

"Miniscule princeps," Eyck told the bartender. He added: "Be
you a wildering terpene."

I was certain Eyck didn't talk like that. He definitely said
something along the lines of, "Poor shadow. Perhaps it's cold?
Add some birch branches to the hearth, friend Ulle."

The wall of incomprehension between the shadow-me and
the human-Eyck twisted every spoken word.

"Jump, brandade," Ulle said doubtfully, and left.

Which, most likely, meant: "I'm not about to waste good kindling on this frozen thing."

I cringed, and said timidly, "There must be some way—"

Eyck signaled for me to be quiet.

Ulle returned and placed a glass of strong red in front of me. Eyck nodded as if to say, "Drink, you Farctory weakling." I was never a big fan of the red color, but in my position beggars couldn't be choosers. I drank.

Red burned my throat. I coughed and croaked: "Bastards . . . !"

"Color me flabbergasted, he resembles a man now!" Ulle said excitedly. "Wow, Eyck, you're one clever meowler."

"Hey, I understood that," I shouted. "Every word!"

Eyck celebrated. "You see! You lost the bet, Ulle. We didn't have to force him: he drank it on his own. I've lost hope that I would get to test this theory. They do possess some kind of a thought process after all."

"What thought process? It's a reflex . . ."

Ulle had always been a skeptic, but Eyck didn't listen to him. He turned toward me and said gently: "Speak, vagabond. What manner of being are you, and why are you bothering us honest folk?"

CANON PER TONOS

We were walking too slowly. I kept looking toward the sky, searching for the first signs of dawn.

"Why don't you fly, friend?" Eyck wondered. "You're a shadow."

Fly! I couldn't even run. The physical laws of our world are ruthless toward shadows; the more I want to get somewhere, the more difficult it becomes to move. The air thickens, the headwind intensifies, my strength flees.

Ulle wouldn't calm down. "I knew there was a reason I never liked that Mauk! To come into a bar and drink from his own flask? Who does that! And he'd sit there and nurse it, and nurse it!"

He grumbled incessantly. At times he'd stop to make sure his shotgun was loaded, catch up with us, deftly kicking up his skinny knees and jumping over the small shoots of fractals, carefully avoiding the more dangerous fractal bushes that branched everywhere, breaking the walls and upturning the pavement.

Ulle squinted at me with little enthusiasm. In his head, Bach and the shadow were two separate things, and these concepts refused to intersect let alone combine.

As to Eyck, he had become gloomy once he heard my story. He looked around suspiciously. He twitched his eyebrows, wordlessly opened his mouth, as though he was carrying on a mental dialog.

Finally, we arrived.

The fractals that took over the nearby buildings seemed not to even notice the Farctory. Their sharp branches reached toward the sky, evenly bending around its cracked walls. I stopped at the entrance, confounded as I listened. Music flowed from behind the small open door at the side of the Farctory gates. It was a slow, viscous, and sad sound. I knew this tune. I'd heard it tens or even hundreds of times through the creak of Grandma Bach's gramophone in cardboard city. An old canon by a Saxon composer whose name I could never recall. I wondered how this music appeared in the real world and immediately understood: the manuscript.

That same manuscript trap I'd once bought from Eyck that whispered a non-existent melody. I experienced the true depth of this melody only now, having become a shadow.

My compatriots couldn't be allowed to come closer. I signaled for them to stop, then cautiously peeked inside.

Of course, we were too late.

"Don't resist. It will only make things worse."

Mauk effortlessly freed himself from the web of the Saxon Canon and calmly watched as the real Bach awkwardly ran against the flow of the conveyor belt.

"You should have drunk the color when I offered it."

Bach pulled his revolver, not knowing that his actions would only accelerate his fall into the abyss. I didn't care about him. Let him fall. Let him wander the maze of the cardboard city. He deserved this. I was only interested in Mauk.

Slowly fighting through the resistance of the intractable air I moved toward the lanky silhouette in a duffle coat. Perhaps there was still time to save him.

But then I saw Hare, helplessly still in the center of the work-shop with the kerosene lamp in his hands. The music Mauk easily shrugged off was an overwhelming load for the boy.

Time stood still. The air was thick as ajoblanco soup. I was drowning, choking. A singular thought pulsed through my trans-lucent head: the explosion the still-real Bach is about to cause by firing into this color-filled space will kill Mauk, and I will never get any answers. Instead, I will open my eyes in the cardboard dungeon again. Open my eyes in the gray world without Barbara.

Screw Hare, whispered some other Bach inside me, yester-day's Bach, haughty and self-assured.

I didn't listen to him. To the accompaniment of the sad ca-non I squeezed past the air particles that almost turned into glass. Slowly, step by step. Trying not to think about how I—incorpo-real and powerless—would manage to move the boy who had turned into a statue.

Out of the corner of my eye I saw how slowly, one after an-other, the bullets flew from the barrel of the revolver. How sparks bit into the color-saturated reality. I wasn't going to make it.

"Why don't you fly, friend?" Eyck whispered in my head. "You're a shadow."

You can be whoever you want to be, agreed the tune of the forgotten Saxon composer.

You can fly.

You can.

You.

Can.

I surged forward, shattering the air glass. I merged with the music. I became wind.

Wrapped in the bundle of yellowed pages and the sound of the Neverending Canon, Hare and I made it into the street a mo-ment before the explosion rocked the insides of the Farctory.

*

THE RUSSLES

The sky brightened, ruthlessly underscoring the unusual darkness of the street.

The circle closed. I was calm. It couldn't be any other way. In a world that rapidly lost its sense, this was the only suitable ending to this story. I turned from the hero of a cardboard western into the subject of an unfinished illustration. The perspective was all wrong, the proportions fell ap`art, and the frustrated artist furiously scribbled fractals onto the page.

Hare was silent. He's always been silent, for as long as I've known him. Eyck walked around grimly, stomping on black sprouts. They mostly reminded me of abandoned marionettes who didn't know how to continue the play on their own. Only Ulle managed to keep it together. It was as though he didn't notice the black cracks, couldn't smell the despair that filled the world.

"Ha!" he shouted, pointing up somewhere. "Would you look at that!"

The explosion had seemingly destroyed the curtain that concealed the Farctory from the fractals. They pounced on the new prey, growing through walls and windows, licking fire with their cold tongues, confidently stalking toward the roof. At the very edge of the roof stood Mauk.

"I guess it's time for a certain someone to answer questions," Ulle said firmly.

He walked up to the Farctory gates. Feeling his approach, a wave of russles spilled out, squinting their contented muzzles at the dawn light.

"Those resilient beasts don't fear anything." Ulle laughed, feigning an attack with his shotgun toward the nearest russle. The rodent turned away calmly and began to gnaw at a fractal.

Ulle turned toward us. "What are you waiting for?"

Hare glanced uncertainly toward Eyck.

"We won't go there," said Eyck. "And you shouldn't either, Ulle."

The old man raised his eyebrows in surprise, then grinned

condescendingly. "Are you scared of a third-rate stage magician in a captain's cap?"

"Some questions are best left unanswered, my dear Ulle. Until the answer is spoken, you're free to remain whoever you want to be," said Eyck.

"Sometimes you speak such gibberish that even a meowler couldn't understand you. No, I prefer clarity." Ulle waved him off and disappeared into the dark, dead Farctory.

Eyck shook his head. He picked up several strips of paper left behind from his silenced manuscript.

"May I take this?" he asked me.

I shrugged.

For some reason I felt guilty. Not just guilt toward Hare, but toward both of them, and even toward old Ulle.

I wanted to ruffle Hare's hair as the means of saying goodbye, but instead I awkwardly waved my hand.

Eyck grinned.

"Farewell, Bach."

Inside the Farctory it was pitch-black and stank unbearably of ash.

The conveyor now resembled a mythical beast, snarling menacingly with scraps of belt and its broken metal carcass. I approached in the hope of finding the hole through which the real Bach fell into cardboard city. But all I could see were the tenacious shoots of fractal, spreading in all directions.

A booming sound came from above. Ulle's soles pounded on the steps. I rushed after him and soon overtook the clumsy old man. Dim rays penetrated through small windows to illuminate our path. The staircase looped curiously past the bends of the dead conveyor. Dark silhouettes of the russles appeared here and there, atop the pipes, on the stairs and grills and the conveyor belt.

Mauk remained standing at the roof's edge, straight and stern in his duffle coat and captain's cap.

"I'm happy to see you, Bach. You're right on time. The most interesting part is about to begin."

His face, however, didn't exude happiness.

I walked over and stood next to him silently. There was no wind.

All the words, all the accusations I'd prepared for this conversation disappeared at once when I looked at the city. Fractals rapidly spread across the streets, covering pavements, buildings, and trees. The ocean turned black. Only the pale sky still somehow argued with the endless darkness, but I saw its sharp branches already ripping into the horizon.

"Here it is, Bach. The fate of any world after the last person leaves it. And I must note, this was a very obstinate person."

"Are you talking about me?"

"Obviously. Who else?"

He followed my gaze. It was still possible to see the figures of Eyck and Hare downstairs: they intently made their way through the maze of fractals.

"Have you not understood anything yet, Bach? Old man Ulle, Eyck, Hare whom you so courageously and pointlessly saved from the fire . . ."

Mauk laughed.

"Keep going. Why'd you stop?" I heard Ulle's voice behind us. He pumped his shotgun.

Suddenly I realized, Eyck was right. It's best not to know some truths.

"Don't, Mauk. Don't say it!"

"Why not? Why remain silent, when a *person*"—Mauk turned toward Ulle, flashing a toothy smile at that last word—"insists."

He took one step, then another. Ulle stood his ground and lifted the shotgun.

"You've remained here too long, Bach," Mauk told me while looking at the old man. "When everyone but you left, the world tried its best to remain the way you were used to seeing it. It built props, imitated a semblance of life. Reality is a very loyal thing, capable of everything for the sake of a person. But then the last person leaves it, the props crumble, and we see—"

Ulle fired.

Lead balls flew slowly, reluctantly. Just as I managed to count them (five balls) they reached Mauk and instantly punctured holes in his duffle coat.

Instead of blood, russles poured from the holes.

I looked to Ulle in horror. The old man's hands trembled, his eyes filled with tears.

I hesitantly bent over Mauk to get a better look at the russles busily leaving the sinking boat. It was an instructive sight.

"Ulle, what are you—?"

Another shot thundered behind me.

At the same time, I heard a sickening squeak of rusty metal. I turned to see Ulle's face fall apart like old plaster. Where eyes, nose, and a smile used to be moments ago, a wheel spun with a rusty squeal of a children's swing. A russle ran busily inside the wheel. I thought: how can such a huge wheel fit into the relatively small head of an old man?

Following the face, his clothes fell apart, revealing a complicated construct made of gears, belts, wheels, and russles.

The automaton was quite clever. Three large wheels, five small ones, with four russles controlling the gear belts and a dozen more on standby.

The russles didn't seem to immediately realize that I could see them. They continued working in concert, the russle-secretary deftly feeding the celluloid punch tape into the sound pickup, with a small speaker obediently reproducing Ulle's stifled sobs. Suddenly the device screeched and began to chew up the tape. Irritated, the russle pressed the pedal twice, shook his small head, and turned . . .

Our gazes met.

The russle jumped down onto the tar of the roof. His comrades followed. Mauk got up, adjusted his coat, and laughed hoarsely.

"Do you understand now, Bach?" he squealed. I imagined a russle, busily pressing the pedal of his sound pickup. "You were the last."

I had an epiphany.

"But you, Mauk, you always knew who you were. What you were."

"Of course. I'm brave enough to accept the truth."

Perhaps, I thought, Eyck and Hare have enough humanity in them to alter the truth. The world that created them was almost dead, but I believed in its largesse.

THE END

How would I have liked to see this world for the last time?

Fluffy clouds, and the sound of an ocean filled with meaning somewhere far away; stern fishermen checking their nets on the shore before they head out to sea; the attendant bird chirping its morning song.

Instead I got chaos growing throughout the city, branching out in fractals, devouring everything in its path.

"I warned you, Bach: think it through. There's no going back. You're in luck; I lie as often as I speak the truth. I'll give you one more chance. I'll answer your question, but only one. Choose carefully."

Mauk walked to the edge of the roof. He moved slowly and awkwardly, shaking and creaking like a broken vending machine. He lit a cigarette. What a weird sight. I pitied the russle in his head.

One question wasn't enough for me. Did I want to know the truth about cardboard city, its low-hanging artificial sky? About the shadows? About the little paper men, doomed to live in those flat stage sets?

Mauk looked at me with understanding, as though he could read all my thoughts down to the last letter. "Don't ask questions the answers to which you already know without me."

"But I don't—"

"You do, Bach. You know. You just don't have the fortitude to admit that to yourself."

The fractals continued their dance. They reached the roof's edge, twirling at Mauk's feet. They pounced upon the sky, shredding it to pieces.

Did this city die because the people left? Or did the people leave because the city was dying?

I could ask why they didn't remember the real world.

I could ask where the border was between cardboard and reality.

"There's no border, Bach. The people make the world real. I love people—they create such wonderful worlds. And then we arrive . . ." Mauk closed his eyes, a dreamy expression on his face. Something squeaked under the duffle coat, as though one russle slapped another. Mauk shook his head. "Your question, Bach."

I could ask why the cardboard world never became real for me.

I could ask about many things.

"Is it true that Barbara—?" I began, but could not finish the sentence. Some words are better left unspoken, so they wouldn't become real.

Mauk frowned.

"Not that, Bach. Not that. Look around. You see how well the chaos is growing? How its fractals bloom, devouring all in their path? It will eat you just like that, Bach. But first—the last piece of the sky, and your chance to follow Barbara along with it."

My paper heart skipped a beat.

"That's possible?"

"Finally. My answer is, yes."

I was troubled by his unexpected altruism. But I understood: there's no choice.

"What must I do?"

Mauk had a long bout of agonizing coughing. Three more russles escaped from the holes in his duffle coat, and I feared that he would speak no more. But he said, hoarsely, "You're a shadow, Bach. Fly."

I frowned. "That won't work. I'll fall."

"Who knows? Sometimes one must crash in order to reach the sky. Make up your mind, Bach. There's almost no time left."

I stepped toward the edge, trying not to look down.

"Here, fortify yourself." Mauk offered me his flask. "The last color!"

That same undiluted one, I realized. A sip. (A barrage of wind knocks me off my feet, I slide along the wet deck, salty cold water whips my face.) Another sip. (Dawn, sand. A wave cuts off the sky and the world as it rises and envelops me; I suddenly realize that I don't need air.)

I adjusted my imaginary coat—where would a shadow get a real one?

"Why are you helping me?"

Mauk smiled his predatory sharp-toothed smile, answering without words: who says I'm helping you?

One must fall to reach the sky.

I'm on my way, my dear.

I squeezed my eyes shut.

I stepped forward.

ABOUT THE AUTHOR AND TRANSLATOR

K.A.TERYNA is an award-winning author and illustrator. She was born in two places at once, one of which is beyond the Arctic Circle. Her fiction has been translated from Russian into six languages. English translations of her stories have appeared in *Asimov's, Apex, F&SF, Strange Horizons, Samovar, Podcastle, Galaxy's Edge*, and elsewhere. Her English-language short story collection is *Black Hole Heart and Other Stories*, from Fairwood Press. As of late, Chekhov the Cat has become K.A.Teryna's co-author. He's in charge of keeping her warm and firmly in her seat. K.A. Teryna's website is www.k-a-teryna.blogspot.com.

ALEX SHVARTSMAN is the author of *Kakistocracy* (2023), *The Middling Affliction* (2022), and *Eridani's Crown* (2019) fantasy novels. Over 120 of his stories have appeared in *Analog, Nature, Strange Horizons*, etc. He won the WSFA Small Press Award for Short Fiction and was a three-time finalist for the Canopus Award for Excellence in Interstellar Fiction. His translations from Russian have appeared in *F&SF, Clarkesworld, Tor.com, Analog, Asimov's*, etc. Alex has edited over a dozen anthologies, including the long-running Unidentified Funny Objects series. His website is www.alexshvartsman.com.

PUBLICATION HISTORY

"Black Hole Heart" originally appeared in *Apex*, June 2017 | "Songs of the Snow Whale" originally appeared in *Reactor*, Dec 2024 | "The Errata" originally appeared in *Asimov's*, March 2023 | "Untilted" originally appeared in *Apex*, November 2017 | "Morpheus" originally appeared in *Samovar*, June 2019 | "Copy Cat" originally appeared in *Strange Horizons*, August 2018 | "The Chartreuse Sky" originally appeared in *Asimov's*, May 2021 | "The Jellyfish" originally appeared in *Future Science Fiction Digest*, June 2021 | "No One Ever Leaves Port Henri" originally appeared in *Galaxy's Edge*, Sep 2020 | "Madame Felide Elopes" originally appeared in *Podcastle*, August 2016 | "The Tin Pilot" originally appeared in *Asimov's*, July 2022 | "Lajos and his Bees" originally appeared in *F&SF*, November 2022 | "The Farctory" originally appeared in *"The Best of World SF 2*, Head of Zeus, November 2022.

OTHER TITLES FROM FAIRWOOD PRESS

*Obviously I Love You
But If I Were a Bird*
by Patrick O'Leary
small paperback $11.00
ISBN: 978-1-958880-37-1

Space Trucker Jess
by Matthew Kressel
trade paper $20.95
ISBN: 978-1-958880-27-2

One Last Game
by T.A. Chan
trade paper $15.99
ISBN: 978-1-958880-34-0

When Mothers Dream: Stories
by Brenda Cooper
trade paper $18.99
ISBN: 978-1-958880-35-7

*Better Dreams, Fallen Seeds
and Other Handfuls of Hope*
by Ken Scholes
paperback $19.99
ISBN: 978-1-958880-32-6

Changelog: Collected Fiction
by Rich Larson
trade paper $20.95
ISBN: 978-1-958880-33-3

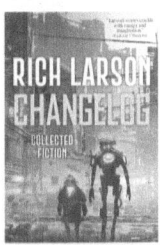

Shifter and Shadow
by Sharon Shinn
trade paper $16.99
ISBN: 978-1-958880-36-4

*A Catalog of Storms:
Collected Short Fiction*
by Fran Wilde
trade paper $18.99
ISBN: 978-1-958880-31-9

Find us at:
www.fairwoodpress.com
Bonney Lake, Washington

www.ingramcontent.com/pod-product-compliance
Lightning Source LLC
Chambersburg PA
CBHW031100020726
47495CB00007B/1968